A Touch of Revenge

Gary Ponzo

Website: garyponzo.com

Blog: strongscenes.com

This book is a work of fiction and the creation of author Gary Ponzo.

Acknowledgements

There are so many people to thank for this book, forgive me if I miss a few. First and last, my family — Jennifer, Jessica and Kyle, without their love I'm not me. My mom for her unrelenting support for my writing. Robert Brown for having the foresight and wisdom to send me down this path. J.A. Konrath for opening up the books and allowing us to see behind the curtain.

A special thanks goes to my beta readers, Jim Ganem, Donald Sprague, Janet Ischy, Bob Moats and Clement Singarajah.

John Locke for his friendship and heavyweight support.

Michael McShane for his guidance and listening to all of my crazy ideas without snickering.

My former and current writing critique group, who've helped me develop my skills, Val Neiman, Wanda McLaughlin, Cindy Goyette, Debra White, Judith L. Pearson, Dave Benneman, Amber Kallyn, Jim Williams, Gabrielle Ruff, Shannon Zweig and Kyle Townsend.

I also want to thank the many readers who've supported me and my work. I appreciate all of your kind words and strive to make every page worthy of your attention.

Chapter 1

The bullet left the sniper's rifle at 3,000 feet per second. Unfortunately, Nick Bracco didn't hear the shot until it was too late. He was sitting on his back porch staring at a pregnancy test his wife had just handed him. It was positive. After eight long years their dream of raising a child was about to come true.

Those plans were made long before the sniper's bullet made it halfway across the small, calm lake sitting in their backyard. It was the same lake that lured them into buying the mature cabin. After years of city living they'd decided to move to northern Arizona and breathe the mountain air.

As the bullet cleared the lake, Nick was focusing on the positive line of the pregnancy test and imagining what it would be like to be a father. Until recently he'd never allowed himself the luxury of relishing the concept. As the head of the FBI's terrorist task force he wasn't sure he'd even survive long enough. Now, though, he beamed with pride. Nick had complied with his wife's desires to get out of harm's way. He left the bureau to become a small town sheriff and raise a family. The happy couple had reached the pinnacle of their dreams.

That's when the bullet hit him in the chest.

* * *

FBI Agent Matt McColm heard the gunshot from a mile away. Before his new partner and girlfriend, Jennifer Steele, knew which direction it came from, Matt knew it was a Remington 700 sniper rifle. He also knew the target.

"Hunters?" Steele asked.

"That's no hunter," Matt said. They were heading down a dirt path on mountain bikes. He twisted his bike around and hustled down the narrow trail toward the source of the shot.

"How do you know?" Steele pumped her legs hard to keep up.

Matt wanted to say, "Because I've been dreading this day." Instead, he pointed to an opening to the right while he veered left. "Go back to the Bracco's cabin," he said. "And call for an ambulance."

Her tires spewed dirt as she sped away.

Matt pulled up on the handlebars and forced his torso down into a rhythm with the stride of his long legs. As he passed the lake to his right, Julie Bracco's wail carried over the water like a wounded animal. There were no trees to buffer the helplessness of her howl. Matt knew Steele was qualified to handle the situation at the cabin. Nick Bracco was probably dead and the thought made him pump even harder. His job now was pure revenge.

Matt realized he could be heading into a sniper's lair, but he banked on the sniper retreating. Adrenalin surged through his bloodstream as he dodged low-hanging limbs and made hairpin turns on the sliver of dirt between the pines. He put the shot at 500 yards to Nick's cabin. There was very little wind. Good shooting weather. From that distance a sniper should get within five inches. The average human head is ten inches. Matt prayed it wasn't a head shot.

As he flew over a rise in the path, gunshots exploded all around him. He dove from the bike and slammed headfirst into a pine tree. When he opened his eyes, he was staring straight up into a fuzzy group of treetops. As his vision cleared, he touched his forehead and felt a knot growing already. His fingers came back gooey red. That's when his Special Forces training kicked in. He took deep breaths and tried to sort things out. There were three shots. Four including the shot at Nick. The full magazine of a Remington 700. The sniper had to be reloading.

The sniper had been impetuous and it was the only reason Matt was still breathing. You don't unload your weapon on a moving target unless it's moving out of range. If the sniper were experienced, he would have used one shot to immobilize Matt, then the other two to finish him off.

Matt rolled to his side and crawled behind a tree. He knew more about a Remington 700 than anyone on the planet. After all, he was the FBI's current sharp-shooting champion. The sniper was using the 7mm Magnum bullet instead of the .308 caliber. There was a distinct difference in the sound which is how he knew the sniper had only four bullets. The .308 caliber held five. The sniper didn't know about his expertise and Matt was prepared to take full advantage of his ignorance.

Matt pulled his Slimline Glock from the holster under his tee shirt. Fully loaded, it held twenty rounds. "I'm all in," he whispered.

A shot blasted just under his right foot and ricocheted over his shoe. Matt quickly tucked in his thin frame and moved farther left with his back to the tree. He ripped off his bright orange shirt. It was worn to stand out for hunters, not snipers.

A second shot blew away the side of the tree, spraying shards of wood across his face. Matt spit out wood fragments and readjusted his position. The shooter was close, inside a hundred yards. The sound of the bullets breaking the sound barrier echoed throughout the forest and brought a creepy urban feel to an otherwise serene mountainside.

Matt knew more than just the weapon the sniper was using, he knew the organization he belonged to as well. Matt and Nick had chased terrorists for a decade with the bureau. During their final mission together, Nick had finished off the leader of the Kurdish Security Force. Matt had always feared someone from the KSF would go after Nick, even after he'd resigned and became sheriff of the Arizona mountain community.

Now, Matt waited behind a pine tree and counted bullets. He needed to use the sniper's impatience against him. He grabbed his shirt and quickly stuffed it with loose leaves and pine needles, then tied the bottom into a knot.

A third shot whizzed past. Close. The one vulnerability of a sniper was the need to be somewhat exposed. The barrel of the rifle needed a clear path to its target. This meant the sniper wouldn't be behind a tree or a rock. He would be flat on his stomach with camouflage as the main source of cover.

The fourth shot came dangerously close. It cracked off a large branch above Matt's head that swung down into his face. Matt deflected the limb, then snapped off a thin piece of the branch and jabbed it into the sleeve opening of his stuffed shirt. He worked on his breathing while he waited for the sniper to reload. He actually heard the bullets clip into the bolt-action rifle.

Matt gripped his Glock with his right hand and swung the stuffed shirt out into the open, quickly, before a trained eye could determine the dupe. It worked. Four quick shots blew apart the shirt full of leaves. He saw the muzzle flashes under a canopy of bushes just fifty yards away. For someone with Matt's skills, the shooter might as well have hung a neon sign around his neck.

Matt jumped up, pointed the Glock at his target and fired once. That's all he needed. The barrel of the rifle flipped upward

on its bipod and remained still. Matt charged up the hill toward
the sniper's den. He was sweaty and shirtless and anxious to see
the son-of-a-bitch who'd murdered his ex-partner. Julie's cries still
haunted the forest as he scrambled the last few steps, his Glock
out in front of him. Matt kicked away the brush and pulled off
the layers of branches that covered the sniper. He tugged on the
shooter's shirtsleeve and rolled over his limp frame. Then he froze.

"Rami," he gasped.

Afran Rami moaned and squeezed both of his hands over
the entrance wound just below his heart. His shirt was already
saturated with blood. He didn't have long.

Matt's mouth went dry. "Where is he, Rami?"

"He'll find you first." Rami tried to grin, but failed.

"Where?" Matt asked again, but it was too late. A pair of dead
eyes stared up at him while an ambulance siren wailed in the
distance. Matt turned and saw the open view the kid had of the
Bracco's front porch. Nick was down behind the wooden railing
and Julie was hunched over him, moving with frantic urgency.

It was starting all over again. Nick had thought the move to
Payson was the answer, but he was wrong. Terrorism doesn't have
a neighborhood. You can't just move away. There are simply hot
targets and cold targets. And Nick and Matt were hot targets.

The ambulance screeched to a stop next to the cabin. Two men
flew out the doors and ran to the porch with their black bags. The
flashing red and white lights seemed out of place at the edge of the
lake. They belonged back in Baltimore swirling against row houses
and illuminating darkened alleys.

Matt took a long look down at Rami's corpse. For the first time
in his career he lamented his marksmanship. He'd wanted to keep
the terrorist alive, just so the warrior could see Matt capture his
new leader.

The familiar squeak of a mountain bike's suspension came
rushing up the path behind him. Jennifer Steele jumped off her
bike and wrapped her arms around his bare torso.

"Are you okay?" Steele asked.

Matt gave her a gentle squeeze. "I'm all right."

Steele pulled away and examined his banged up face. "That's
a relative term."

Matt wiped his forehead and came back with bloody fingers.
He'd been going so hard, the adrenalin had disguised the pain.

She looked past him at the corpse. "Who is he?"

Matt looked down. "Afran Rami."

"He's with the KSF?"

"Yeah," Matt said. "Temir Barzani's nephew. Barzani probably offered him the opportunity to kill Nick."

"You mean *try* to kill Nick."

Matt snapped his head to face her. Steele's wobbly smile said it all. She pointed to a spot between her left shoulder and her left breast. A spot where no major organs resided. A survivable spot, even from a 7mm Magnum.

"He's alive?" Matt said.

Steele shrugged. "You don't want to see the exit wound, but he's going to make it."

Matt thought for a moment. "I need to see him."

"I'm sure he's on his way to the hospital by now."

Matt nodded absently, trying to figure out the best way to proceed. Without Nick by his side, he was at a momentary standstill.

Steele tilted her head. "What are you thinking?"

"Did Nick say anything?"

"Yes," she said. "He was in shock, but he urged me to get to you. He wanted you to know that it wasn't a pro. Otherwise, he said, he'd be dead already."

"What else?"

Steele shook her head. "He's lying there practically bleeding out and he's telling me to go back and help you. Like I need incentive."

She turned sad and Matt gathered her in his arms. "It's all right," he said.

She dug her face into his neck and sighed. They stood there embracing for a moment, letting their heartbeats settle into a steady rhythm.

Then Steele said, "It's just starting, isn't it?"

Matt smoothed her hair and never even considered lying. "Yes."

"How well do you know Barzani?"

"Well."

"Are you better than him?"

"Yes."

They clung to each other, sorting things out in their heads.

Finally, Steele pulled back and said, "You can't kill every terrorist in the world, you know."

Matt smiled. He leaned down and kissed her on the forehead. "I'll try to remember that."

Chapter 2

Payson Memorial Hospital was a small forty-bed brick building which sat on a hill at the east end of town. Nick Bracco's room seemed appropriately dreary with the window blinds narrowed and the overhead fluorescent lights beaming. It was the following morning and Nick was still sleeping off the effects of the anesthesia.

Matt sat cross-legged and watched Julie Bracco gently sweep loose strands of hair out of her husband's face, while Jennifer Steele sat next to him, her tablet computer on her lap, reading the latest FBI updates. She nudged Matt and handed him her tablet. The front page of the *Washington Post* was displayed on her screen. The cover story was about the murder of FBI agent Dave Tanner last night. Matt took a breath and tried to take it all in. Dave was their teammate back when they were terrorist specialists. It didn't take much imagination to understand why Nick and Dave were targeted. The KSF was trying to eliminate the team which had silenced their leader. He read the full article, but there was no word about any of the other three members of the team being singled out.

He handed Steele back her tablet and shook his head, letting her know it wasn't time to tell Julie about Dave. Matt's mind raced as he watched Nick, eager to see a sign of him regaining consciousness. He desperately needed his ex-partner's help and he tried to will Nick awake with the weight of his stare.

"You look worried," Julie said.

"Does that bother you?"

"Actually, it does. You're his guardian angel. If you're worried, what should I be feeling?" Her voice cracked on the last word.

"I'm not worried, Jule," Matt said. "I'm just working it out in my head."

"He already knows who's behind the shooting," Steele said absently while tapping her keyboard.

Julie's eyebrows rose as she looked at Matt for an explanation. Matt glared at Steele.

"She deserves to know," Steele said. "Nick would tell her."

"Who is he?" Julie asked him.

Matt sighed. He knew Julie too well to give her the company line. "His name is Temir Barzani. He was one of Kharrazi's top lieutenants. When we raided the KSF's safe house, Barzani was one of the few who escaped. That always bothered me."

"And he wants Nick dead for killing Kharrazi?"

Matt shrugged.

"How many members of the Kurdish Security Force are still roaming around the area?"

Matt had to think. "If I were to guess, I'd say ten. Maybe less."

Julie looked away. She appeared to be struggling to hold it together.

"Jule?" Matt said.

Julie focused on the bed sheets. "It's just never going to end, is it?"

"Jule, listen—"

The door opened and the deputy who was guarding the door stuck his head inside and said, "There's a Tommy Bracco here."

Matt lowered his head and sighed. "Great."

Julie's face brightened. "Yes, send him in."

A dark-haired man wearing a brown leather jacket walked in with a purple toothpick dangling from the corner of his mouth. He immediately frowned at the sight of Nick in bed. Julie jumped up and threw her arms around him.

"I'm so glad you came," she said. Tears glistened in her eyes.

"Like I'm gonna sit in Baltimore while someone takes pot shots at my big cousin here."

Matt covered his face with his hand. Tommy coming to Payson only made his job that much tougher. It was a family hurdle he'd jumped through in the past and he wasn't eager for an encore.

Tommy Bracco pulled back from Julie's embrace and smiled. "You still got the prettiest eyes I ever seen."

Julie blushed.

Tommy's face turned severe as he moved toward the bed and examined Nick's bandaged shoulder. Nick had a tube coming from the crook of his elbow and his mouth hung open helplessly.

Tommy pulled the covers up a little and said, "How is he?"

"He'll recover," Julie said. Her voice sounded braver now that Tommy was there. It was a naïve confidence Matt never fully understood. He simply chalked it up to a Sicilian thing. Something

Matt always contended with whenever Nick's family was involved.

Tommy meticulously made his way around the bed, tugging on the blanket, moving Nick's limp arm to a more masculine position, pulling up on his blue gown to cover his shoulder. As he tended to Nick's appearance, he glanced at Matt briefly, just long enough to let everyone know who he was about to speak with.

"I just want one thing from you," Tommy said, adjusting Nick's pillow. "I want a name."

Matt stuck a piece of gum in his mouth and began a slow chew.

Tommy let it go almost a minute before he stopped fussing over his cousin, then pulled his purple toothpick from his mouth and pointed it at Matt. "Let's you and me take a little walk."

Matt stood. His six-foot-three frame loomed a good three inches over Tommy. He chewed his gum with more fervor.

"Knock it off," Steele said. She dropped her tablet onto the chair next to her and stood between the two combatants. "Both of you want the same thing so let's not allow testosterone get in the way."

Tommy smiled a big affable smile. He returned his toothpick to the corner of his mouth. "I always did like you," he said to Steele. "You've got . . . uh . . ." he snapped his fingers, "what's the word I'm looking for?"

"Chutzpah," Julie said.

"Yeah, that's it, chutzpah."

Now everyone smiled except Matt. Here was Tommy being Tommy, getting everyone comfortable with his streetwise humor, acting dumb, playing the innocent buffoon. It was something he did so well, Matt almost fell for it. But Matt had seen Tommy operate and there was nothing innocent about his motives. He never made a move that wasn't calculated.

"Why can't you two work together?" Julie asked.

"Come on, Jule," Matt said. "Be sensible. I know he's family, but . . ." he waved his left arm toward Tommy. "He's also part of a different family. A family that doesn't have a lot of respect for the law."

"Oh really?" Julie folded her arms. "I'm curious. When Kemel Kharrazi was terrorizing our nation and killing innocent civilians, who did you and Nick go to for help to track him down?"

Matt just shook his head. Some decisions came with ghosts, but that one was going to haunt him a lifetime.

"And who did the FBI go to when they needed underground information about the blasting caps?" Julie continued. "And why did . . ."

Julie went on, but Matt didn't need to hear any longer. He knew the direction she was headed and Matt's argument was tepid compared to the solace Tommy's presence offered. After all, her husband was just a few feet away recovering from a gunshot wound.

Matt moved to the window, pulled up the blinds and looked out over the stretch of grass that surrounded the hospital. A camera crew from a local TV station was setting up their equipment in the parking lot. The sheriff had just been shot and it would certainly remain the lead story for another day or two. A slow parade of cars meandered past the news crew, while pedestrians were pulled aside by a female reporter eager for a scoop.

Matt still felt like a foreigner in the mountains of Arizona. He wouldn't be there if not for reuniting with Steele . . . or his ex-partner deciding to leave the bureau for a simpler life. Matt wasn't sure which circumstance drew him more.

He felt Steele's fingertips on his shoulder.

"Tommy just wants to help," Steele said.

"I know what he wants," Matt said to the window.

The truth was, Matt didn't know how hard to press. He missed Nick's direction. Nick and Tommy were closer than most brothers. It would be so much easier if Nick were lucid enough to share his thoughts.

A hearse slowly made its way around the perimeter of the parking lot. It was there for Afran Rami's body. Something about seeing the hearse gave him a sudden sense of perspective and he reached over his shoulder to touch Steele's hand on his back. She responded by leaning closer. He'd never thought about spending his life with the same woman before he'd met Steele. Now he was getting caught up in the moment. The hearse slowed as it passed in front of the room. Hodgen's Funeral Home was stenciled on the side of the door. Matt got a good look at the driver as he went by.

"Maybe we should all go and have ourselves a talk," Matt said.

"Now you're making sense," Tommy said.

* * *

Kemin Demir slowed the hearse to a crawl as he observed the reporters doing the dance of the news story. Nothing excited Americans like a juicy story. And Kemin was prepared to give them a grand one. The sheriff who was shot would be killed while recovering from an assassination attempt. An assassination which would have been successful had Kemin fired the rifle and not Temir Barzani's nephew. Unfortunately, Kemin wasn't in the position to question the decisions of his leader.

Barzani was clever enough, however, to allow Kemin to finish the job that his nephew couldn't accomplish. Nick Bracco and his partner were both going to pay for killing Kemel Kharrazi, the greatest leader the Kurdish Security Force had ever known. The KSF needed to appear cohesive and there was no better way than retribution.

Kemin parked the hearse in the exact spot the regular driver had instructed—just before Kemin slit his throat. The ceramic knife he carried was sharp enough to decapitate a two-hundred pound man, yet light and invisible to a metal detector.

Kemin got out of the hearse and pushed the buzzer next to the large white door in the rear of the building. A moment later, a man in blue scrubs and a fabric mask dangling around his neck glanced at the hearse and waved Kemin in.

"You here for the Rami kid?" the man asked.

Kemin nodded.

The man gestured to a silver gurney where a teenage boy lay naked. Rami was a severe shade of white, as if his entire body was sucked dry of blood. The room was dark, but for the silver spotlight which hung directly over the kid's body. The place smelled like a giant pail of antiseptic cleaner.

"Hey," the man said. "Where's Larry?"

"Sick," Kemin said. "I just started on Tuesday, so this is all new to me."

The man seemed to understand, and as expected, he appeared eager to show Kemin how much he knew. These Americans and their bold appetite to exhibit their knowledge.

"Do you have the paperwork?" the man asked.

Kemin produced the proper sheets of paper and the man pointed to a doorway. "Through that door and up the stairs to the

Administrator's office. Ask for Merle. He'll sign the papers for you, then come back and I'll help you load the body."

Kemin smiled. "Thanks."

Once he was inside the guts of the hospital, he knew precisely where to go. His informant had scouted the vicinity hours ago and relayed all of the necessary information. One deputy was guarding Bracco's door and two FBI agents were inside the room with Bracco's wife. They would not be expecting such a brash attempt and Kemin was salivating at the opportunity to surprise them.

Adrenalin rushed through his veins as he walked up the stairs and entered the second floor of the patient rooms. He spotted a directory and counted down the numbers on the doors like the launch sequence of a rocket ship. When he was within thirty feet of Bracco's room he spied the deputy sitting on a chair next to the entrance. The man appeared tired. His legs were spread and his arms were folded across his chest. At first Kemin thought the deputy was examining something on his shirt, but as he got closer he realized the man was asleep. His eyes were completely shut and his chest rose and fell with the cadence of a deep sleep. It alleviated the need for Kemin to slit his throat.

Kemin took a deep breath and grasped the ceramic knife inside his coat pocket as he leaned against the oak door and pushed himself into the room. Two steps inside the hospital room and he knew right away he was in trouble. Nick Bracco wasn't in the bed as expected. Instead, a man wearing a brown leather jacket sat on the end of the bed with a purple toothpick in his mouth. The American gangster. The same man who helped the FBI locate Kemel Kharrazi.

"How ya doing?" the man said. "Glad you could make it."

Kemin was about to charge the man when he sensed a presence to his right. Sitting on a plain, armless chair was the FBI agent, Bracco's old partner. He was aiming a pistol at Kemin and seemed ready to fire it.

"I wouldn't move any further if I were you," the agent said. He was wearing an FBI windbreaker and jeans. Kemin looked around and found no other agents.

"I am here to kill you and your partner," Kemin announced.

The gangster laughed. "He's got large ones, G-man. You have to give him that."

"Take the knife out of your pocket and drop it on the floor," the FBI agent said.

Kemin thought about his options. He could lunge at the gangster and kill him before the gunshot would put him down.

"Now," the agent said. "Or I start firing."

Something in the agent's voice convinced him to drop the knife. He knew the agent was more of a cowboy than most and it wasn't time to start an attack. Not yet.

"Kick it my way," the agent insisted.

Kemin kicked it to him and watched the agent pick it up.

"What else do you have?"

What more did he need? A good knife and two of the best hands in the KSF.

"Nothing," Kemin said.

The gangster hopped off the bed and walked around Kemin as if inspecting for disease. Kemin felt his wallet being pulled from his back pocket so quickly, he had no time to respond. The gangster returned to the bed and sat.

"Let's see what we have here," the gangster said, rummaging through his wallet. The man was so close he almost took a swing at him.

"Look at me," the FBI agent said. When Kemin turned, he saw no emotion in the agent's eyes.

"Where's Barzani?" the agent asked.

Kemin had to stifle a laugh. "What are you going to do — put me in jail?"

"I'm going to get the answers, one way or another."

Kemin smiled. He didn't have a thing to say. The agent could pull every finger from his hands and it wouldn't have an effect on Kemin's desire to talk.

The agent walked up to Kemin and patted him down. Once he was convinced Kemin was free of weapons, he stood directly in front of him and stared. His jaw was tight and his eyes held fire.

"What are you doing?" the gangster said.

The agent didn't respond.

"What, you gonna slap him?" the gangster said. "You think that's gonna get him to sing?"

"Shut up, Tommy" the agent said.

Suddenly, the gangster had a pistol in his hand. From behind the agent, the gangster clocked him hard and the agent went down. The agent's pistol came loose and ended up just a yard from Kemin's feet. Kemin cursed himself for not being prepared for the opportunity. By the time he realized what was happening, the gangster had recovered the agent's pistol and waved one of them at Kemin and the other at the agent.

"Sit down," the gangster ordered the agent.

The agent sat on the floor and rubbed the back of his head. "What the fuck are you doing?"

"I'm doing whatever it takes to get to the bottom of this. It's obvious this dipshit didn't order my cousin to be killed, so I need to find out where the asshole is."

"Listen—"

"No," the gangster barked. "I'm done listening. Now it's time for me to act." He waved the tip of the pistol to a chair in the corner of the room. "Sit over there and watch."

The agent got to his feet and sat down.

The gangster ordered Kemin to sit down a few chairs away from the agent and Kemin complied. It concerned him that the gangster seemed to be in charge of things.

The gangster sat back on the bed and placed one of the guns next to him while sifting through Kemin's wallet with his free hand. He pulled a card or folded piece of paper from his billfold, then tossed it on the bed as discarded junk. Kemin knew there was nothing of true value there.

The gangster hopped off the bed and appraised Kemin without a trace of fear.

"Okay," the gangster said. "You're not going to tell him anything because he can't do anything to you. I mean he's got that whole Constitution thing hanging over his head all the time." The gangster looked over at the agent. "Am I right? It's a fucking wonder people even pay their speeding tickets anymore."

The gangster turned toward Kemin once again. "There's nothing he could do to you physically that could matter in even the slightest."

Kemin almost nodded. The gangster was getting at something.

"So," the gangster said, "what could I do to motivate you?"

Kemin sat silent.

The gangster leaned back on the bed again and continued his fascination with Kemin's wallet.

"How about money?" the gangster continued. "Is that of any use? Nah, supposedly you guys are rolling in dough. Torture? Naw, too unreliable. You'd probably tell me anything I wanna hear."

Suddenly the gangster's face brightened as he uncovered Kemin's fake visa."

"I forgot, you're from Turkey?"

Kemin remained still.

"Holy cow," the gangster said. "What are the odds? It turns out I gotta couple of friends vacationing over there right now. Well, it's more of a business trip," the gangster winked at Kemin. "If you know what I mean."

The way the words came out, Kemin stiffened a bit.

"Don't do this, Tommy," the agent protested.

Kemin wasn't sure what he was talking about.

The gangster pulled a picture from Kemin's wallet. It was a photo of his children from a couple of years ago. They were two and four then. He held it up for Kemin to see.

"One boy, one girl." The gangster smiled a paternal smile. "You must be proud."

Even though they were both half a world away, Kemin's throat became dry. He licked his lips. This turned the gangster's paternal smile into a sinister leer.

"Cut it out," the agent said, more forceful this time.

The gangster grabbed an open laptop computer sitting on a vacant chair and looked at the screen. "Let's see here," he said tapping his fingers on the screen. "It says here, Kemin Demir, twenty-seven-years old. Birthday, July ninth, oh, here's an interesting item—last address in Turkey."

"That's confidential information," the agent barked.

The gangster leaned back onto the bed and casually opened his cell phone. He began to dial a series of numbers. Too many numbers. As he dialed, he said, "I wonder what time it is over there?"

Kemin felt his heart pound in his chest.

As the gangster put the phone to his ear, the agent said, "Tommy, knock it off."

The gangster ignored him as he spoke into the phone. "Gino, what's up?"

There was a pause, then the gangster said, "Hey, where are you again in Turkey?" Another pause. "Ankara?"

The gangster looked down at the computer. "Is that anywhere near Sincan? . . . Oh really, not far at all . . . Listen, is the Butcher still with you? . . . Good, and he brought his tools? . . . Oh, good."

Kemin felt his knees become weak.

"Hey," the gangster continued, "what's the weather like over there? . . . Oh wow."

The gangster held his hand over the phone and looked at Kemin. "It's raining cats and dogs over there."

Kemin had spoken to his wife just an hour ago. He could hear thunder throughout the entire conversation.

"Well, don't step in any poodles," the gangster said, then laughed uncontrollably.

Kemin tried to swallow, but came up empty.

"Listen, I have some good news for the Butcher." The gangster stared at the picture of Kemin's two children as if it were the Mona Lisa. "Tell him I have some fresh meat for him."

The gangster held his hand over the phone once again and addressed Kemin. "The Butcher is a pedophile. A real sick bastard, but hey, he knows his way around a carving knife." He returned to the phone. "Yeah, tell him it's exactly the cut he likes." He casually glanced back down at the tablet. "The address is—"

"Wait!" Kemin shouted. He looked over at the FBI agent. "Are you going to allow this?"

The agent said to the gangster, "Any information you acquire now is tainted. It will never hold up in court."

The gangster continued without hesitation. "It's three, nine, four—"

"Stop!" Kemin came to his feet. With the reflex of a cat, the gangster pointed the pistol at his chest.

"Sit down, asshole," the gangster said.

Kemin sat.

"Not you, Gino," the gangster said into the phone.

Kemin struggled to gain a normal breath. Part of him wished this was all a big game they were playing, but he couldn't afford to guess wrong.

Kemin looked down. "I'll tell you what you want."

The gangster continued his conversation as if he didn't hear him.

"I said I'd tell you what you want," Kemin repeated, louder this time.

The gangster paused. He looked at Kemin with dark eyes. "You're interrupting my phone call."

"That's right," the gangster said to the phone. "Three, nine, four, Evins Street. Sincan. That's right."

"They're deep in the woods," Kemin blurted, desperate. "I can give you exact directions. I can take you there."

The gangster looked over at Kemin annoyed and kept talking. "That's right, Gino, tell the butcher to take his time. Work close to the bones."

"Tommy," the agent said. "He's talking to you."

The gangster pulled the phone down to his chest momentarily. "What, you think he's telling me the truth?"

"I am," Kemin insisted. "I am. Please tell them to stop."

The gangster frowned. Then he slowly raised the phone to his ear. "Listen, Gino, I'll call you back. Wait about forty-five minutes and you don't hear back from me, tell the Butcher to knock himself out."

The gangster snapped the phone shut and sneered at Kemin. "This better be good."

Chapter 3

Anton Kalinikov sat at the coffee shop against a window and read the Washington Post with his legs crossed. The front page was consumed with the death of FBI agent Dave Tanner who was murdered in a nightclub parking lot the night before. Kalinikov read the details with extreme interest. He found some discrepancies with the timeline, but otherwise was satisfied with the reporting. There was no mention of witnesses or potential leads. Kalinikov was still amazed at the amount of details the American press would release to the public.

He waited for his coffee to go cold before drinking. It was how he was raised to drink the beverage back in St. Petersburg. Back before he was recruited into the KGB. Back when the Soviet agency was the most effective information-gathering organization in the world. The perception of the killers who saturated the KGB was highly exaggerated compared to amount of spies it had. The number of pure assassins never actually reached double digits. It made Kalinikov's skills that much more valuable.

Kalinikov was there when they shut the office down for good in the early nineties. Once his job had been eliminated, he began freelancing. To be safe he traveled to distant continents. Places where the authorities had a very low level of sophistication. It's the reason he'd never worked in America before this trip. Not that he was afraid, just smart. He could assassinate a Brazilian official with a half-hour notice. Very low risk, yet the compensation was still quite high for the job. An FBI agent, however, required some heavy preparation. Four FBI agents required four times the work, which is why at his age he demanded the huge sum to be cajoled into making the trip. It would be his final job before retiring and he needed enough to send him off to a warm island paradise.

His cell phone vibrated. He pushed a button and saw the text message:

TRANSFER HAS BEEN COMPLETED.

Kalinikov smiled. One quarter of his compensation was now in his Swiss bank account. He pushed another couple of buttons and confirmed the transfer. Next, he unfolded a small piece of paper with four handwritten names and crossed off Dave Tanner's name. Even though Kalinikov hadn't been to America, he was keenly aware of his targets. All four names listed were the FBI agents who'd made up a squad of six counter-terrorism specialists known as, "The Team." There were two other members in Arizona, but they were none of his concern. His responsibility remained with the four agents in D.C.

Kalinikov didn't care about who or why, as long as he got paid. From his only phone conversation with his employer, he'd discerned a Kurdish accent. After the death of Kemel Kharrazi it was easy to imagine the reason these four men's fates were to follow that of the Kurdish terrorist's.

Turning the page, he noticed another small article of interest. A report of an assassination attempt on an ex-FBI agent who was now a sheriff in Gila County, Arizona. Apparently the suspect was a young Kurdish terrorist who had been shot to death by the agent's ex-partner. Kalinikov shook his head in disgust. Everyone wanted to be an assassin but nobody was willing to put in the time to become a professional.

By now the FBI knew these two incidents were not a coincidence. It concerned Kalinikov, but not too much. He was far superior in his abilities to fall prey to a tail or be caught finishing his work. It always came down to routine. The same routine which caused the next name on his list to become vulnerable. FBI agent Mel Downing's weakness was his sweet tooth. Every day after work he would walk into this very coffee shop and buy a chocolate muffin to eat on his way home. His wife was a meddling woman who'd watched every calorie the poor guy ate, so Downing would get in a last sugar fix before he went home to his mate's scrutiny.

Kalinikov checked his watch, then looked up in time to see Downing enter the coffee shop and move to the sales counter. The assassin waited patiently as the clerk picked up one of the two remaining chocolate muffins with a pair of tongs and placed it in a bag. The same two muffins which Kalinikov had ordered, then laced with a slow-working poison, then quickly returned the muffins for two chocolate scones instead. He'd laced the muffins so quickly, so adroitly, that he'd never even left the counter. He needed the clerk to know they were untouched as he apologized for his mistake and assured they were still fresh for another client. The clerk, in a hurry, placed the two muffins back in the case.

Now, Agent Downing was scanning the room. He was trying to be inconspicuous, but Kalinikov could sense the anxiety in his eyes. Downing couldn't possibly recognize him. Kalinikov had always worn a disguise and never left a true surveillance image behind any job he'd ever done.

Downing took the bag from the clerk and smiled. As he left the shop, he dipped his hand greedily into the bag and stuffed his mouth with the delicious toxin. The amount of ricin powder he'd already swallowed was lethal. The vomiting and diarrhea would begin within a couple of hours, then severe dehydration followed by low blood pressure. Unless he'd had every major organ transplanted within the next forty-eight hours he'd be dead.

Kalinikov watched the man walk blissfully down the sidewalk toward home. He crossed Downing's name from the list and took a sip from his cold cup of coffee. He shook his head. Human beings thrived on routine. It gave them comfort in its ritual. But in the hands of someone with Kalinikov's experience, routine could be very lethal.

* * *

Before he even opened his eyes, Nick Bracco heard his wife's voice. She seemed to be stifling a giggle.

"Can you imagine?" Julie said. "I'd have paid anything to be there."

When Nick's eyes gained focus, Julie was at the foot of his bed in an animated discussion with Jennifer Steele.

"Who knew those two brutes could act?" Steele said.

Julie turned to see Nick trying to prop himself up on his elbows.

"No, no," Julie ran over and rested her palms on his torso. "Stay down, baby."

Nick's left shoulder pinched him with a searing burn that sent a nauseous spike to his throat. He swallowed it down, then allowed gravity to settle his head back to the pillow.

Julie smiled down at him. "How's my boy?"

Nick fought a drug-induced stupor. "How long was I out?"

"You slept through the night," Julie said. "The surgery went fine. The best thing you could do right now is rest."

Nick's patchy memory sprung to life. "Who shot me?"

Steele came around Julie to face him. "Afran Rami."

"Rami?"

"Apparently the KSF is bitter."

Nick nodded. "Where's Matt?"

That brought a smile to both of the women's faces.

"Yeah, well, he and Tommy are sort of working together."

Nick squinted.

"You see," Julie said, "while you were recovering, Kemin Demir stopped by."

Nick's eyes widened.

"It's okay," Julie said. "Matt and Tommy took care of it."

"Tell me about it," Nick said.

Julie looked at Steele and Matt's new partner seemed to give it some thought.

"They played good cop, bad mobster," she said. "I guess Matt knew about a weakness."

"His kids," Nick said.

Steele's mouth opened. "How did you—"

"We were together for ten years. There's very little that only one of us knows."

"Yeah, well, they got Kemin to lead them to the KSF safe house."

Nick lurched upward, but an acute sting in his shoulder forced him back down.

"They're liable to walk into a trap," he said with a short breath.

Steele's eyes showed concern. "They know," she said.

Nick looked out the window and tried to focus. Barzani couldn't have many soldiers left. Afran Rami was his youngest and his nephew. He must've begged his uncle to be the one to kill Nick Bracco. The kid was inexperienced with rifles, so it was a tactical mistake to send him in the first place. But Barzani was loyal to a fault.

"Nick," Steele's voice became somber. "Dave Tanner is dead."

Nick put his head back on the pillow and closed his eyes. He didn't need to hear any details, he already knew who and why. He thought of Dave's wife and daughter and sighed. The team had become a target. Barzani had enough money to hire every hit man in America to track them down and get revenge for killing their leader.

Nick sat up on his elbows and thought about the rest of the team. "Anyone else?"

Steele shook her head. "Everyone else is fine."

Julie's face wilted with apprehension. With her hand she held her stomach as if trying to protect her unborn child. Nick reached over and touched her arm.

"It's okay, Sweetie," he said, looking as confident as he could while wearing a baby-blue hospital gown. "We'll take care of this."

Julie bit her lip and nodded, but Nick could see the memories coming back to her. The death of Don Silkari while trying to stop the KSF from destroying the White House. She must've known the arduous task ahead of them and wondered where it might stop. Nick sat there wondering the same thing himself. But he knew Barzani was the key. If he found him, he would cut the head off the KSF's American team.

* * *

"Something's wrong," Temir Barzani said. He wore olive fatigues and stood at the head of the kitchen table to address his soldiers. Inside the log cabin were seven KSF members who were assembled around the long, oak table with complete focus on their leader.

"It's thirty minutes past his contact time," Barzani said. "We must assume he's been captured, or worse."

"Worse?" a soldier asked.

"Yes. He could have given up our location."

A murmur of disagreement filled the small room. The tepid chatter was silenced by the loud thud of a fist pounding on the table. All eyes returned to their leader.

"Now," Barzani said, "until we hear from Kemin, we must prepare for uninvited guests. Secure the cabin."

"But, Sarock, if Kemin is merely late, he might—"

One glare was all it took for Barzani to receive the desired submission from his subordinate. Barzani had two requirements from his team while they occupied American soil: Speak only English and never second-guess his orders. Both rules came from the greatest leader the Kurdish Security Force had ever known, Kemel Kharrazi. Since Kharrazi's demise, Barzani had been forced into a leadership role he reluctantly assumed. It was a suicide mission they were on, but Barzani kept that to himself so he could receive the full thrust of obedience he needed to succeed.

Barzani appraised his soldiers with a stern eye. "Why are you still gathered here? Prepare for intruders. Now!"

The kitchen buzzed with screeching wooden chair-legs and shuffling feet as the team headed toward their assigned posts. Barzani would not make the mistakes his predecessor had made. He would leave no opportunities to thwart his plans. Especially from the FBI agents who'd destroyed Kharrazi.

One of the soldiers stayed by his side awaiting instructions. The man was his finest lieutenant, Hestin Jirdeer, who was the one person Barzani trusted above all others.

Jirdeer waited until the room cleared before he said, "Rami was a brave soldier."

Barzani understood the meaning. Rami did everything he could to become just like his uncle, but he was too inexperienced to take on such a task. Barzani wondered whether he'd undermined his authority by making such a brash decision, or whether he was displaying his willingness to lose his own nephew to prove a point.

As if Jirdeer could sense his concern, he looked his leader in the eye and said, "It was the right choice."

Barzani appreciated the gesture. He nodded.

"And so was Kemin," Jirdeer said. "However, these men are not to be underestimated."

Barzani looked at his lieutenant with a questioning expression. "You have already sent for the assassin?"

"Yes, Sarock. We may be low on manpower, but we have an excess of funds. These funds can pay for someone else to achieve our goals here. I think this man is a good choice."

Barzani looked down at his computer screen where he'd just transferred a half a million dollars to pay for the deaths of the remaining FBI agents who'd conspired against them.

He pointed to the screen. "Is this man as good as The Russian?"

Jirdeer hesitated. "It is doubtful anyone could be so good, Sarock."

That was a very true statement. The Russian had no equal. It's the reason they'd decided to overpay him. Vengeance had no price tag.

Barzani heard the bustle of footsteps overhead. His men were acquiring positions for battle. At one time there were more than two hundred KSF soldiers in the United States. This was before the American FBI agent had tricked their great leader and ruined their plans of forcing U.S. troops from their homeland in Turkey. A place where Kurds made up twenty percent of the population, yet after thirty years of negotiating with the Turkish government for autonomy, their language was still barred from schools and official parliament meetings. The time for negotiation was clearly over. It was time to make the United States pay for their support of the Turkish government. But more importantly to Barzani, it was time for revenge.

"Do you trust this man?" Barzani asked.

"No," Jirdeer said. "But he is no friend of law officials."

Barzani grinned. He always valued his lieutenant's directness. There was never any worry of pretense. He pulled a key from his pocket and handed it to Jirdeer. "Take whatever you need."

As Jirdeer reached for the key, Barzani pulled it back. "Make sure he gets the woman. I want this agent to suffer. I want him to understand what losing a family member is like."

Jirdeer took the key. "As you wish, Sarock."

* * *

"Why are we stopping?" Tommy asked from the back seat.

Matt had slowed the sedan and pulled to the curb of the suburban tree-lined street. "We wait here for backup. Luke is picking up Jennifer."

"What are you talking about?" Tommy said. "I wanna get this rat bastard while I still got venom running through my blood."

"They've got six, maybe seven soldiers up there. We're not going to accomplish our goals alone."

"I gotta tell ya." Tommy shook his head. "Taking orders is not my strong suit. It's the reason I never got married."

"Relax. They'll be here in ten minutes."

Kemin's face grew smug in the passenger seat.

"The fuck you so happy about?" Tommy blurted.

Kemin's smile disappeared. He seemed reluctant to engage Tommy in dialogue. As if he might give Tommy more information than he'd already had.

Tommy stepped out into the cool autumn air.

"Where are you going?" Matt said.

"I'm taking a little stroll."

"Get back in the car!"

Tommy dug his toothpick in between two back molars and

took in the surroundings. Nice rolling hills. The houses were separated by acres of trees. No two homes looked alike. Nothing like the endless parade of row houses that framed the bowling-lane streets back in Baltimore.

"I like it up here," Tommy said.

"Good, now get back in the car."

Tommy looked down at Kemin in the front seat. "How far away are we?"

Matt jumped out of the car and slammed the roof. "Dammit, Tommy, we do this my way."

"Your way put my cousin in the hospital. I'm not so impressed —"

"I'll take you," Kemin interrupted.

No one spoke.

"You two fight like old women arguing over a soup recipe," Kemin said.

Tommy smiled. "See, even the terrorists are accommodating up in the mountain air." He opened the passenger door and gestured Kemin to get out.

"Tommy," Matt said. "You're screwing this whole thing up."

"Let me tell you something, G-man." Tommy pulled on Kemin's arm until he was out of the car. "A kind of operation like these guys have, they've got a system. This putz is overdue for his call-in. They know something's wrong. If we wait until those two get here they could be gone."

Matt seemed to consider the idea.

Tommy raised his eyebrows to emphasize his point. "You see, I understand these guys better than you think. We don't have time. At least let's get close and be ready to stop them if they try to bolt."

Matt lowered his head for a moment, then slammed his door shut and came around the car. "All right. We get to within five hundred yards and that's it. I'll monitor them with my field glasses."

"Is that the same as binoculars? You government types always trying to complicate things."

Matt shook his head in disgust and motioned for Kemin to show them the way.

Tommy took out his pistol and held it waist high. "Don't get cute, unless you can run faster than a thousand feet a second."

Kemin took slow, deliberate steps and seemed to be searching for markers along the way. Tommy didn't like the way Kemin observed the leaf-covered floor of the forest. It gave him an uneasy feeling, like when someone had a winning hand at a poker table.

Tommy was about to tell Matt about this when his world fell out from under him. He plunged to the bottom of a massive hole with enough force to empty his lungs. He gasped for air as tears filled his eyes. The back of his head throbbed from the impact. He tried to make sense of what just happened. He looked up and eight feet above him were long strands of branches with leaves glued to them. They covered up the opening. A couple of the branches came down with him into the hole.

He heard Matt shout. Then, two gunshots pierced the forest.

Matt stopped shouting.

Tommy groped around the hole for his gun, but it wasn't there. His breaths were coming in quick spurts. It was dark and the dirt was cold and moist. The gun, where did his gun go? His question was answered when he looked up. Kemin leered down at him with his arm extended. In his hand was Tommy's gun.

"Great," Tommy said, catching his breath. "You found my gun. Thanks."

"Throw me your cell phone," Kemin said.

"What's the matter all of a sud—"

"Give me your cell phone or I kill you like I did the FBI agent."

"See, I just don't see myself doing that."

"Goodbye, you stupid, stupid man." Kemin stretched out his shooting hand and smiled a wicked smile. Tommy sat motionless. He shut his eyes tight and waited. When the shot came, it was quieter than he'd expected. As if Kemin had moved farther away. He waited for the pain, but it didn't come. When he opened his eyes Kemin was gone. He couldn't put it together in his mind until he saw a different face come into view above him. It was Matt. His face was dirty. His gun was by his side.

"You okay?" Matt said.

"How?"

Matt pounded his chest with his fist and the unmistakable sound of Kevlar rung out. "I slipped it on before we left the hospital."

"You know something?" Tommy said. "I'm beginning to have a crush on you."

Chapter 4

Joe Tessamano sat down on the barstool at the Winchester Saloon and raised his index finger to the female bartender. "Draft Bud," he said.

The woman gave him one of the best tip-grubbing smiles he'd ever seen. She was half his age, but that didn't stop his imagination from drifting away. He watched her in those tight jeans as she poured his beer and placed it on a cocktail napkin in front of him. He slid a twenty dollar bill toward her and said, "Keep it."

She beamed and Joe smiled back. He took a sip of his beer and looked around the darkened bar. It was his first trip to Payson since he'd moved to Scottsdale from the east coast. Scottsdale was oozing money, with oversized trucks and hot moms driving convertibles and everything else this little mountain town wasn't. But he hadn't driven the hour and a half for pleasure. This was simply a business trip. Or at least it had the potential to be a business trip should the circumstances present themselves.

He reached into his shirt pocket and pulled out a hand-rolled Dominican cigar. The Cubans had the best tobacco, but the Dominicans knew how to roll better than anyone he'd ever seen. He licked his lips, then placed the cigar in his mouth. The female bartender gave him a firm look.

"Don't worry, darling," he assured her. "I'm just getting it lubed up for later."

She grinned and Joe winked back.

A thin man with dark skin and thick mustache sat next to Joe. "Are you Joseph?" the man said with a Middle Eastern accent.

Joe didn't like the guy already. He was stiff and uncomfortable and

drawing attention to himself just by his formal behavior. He'd called him Joseph as if he'd learned his name from looking up Joe's driver's license.

"Joseph?" Joe said. "That's who you're looking for?"

The man nodded. "Yes, please."

If Joe didn't suspect the guy was carrying an envelope full of money he would've just shot him right then. Joe looked around the shadowed room, pool tables and dartboards filled the east side of the bar. Lynyrd Skynyrd blared from an antique jukebox. He gestured toward a booth on the other side of the bar. The two of them slid in on opposite sides.

"What exactly are you looking for?" Joe said, blunt and not caring how it sounded.

The man swiveled his head around, then said, "We need someone eliminated."

"We?" Joe said. "Who's we?"

"I mean me," the man tried to recover.

"No, you said we. So tell me who I might be working for and maybe I'll listen."

The man with the mustache just stared. It wasn't a deep thoughtful stare, just a blank expression like he hadn't considered the possibility the assassin would ask any questions.

Joe got out of the booth and patted the guy on the arm as he passed. "See ya, pal. Good luck finding someone stupid enough to work blind."

He'd only taken four or five steps before he felt a hand on his shoulder. "Please," the man said, "let me explain."

Joe had no intention of leaving. He was way too intrigued to let this guy fly the coop, but he wasn't going to be bullied by an incompetent negotiator.

They returned to the booth and Joe twisted the tip of his cigar between his lips, waiting for an explanation. The man looked down at his hands folded on the table.

"Do you know the name Kemel Kharrazi?" the man said.

"Of course."

"Well, when he died he left behind some loyal followers." The man looked up at Joe as if that might be enough. Joe kept his mouth shut which he knew would force the imbecile to keep talking.

"And some of these followers have a grudge against the person who murdered their leader."

Joe wanted to tell the guy that Kharrazi wasn't exactly murdered, but that was beside the point. As far as he knew Kharrazi was trying to escape an FBI manhunt when one of their agents tracked him down to a path in the woods of Payson and won a game of chicken against the terrorist. The two of them were supposedly racing head-on toward each other with trucks when

Kharrazi turned into a tree and died from the collision. But Joe still stayed quiet and watched the man raise his eyebrows as if Joe should finish the story on his own.

"I'm listening," Joe said, playing stupid just to watch the guy squirm.

"So," the man said. He looked around the room. Only a few people were playing pool and two old-timers were watching an east coast football game at the bar. It was noon and the Winchester wasn't exactly a lunchtime type of place. "We're part of a group of people who support the Kurdish search for a nation of their own."

"The KSF," Joe said.

"I didn't say that."

Joe shrugged. He wasn't particularly political, but you had to be living in a cave not to know who the KSF was. "All right, who's the target?"

The man drew a thin envelope from his pants pocket and laid it in front of Joe.

Joe opened the envelope and saw the picture inside. He had to hide his surprise.

"You know her?" the man said.

Joe nodded, but kept it straight. "I never met her, but sure I know her. Most people around here would."

"Are there any problems?"

Joe lifted his glass and took a long pull on his beer. Now's when the negotiations began and it was one of the few pleasures Joe missed about the business.

"Well," Joe began, "I've been retired almost ten years now. I'm not exactly chomping at the bit to take any unnecessary chances, if you know what I mean."

The man was paying full attention, which was good.

"Plus, this isn't your ordinary get-rid-of my-ex-wife kind of thing," Joe added.

He thought he saw the man twitch at the idea Joe might decline the job.

"So, I don't think this is something worth the risk," Joe finally said.

The man reached into his jeans pocket and pulled out a lumpy envelope and placed it in front of Joe.

"I give you ten thousand right now," the man blurted. "The other forty when you're done."

Joe looked at the envelope, then up into the man's jittery face. "When does this need to be done?" he asked.

"By tomorrow."

This time Joe didn't hide his surprise. "Tomorrow?"

"Yes."

Joe picked up the envelope and felt it like he was testing a ripe cantaloupe. Then he put it on the seat next to him.

"Tell you what," Joe said. "You give me that other envelope you're carrying with the forty and maybe we can agree on something. But you'll give me another fifty when I'm done."

"Another fifty? That's one hundred — that's double what we agreed."

Joe pointed his cigar at him. "We didn't agree on jack shit. I said I'd listen to your proposal, that's all. Now, those are my terms. I don't need any of this to live a full and happy life."

Joe gave the man his hundred-thousand-dollar smile and waited.

Finally, the man pursed his lips and pulled a larger envelope from his pocket and handed it to Joe. "Okay. By tomorrow."

There, Joe thought, sticking the cigar in his mouth. *That wasn't so hard, was it?*

Chapter 5

Matt tossed Kemin's corpse into the hole, then he and Tommy continued their search of the KSF's safe house. They weaved their way through the dense woods twenty yards apart, both seeking traces of the unordinary. Something that was out of place in the serene, suburban cabin community.

Matt made eye contact with Tommy and watched him shrug.

"I'm a city boy," Tommy said. "I don't even know what to look for."

They walked further, slowly, listening to the leaves crunch under their steps. Five minutes later Matt held out his hand and snapped his fingers. Tommy stopped. A bush moved fifty yards ahead of them. It was the type of movement only a trained sniper would notice. It wasn't wind.

Matt motioned Tommy to take cover and Tommy slid behind a large tree with his pistol by his side. Matt dropped to his knees, tucked behind a fallen log. His eyes focused on one spot, while monitoring his peripheral vision. There was unnatural movement all around them. Bushes, tree limbs, leaves along the forest floor. He could sense the danger and tried to quantify his targets. He counted at least six. That meant there were more than ten. Not a number even he could overcome.

Tommy poked his head out and searched for something he would never see.

"Get back," Matt said.

"I don't see nothing."

Matt sighed. All of his sharp-shooting prowess wasn't going to get them out of this. The only thing that gave him hope was the fact that these weren't terrorists. They were too organized. Too much training as a team. Terrorists weren't good at playing together. These were professionals. They acted like Special Forces, but that couldn't be right. The FBI SWAT team had the only pros around and they were down in Phoenix two hours away.

"Hey," Tommy said. "What're we waiting for?"

"Drop your gun," Matt said.

Tommy cocked his head. "Come again?"

"Drop your gun and raise your hands up high."

Tommy just squinted.

"Listen to me. If you don't do what I tell you, you'll be dead in a few moments."

Matt dropped his Glock and slowly walked out from behind the tree. He placed his hands on his head and motioned for Tommy to follow his lead.

Tommy hesitated.

"If not for me, Kemin would have finished you off an hour ago," Matt said. "Trust me. I know what I'm doing."

Tommy grimaced. He dropped his pistol and walked into the open with his palms on his head.

"You'd better," Tommy said.

It only took a moment to prove Matt's theory. A male voice called to them from a spot thirty yards in front of them.

"Keep coming," the voice said.

They sprang from the left, the right and the treetops. In less than twenty seconds a dozen soldiers in camouflage gear surrounded them with automatic weapons and blackface. The clicks of chamber rounds echoed in the quiet of the woods.

Their leader was easy to spot. He was the one who maintained a leisurely stroll while everyone else knelt into a perfect attack position. The leader must've been pushing sixty, but he seemed fit and alert.

"FBI," Matt said, holding his hands lower and waiting permission to remove his credentials from his pocket.

The man nodded.

Matt pulled out his creds and watched the man examine it for a moment, before returning it to him. The man glanced at Tommy.

"He's working with me. An informant," Matt said.

The man seemed to buy it. He held out his open palm to Matt. "Name's Buck Martin."

Matt shook his hand. "Matt McColm. This is Tommy Bracco."

Buck shook Tommy's hand.

"Which unit are you with?" Matt asked.

"Well," Buck said, "we're not exactly with the military. We're private contractors. Iron Mountain, USA."

"Mercenaries? In Payson, Arizona?" Tommy said.

"Soldiers of fortune, if you wish," Buck said. "The fortune is paid to us all over the world. Even here in the states."

Matt gestured toward the soldiers still training their M4s at him and Tommy. "Any chance of getting them to relax?"

Buck nodded. "Stand down, boys."

In unison the soldiers placed their weapons to their side.

"May I ask exactly what you're being paid to do?" Matt said.

Buck seemed to mull it over in his head. Finally, he said, "We're contracted to rid the area of residual terrorists. They're believed to have dug in and waited out the original eradication."

"You're in luck. I'm one of two the resident agents here in Payson. I was here during the original eradication. My partner and I came over from Baltimore and —"

"Nick Bracco," Buck said. "Yes, I know all about you. Unfortunately, we're not set up to work with outside agencies. We're much more effective on our own."

That stopped Matt. He'd never heard of any law enforcement turning down help. But these guys weren't the law. They were more closely related to hired assassins.

"You mind if I ask you something?" Tommy said.

Buck nodded.

"You know where this safe house is?"

Buck paused. "That's privileged information."

"Oh that's fucking rich," Tommy said. "You see, that little hesitation tells me you don't know squat. We're in the middle of nowhere searching for a group of foreign soldiers and you're too privileged to accept our help?"

Tommy walked around Buck and said to Matt. "C'mon. We're running out of time. These terrorists already suspect something is up when they didn't hear from Kemin. Let's not give them a reason to skip town."

"Where do you think you're going?" Buck snapped.

Tommy dug a bright orange toothpick into the corner of his mouth. "The fuck you gonna do about it, pops? You gonna shoot an FBI agent and his informant? That your plan?"

"I can't let you interfere with our mission."

"Your mission?" Tommy sneered. "Let me tell you about my little mission. I got a cousin in the hospital from a gunshot wound ordered by someone hiding in these woods. My mission is to stomp my shoe on his throat until he understands my feelings about the matter. That's my mission."

Tommy walked over and picked up his gun, then retrieved

Matt's gun and handed it to him.

"Let's go," Tommy said.

Matt stood there for a moment, weighing his options.

"For crying out loud," Tommy bellowed, "they ain't gonna shoot us. Let's get out of here."

Matt followed Tommy. He looked straight ahead and never wavered, even when Buck hollered for them to stop. Tommy was right, they weren't going to shoot an FBI agent—were they?

Buck gave a command that Matt didn't quite hear. He kept pace with Tommy. The clatter of rifles and machine guns rushing into firing position echoed through the forest. Matt's pulse quickened.

Buck growled another command to his troops.

Matt kept walking.

"One more step and you're both dead men," Buck yelled as clear as if he were a foot away.

Tommy kept going. He waved a middle finger over his shoulder as he continued his stride.

Matt stopped, but didn't turn around. His instincts told him they were bluffing, but he wasn't willing to wager his life on it.

Matt turned to face the troops who looked very much like a firing squad.

"Are you going to shoot me?" Matt asked.

"You bet your ass I am," Buck sneered.

A female voice called from behind Buck's men. The voice was cool and calm. It was Jennifer Steele. She held out her 9mm. Next to her was Deputy Luke Fletcher aiming his rifle at Buck.

"I wouldn't do that if I were you," Steele said.

Buck turned and scoffed at the sight. His men turned their weapons on the two law enforcement officials. "This is your posse, Agent McColm?"

Matt grinned at the sight of Steele coming to save him. "Yeah," he said. "You can call it that."

Buck's amused face turned sour, then he approached Steele with a slow, methodical gait.

"We're contracted to do a job," Buck said, and left it at that.

Steele nodded. "Give me a reason why I shouldn't take you all in for treason?"

"Because," Buck said, "we're all on the same side here."

"Is that what you're calling this?"

Buck sneered at Steele while pointing at Deputy Fletcher. "Is that supposed to scare me?" He made it a point to look at his crew, who were all standing with one eye in their sight, focusing their automatic weapons directly at the deputy. "I mean, what's he going to do, shoot every one of my crew before his body gets pulverized with bullets?"

"No," Steele said. "He's just going to shoot you."

Buck frowned, then gave a nod to his soldiers and they lowered their weapons.

"We have a job to do here," Buck said in a low voice.

Steele put her gun down. "Does your job include threatening an FBI agent?"

"We have a contract with the State Department."

"So?"

Buck looked back at Matt as if he might understand his authority best. "Our contract affords us complete immunity while on our mission. Which includes unlawful deaths."

"What?" Tommy blurted. He looked at Matt. "Is that even possible?"

Matt took a breath and exchanged glances with Steele. They both knew how these private forces worked. If it were a Black Budget Contract, Buck's team could shoot anyone they wanted, whenever they wanted, without any ramifications.

"Yeah," Matt said to Tommy. "It's possible."

Tommy pulled out his cell phone and glanced at the time, then shoved it back into his pocket. He looked at Buck. "Listen, you're a real pisser to chat with, but we've got a terrorist to catch."

"He's right," Matt said. "We have a live target around here."

"Yeah," Buck said. "That's our target."

"Well then let's all get it done," Tommy said.

Matt chewed on his lower lip, searching for a way to make it work. They might be able to combine forces, but there could be only one leader.

It seemed Buck had sensed the same predicament. "All right," he said, "let's join forces and find these guys, but," the experienced soldier glared at Matt, "I'm the one giving the orders here."

Matt shook his head. "I can't do that."

"Tell me," Buck said.

Matt apprised the group of mercenaries who watched intently. "You guys are good, no question."

"The best," Buck said.

"And your equipment is superior."

Buck nodded in agreement.

"But when it comes to terrorists you forget to ask the most important question. Why."

"Who gives a crap why?" Buck snorted. "Let the man upstairs figure that one out for them."

"But you don't track a terrorist the same way you track a drug dealer, or a serial killer."

"Sure you do," Buck said, looking over his men for a moment. "Bad guys are bad guys. You think you're something special just because you and your partner took care of Kemel Kharrazi?"

"No," Matt said. "We just have more experience with this organization."

Buck stretched out his thick neck and sneered. "You think I'm some dumb hick who doesn't understand his adversary?"

Tommy pulled the toothpick from his mouth and pointed it at Buck. "Yeah, I think you're on to something there, killer."

Matt shot Tommy a look and watched him shrug.

"For your information, I happen to know quite a bit about these KSF turds," Buck said. "I know they're tunnel-diggers. I know they don't follow any particular religious sect. And I know they're a little lost ever since your partner won a game of chicken with their leader a few months back."

"That's good," Matt said, moving left toward a particularly thick pine. "Did you know they don't send out scouts with guns?"

"What?" Buck said, looking confused.

"I mean they send their lookouts with knives so they aren't tempted to fire a weapon in the open theatre and give away their position," Matt said, looking straight up the wide pine tree. "Isn't that right, Semir?"

With choreographed speed, Buck's team swarmed the tree where Matt stood and took military positions, their machine guns clattered as they flanked their target, pointing straight up the tree trunk.

There was a small man at the top of the tree with green fatigues and green face, effortlessly blending into the scenery. His legs were wrapped around the pine like it might blast off without him. He looked resigned to his fate as he faced the squad of trained soldiers.

Matt smiled at Buck and said, "Tell me more about these tunnel-diggers."

Chapter 6

President John Merrick sat on the couch reading the daily CIA report on his tablet when the door to the Oval Office opened. There was only one person who would enter the office without knocking.

"Hey, Sam," Merrick said while scrolling the page with his finger.

Secretary of State Samuel Fisk sat on the black leather couch across from him. The two couches faced each other with a rosewood coffee table between them. On the table was a pot of coffee, crackers and a plate of fresh fruit.

Merrick held out his hand and rubbed his fingers together. A moment later he felt a crumpled up five dollar bill in his palm.

"Asshole," Fisk murmured.

"I told you that point guard was underrated," the president said with a smirk.

Fisk filled a small plate with melon chunks and used a toothpick to pick them off the plate like he was spear fishing.

Merrick kept rummaging through the report. "You're going to eat five dollars worth of my food, aren't you?"

"What else would I do?"

Merrick saw Arizona mentioned in the report and it reminded him why Fisk was there.

"So, how's Nick?" Merrick said, listening to Fisk stuff his mouth with cantaloupe.

"He's okay," Fisk said, chewing. "There was minimal structural damage to the shoulder. Should be out of the hospital by tomorrow."

Merrick sighed with relief. He scanned the screen while maintaining his thoughts. "How much support can the bureau offer him?"

"Not much," Fisk said. "With this airport stuff going on, they need to be proactive."

"Does Nick know about LAX?"

"No, but Walt's on his way there right now to fill him in."

Merrick examined the report, searching for anything which

could confirm or deny accusations the Kurdish Security Force was on the verge of detonating a bomb at the Los Angeles Airport.

Without looking up, Merrick added, "We need to get Nick whatever he needs. I can't have these guys getting personal with our FBI agents. Especially not those two."

Fisk poured himself a cup of coffee.

"What about Dave Tanner?" Merrick asked.

"Professional. Two shots to the back of the head."

Merrick winced at the notion. "So Barzani sends his nephew to go after Nick, but Tanner is a killed by a pro here in D.C.? Any leads yet?"

"Nothing."

"Any doubt Barzani had Tanner killed?"

"No."

Merrick looked up at Fisk. "I spoke with Tanner's wife." He shook his head. "I've been making too many phone calls like that, Sam."

"We need help from our allies," Fisk said. "They need to step up."

Merrick thought about the man waiting in the lobby. As president, Merrick had learned to be the ultimate multi-tasker. Instead of dental visits and basketball practice, however, he had to console FBI agents' widows while keeping an eye on the senate majority leader's budget proposal.

Merrick looked over Fisk's shoulder and gestured with his head. "How far can I push this guy?"

Fisk took a sip of coffee, then placed the cup on the table and stared intently at Merrick. "We're not reducing our troops in Turkey, right?"

"No."

"Because it would send a terrible message—"

"No," Merrick held up his hand. "I'm not bending here, Sam, so just relax."

Fisk took a breath. The silence hung between them while Merrick returned his attention to the CIA report which was completely barren of any valuable information. Sometimes he would read dozens of pages of material which he knew in his heart was prepared by someone simply trying to impress him with their ability to write a report.

Finally Fisk said, "Truth be told, the Kurds have a strong case.

It's just their delivery method is a bit violent."

At that Merrick glanced up. "You think?"

Fisk shrugged. "This goes back decades, John. You're not going to settle it with a half-hour conversation."

Merrick scrolled again. "Wow, talk about bringing a guy down. I won't tell you about my plan to cure cancer over lunch."

Fisk reached over and snatched a toothpick with a piece of cantaloupe attached. He dropped the melon in his mouth and chewed. When he was done chewing he said, "They don't have much to offer."

Merrick looked up. "Excuse me?"

Fisk pointed his thumb over his shoulder to the closed door.

Merrick understood. The Turkish ambassador was waiting for a meeting with him. Turkey had little to offer the United States. They didn't even produce enough oil to satisfy their own needs. Their biggest exports were boron salt and copper. Not exactly a powerful trading partner. What they did have, however, was the most world's most dangerous terrorist organization operating in their backyard, which made them a necessary component to the fight on terrorism.

Merrick waved the back of his hand at Fisk. "Get out of here and send that twerp in."

Fisk grabbed another melon piece and slowly got to his feet. They'd known each other for three decades, so Merrick could talk to him like that without worrying about hurting his ego.

Merrick took his tablet and sat tall behind his desk. He wanted the ambassador to sense the full brunt of his authority.

A few seconds after Fisk left, there was a three-bang knock on the door signaling the arrival of a scheduled guest. Necmetin Ciller stepped into the Oval Office. He was tall, thin and fidgety as he approached to shake Merrick's hand. Merrick gestured to a seat in front of the massive presidential desk.

Ciller took his seat and gripped the armrests as if they might take flight.

"How are you, Mr. President?"

"Not so well," Merrick answered. "I'm finding some of your residents taking shots at our government agents."

"They may be residents of Turkey, Mr. President, but I assure you they are not representing our nation in any way."

"But you have the ability to do something about them."

"Sir, I promise you we have done—"

"Do more."

"Mr. President, you must understand, these are not reasonable people. They will not adhere to any agreement."

Merrick came to his feet and began a slow pace behind his desk. "I'm going to tell you something, Mr. Ciller. I can relate to the Kurds here. These people deserve a place to call home. A territory of their own." He turned in time to see the ambassador's face cringe.

"And I have come to an important decision," Merrick continued his methodical pace back and forth, hands in his pockets. "I'm considering the withdrawal of our peacekeeping troops in Turkey at the first of the year."

This had the ambassador on his toes, leaning forward in his chair, almost ashen.

Merrick paused, arching an eyebrow. "Does that concern you?"

"Mr. President, please. This is such a radical move. Don't you think you should consult with the Prime Minister before making such a bold decision?"

Merrick stopped to look outside the bulletproof window. From his vantage point he could see over the South Lawn to the Rose Garden. The view helped to calm him. Nick Bracco was the FBI agent who stopped the last session of terrorist attacks on American soil and Merrick was in no mood to allow the KSF another chance to murder him. Before he even knew what he was doing Merrick was rolling up his sleeves, involuntarily, his temper rising with the thought of his best terrorist agents becoming targets.

Merrick turned and saw the concern on the ambassador's face.

"The United States could be a very good friend to have, Mr. Ciller."

"Yes, Mr. President."

"And good friends tend to be there when you need them."

"Yes," came the anxious voice.

"Well, Mr. Ciller, should Turkey decide they need America to be its close ally, they need to act like it."

The ambassador nodded.

"Because you don't want America to become that friend who merely sends you a Christmas card each year detailing what their family has done over the past twelve months."

The ambassador shook his head.

Merrick leaned over his desk, fists on the wooden structure, jaw tight, the American flag over his right shoulder. "Temir Barzani is in our country killing our government agents. I need you to tell the Prime Minister that I've run out of patience. You either sign a peace agreement with the Kurds, or find a way to diffuse Barzani's power here in the states."

"Mr. President . . ." the ambassador stopped when he saw Merrick tilt his head in a disapproving manner. He seemed to know he'd spoken too soon.

"Or I will remove our troops and put you on our Christmas card list," Merrick said in a low controlled voice.

The ambassador said nothing

"Go, Mr. Ciller. Go tell the Prime Minister about our meeting here."

Ciller got to his feet. He seemed to question whether to shake Merrick's hand, then decided not to. As he backed away from the president, he seemed appropriately shaken up.

Merrick raised his eyebrows. "It's time to get creative, Mr. Ambassador."

The ambassador nodded and appeared to understand what the president was suggesting.

"Yes, Mr. President."

When the ambassador turned to leave, he kept nodding, with an expression of comprehension on his face. Merrick was glad to see that because he had no idea what he himself meant by the comment. He'd only hoped Mr. Ciller was frightened enough to translate effectively.

* * *

Matt allowed the Iron Mountain team to interrogate Semir Jetake, which he knew would do nothing but buy him time to strategize. Buck Martin and two of his commandos had Semir handcuffed and on his knees in a subservient position, while they grilled him for information. Matt and Tommy stood twenty yards away and watched the proceedings with disgusted expressions while Jennifer Steele and Luke Fletcher checked their cell phones for messages.

"He really thinks that guy is gonna squeal on his terrorist buddies?" Tommy asked.

Matt grimaced as Buck backhanded Semir's face. "He's stuck in his ways. Nothing I say is going to change his mind."

"Well, someone better," Tommy said. "Or that kid's gonna get killed for nothing."

The two of them watched Buck spit into Semir's face.

Matt shook his head. "He's making it worse. We need to shake these guys before they start using loudspeakers to announce their intentions."

Tommy waved his hand at the soldiers surrounding Buck. "You gonna pick a fight with those guys?"

Matt was outnumbered, but he couldn't just stand there and watch them murder the young Kurd just because Buck's team had immunity. He looked around at the faces of Buck's men and realized who they were. They'd all joined the service for the right reasons and Matt hoped those reasons still lurked beneath the surface.

He approached the interrogation and briskly yanked Semir to his feet. "Let me take a crack at this," he said.

"Do your best, Agent McColm," Buck sneered.

Matt pulled Semir away from the circle, dragging him into the nearby woods and shoving him up against a tree. With a menacing expression he whispered, "You have a question you haven't asked yet."

Blood trickled down the side of Semir's face while his eyes roamed wildly.

Matt showed him clenched teeth and gripped the kid's shirt with both hands. He pulled Semir close, inches from his face. In a threatening hush, he murmured, "Don't you want to speak with an attorney?"

Semir seemed disoriented. He simply shook his head, appearing leery of Matt's intention.

Matt would've rolled his eyes if he didn't have to look so intimidating.

"Semir," Matt whispered, "I'm trying to help you here. If you ask for an attorney I can take you away from this maniac."

The young soldier took rapid breaths and looked into Matt's eyes as if the answer might be right there for him.

"This is not a trick question, Semir. If you want I'll give you back to the old man and let him finish you off. Otherwise, you ask me for an attorney and I'll take you into custody. You get to live.

Maybe even see your two little boys again." Matt lowered his head and winked.

Semir swallowed hard. He looked over at Buck and watched the guy standing there with his thick arms crossed, examining every move. With the slightest of voices, he said, "Yes."

"Yes, what?"

He looked back and forth between Buck and Matt as if gauging his options. He was clearly under duress and not thinking properly.

He managed to whisper, "I would like an attorney."

Matt jumped back and slapped his hands together in disgust. "Shit."

"What?" Buck asked.

Matt looked over at the group with rage on his face, then pointed to Semir. "Tell them what you just said."

Sweat saturated the boy's temple as he danced in place, his hands still tight behind his back. "I would like an attorney?" he asked with complete uncertainty.

Buck placed his hands on his hips and glared at Matt. "Oh really? That just came to him?"

"Hey," Matt said, grabbing Semir by the back of his shirt and heading down a path toward their car. "He's got rights. I'll take him in and get a statement."

"Hold it," Buck barked.

Matt didn't hesitate. He threw Semir to the ground, then marched over to Buck, sensing the machine guns coming into a ready position around him.

"I trained at Fort Bragg," Matt said looking around at the commandos, letting them know he's one of them. Special Forces. A brotherhood that didn't wash off even after you were discharged. Then he took in Buck's glare. He gestured toward Semir on his knees. "He's coming with us. We're going to question him using the techniques allowed under the constitution." He looked around again at the soldiers. "You remember the constitution, right? Remember that oath you all took to defend it? Because I remember it. It was our creed. So if you're going to shoot me go ahead. I'm not afraid of dying. Just try living the rest of your lives with cold-blooded murder on your conscience."

Buck looked around and saw his team loosen their grips on their weapons. It was subtle, but it was there. They weren't about to kill one of their own. Not over this.

Matt nodded to the rest of his team and watched them fall in behind him.

"I'm taking my suspect into custody," Matt said. He eyed the soldiers surrounding their leader. "You guys follow him," Matt said as he pulled Semir down the path. "He'll get you killed before sundown."

Chapter 7

It was late afternoon by the time the team arrived at the county Sheriff's office. The complex was a one story block building with a gravel parking lot and a flagpole jutting out from a circle of red bricks. You had to pass Old Glory on the way into the building which made Matt smile, reminding him of the entrance to the Baltimore field office. Except this was no FBI building. This was merely a small satellite office to the main sheriff's office in Globe. Twelve hundred square feet of block walls and linoleum flooring. They didn't even have a receptionist to answer phones.

Steele, Tommy and Luke entered first while Matt kept a grip on Semir's arm. Luke opened the single jail cell and Matt shoved Semir into the empty space before turning to see Julie Bracco by herself, cleaning sandwich crumbs from the vacant receptionist's desk.

"What are you doing here?" Matt asked.

Julie rolled her eyes and gestured toward the closed door to the inner office. "Guess who's back, playing sheriff?"

"Are you kidding me?" Matt said. He noticed the frustration in Julie's eyes and wanted to retract his comment the second it left his mouth.

"Listen," Julie crumbled up the sandwich wrapper with more muscle than necessary, "do you really think he's going to sit at home nursing a wounded shoulder while a terrorist is out there trying to kill him?"

She turned to throw the wrapper in the garbage and Matt followed. He wedged himself in front of her and held her arms to face him. She was a rock. Her body trembled in his grasp, but she kept her composure. Matt crouched down to be at eye level. "Jule," he said with his most professional face, "we'll get this done just like we always do. Understand?"

Julie's face tightened. It seemed to be the same fight she'd always contended with as an FBI agent's wife — be brave, but not naive.

"I understand," she said, stepping out of his grasp. Then she tried to act busy cleaning the remaining lunch items on the desk.

Matt let her go. He made eye contact with Steele and saw compassion on her face. As if thanking him for trying to settle Julie's nerves. He smiled back at her.

* * *

Nick had two large computer monitors side by side squeezing out the small globe and adjacent Arizona and American flags to the brink of his desk. Two tall filing cabinets sat against one wall while a scattering of folding chairs took up the rest of the space in the office.

With his sling hugging his left arm to his chest, the fingers on his right hand plucked the keys of his computer keyboard. He had Google Earth humming on the left screen, scanning for something out of place in the Payson area. Barzani was close by and somehow Nick needed to find him first, before he became another statistical accomplishment of Barzani's revenge crusade. His mind felt slowed by the lingering effects of the anesthesia, but he kept grinding out ideas, piece by piece.

He heard the commotion in the outer office and figured the team had returned.

Tommy was the first to barge into the inner office like he was the governor. "Don't you know when to lay low?" Tommy said, stopping in front of Nick's
desk and folding his arms.

"I guess not," Nick said.

A massive black bear hung on the wall, stuffed and staring down at them with a mouthful of sharp teeth.

Tommy pointed at the animal. "That something you—"

"It was there before I got here," Nick said, lifting his attention from the computer screens and watching Jennifer Steele, Luke and Matt come into his office.

"Well," Matt said, "you can cross Semir off the list."

"Tell me about it," Nick said.

They did.

Jennifer Steele brought Nick up to speed with her and Luke's liberation of Matt and Tommy from Buck Martin and his Iron Mountain team. Matt added the capture of Semir and explained the battering Buck gave the kid.

"He okay?" Nick asked.

"He's fine," Matt said. "Luke bandaged him up on the ride over here."

Tommy dug a purple toothpick in his mouth. "So are you gonna tell me about this Barzani guy?"

"Well," Nick said, leaning back in his chair, "he's smart. He graduated from Georgetown with a Political Science degree. That's where he met Kharrazi. When Kharrazi had his . . . uh, car accident," Nick tried to keep the satisfaction from his face, "Barzani took over. The thing is, he's not as brash as Kharrazi, but he's more progressive. He's very tech savvy. He'll keep his hands clean and let some of his underlings do the dirty work."

"So this Barzani guy sets up camp here just to kill you?" Tommy asked.

Of course it was the perfect question to ask and if an eavesdropper were to listen to Tommy's inquisitiveness they might mistake it for dumb curiosity. But Nick knew nothing could be further from the truth. Tommy might have dropped out of high school, but he could read a situation better than any Harvard psychology professor. It was one of Tommy's true gifts. He'd been underestimated his whole life and loved every minute of it.

"That's what I'm trying to figure out," Nick said. "Why did he send his nephew to take a shot at me? If he was serious, he would've sent a true sniper."

"This guy a religious fanatic?"

"No, these guys aren't jihadists. They're on a mission. There are over twenty million Kurds living in Turkey, Iran and Iraq. They're the largest ethnic group in the world without a country. They want to declare a portion of Kurdistan a sovereign nation for Kurds."

"So, what's wrong with that?" Tommy jabbed his toothpick in between two molars.

"What's wrong is Turkey asked for the U.N. to send troops to help subdue the KSF from ravaging villages. The Kurds want the U.S. to withdraw its troops so they can take control."

Tommy sucked on his toothpick and seemed to take it all in.

Nick turned to Matt and sighed. "I spoke with Trish Tanner."

Matt's lip curled into a disgusted look of anger. Dave Tanner was one of their teammates and they'd spent years chasing terrorists together. "How is she?"

Nick shook his head. "Not good. She was upset and spitting

some creative words my way." Nick rubbed the back of his neck and looked up at Matt. "She begged me to kill Barzani. She said, do it for Dave."

"Who's Dave?" Tommy asked.

"Dave Tanner," Nick said. "You knew him, he was part of our team back in Baltimore. He was murdered last night."

"Damn," Tommy said. "They're turning the table on you guys, making you the targets this time."

"Yeah," Nick said. He looked around the room at the rest of his current team and assessed their chances of catching Barzani. He needed help, but he didn't know from where.

Nick looked at Matt. "You still have the password to the counterterrorist team's file?"

Matt shook his head. "Not since we came here."

"Shit," Nick grumbled.

"Call Walt," Matt said. "He'll give it to you."

Nick considered the idea when a voice came from the doorway. "Someone looking for me?"

A large, dark-skinned man stood with his arm around Julie, who beamed her delight at his presence. Walt Jackson strode into the room like a giant leopard, moving his six-foot-five frame with the elegance of an Olympic athlete. Which he was before he became the Special Agent in Charge of the Baltimore field office. He held a brown brief bag under his arm.

Julie said, "I found this man roaming the parking lot," then she disappeared and closed the office door.

Matt was the first to greet Walt, first shaking his hand, then being pulled into a bear hug.

"Good to see you, Walt," Matt said.

"Yeah, well I couldn't exactly stand still while a couple of my old agents became targets."

Nick moved around the desk now and Walt was careful to keep his greeting to a two-handed handshake, dropping his bag on the desk.

"How are you?" Walt asked, sincere as always.

"I'm fine," Nick said, glancing at his shoulder. "A flesh wound is all."

Walt frowned. "Yeah, right."

Nick made some introductions, then directed Walt to the only chair which might hold his large frame — the chair behind Nick's desk.

Walt sat down with a grunt. He had bags under his eyes. "Been traveling all day," he said stretching out his legs.

Tommy must've sensed a law-enforcement meeting coming on as he edged toward the door.

Before he took a second step, Walt said, "Sit down, Tommy. I could use some of your help here."

Tommy's chest pumped out at the comment. He grabbed a folding chair to sit on, then resumed his toothpick routine.

"I hope you didn't come all the way here just for me?' Nick asked.

The sun momentarily hid behind a cloud while Walt looked down at his shoes. "You know about Dave, right?"

Nick nodded.

Walt said, "I don't like the timing." He reached over and grabbed his bag. He came out with an eight-by-ten glossy of Dave's body. He handed it to Matt and watched his ex-partner grit his teeth.

When Nick got the photo, he wanted to hand it to Steele before he even looked it over. Dave appeared to be in an alley lying face down looking away from the camera. His neck was twisted at an odd angle as if he'd fallen on a rock. Steele took the picture and spent more time than Nick did before handing it to Tommy.

"Professional," Tommy said.

"That's right," Walt said. "Two bullets to the back of the head."

"He owe anyone any money?" Tommy asked.

Walt raised his eyebrows. "Yeah, actually he did. He was down heavy to a bookie in D.C. It made us wonder if that direction was a possibility."

"How much?" Tommy asked.

"Five grand."

"Uh uh," Tommy said. "Not enough to get slammed like this."

"Tell me," Walt said.

Tommy leaned over to put the photo on the desk, then said, "There's a ten grand rule in D.C. Everyone abides by it. Someone runs their debt up to nine grand and they stop playing or leave town. No one's dumb enough to go over the limit."

"Maybe he was dealing with someone who didn't know the rules?"

Tommy waved his toothpick at Walt. "Nah. The street wouldn't allow it. Too many steps to booking inside the beltway. The SEC practically regulates the damn thing."

Walt smiled. "Thanks, Tommy." He turned to Nick and made it a point to look at his shoulder as he spoke. "So like I was saying, I don't like the timing."

Nick stared out the window and thought about Dave Tanner's wife and kids. For a brief moment he remembered that he himself had a child on the way, but he quickly brushed away the thought like a housefly.

"Any idea who did it?" Nick asked.

Walt leaned his head back. "That bothers me. We've practically had that scene scrubbed with a microscope and came up with nothing. No prints which matched anyone in the computer, no witnesses. Nothing."

"Barzani paid a professional, no doubt," Nick said.

"He's the ultimate delegator," Matt chimed in. "What about the rest of the team?"

Walt cocked his head, "Those three? You see them hiding in a safe house while the rest of the office goes after Dave's killer?"

Matt shook his head.

"Exactly," Walt said. Then he squirmed a bit trying to get comfortable. "I need to tell you, there's credible evidence the KSF is attempting to detonate a bomb at LAX."

"How credible?" Nick asked.

Walt seemed to understand the question. He shrugged. "It's not strong, but it's LAX and we can't afford to be wrong about it."

"So there go our resources," Matt said.

There was a twinkle in Walt's eye as he watched his two star pupils putting the puzzle together.

"That's right," Walt said. "That's where I'm headed right now. I won't be able to offer you much support. They're not threatening anything around here."

"Except us," Nick said.

"What about the Army, the National Guard, Hostage Rescue?" Steele asked.

Walt sighed and went for the obvious retort. "The military is a bulky sword," he said. "What this requires is a scalpel. A small tactical team of professionals."

Walt looked around the room, his eyes landing on Steele.

"That's where you come in. They're going to need your help here."

The room stayed silent while Nick considered the challenge of going after Barzani with the inhabitants of that small room.

Walt let out a big breath, like he was holding it in for just such an occasion. He edged forward on the chair and counted off on his fingers. "First of all you'll have full access to our tech squad. You need a license plate run or a satellite image, you got it. Second, I've sent for a couple of agents to come up from Phoenix. They can set up a safe house for Julie until we can resolve this mess. Third, I'll have a specialist sent up with those guys. Someone with gear to help track Barzani. And finally . . ." Walt looked at Nick and Matt. "Do what you two do best. Use your instincts."

Nick and Matt nodded.

"So," Walt said, repositioning his stiff legs. "What do we do?"

"Start with what we know," Matt almost chanted. It was the same question Walt would ask during every briefing and induced the same response each time.

"And what do we know?" Walt asked.

"Barzani has been here for six months," Steele said.

Walt smiled. "That's right, Jennifer. What does that mean?"

"It means he's had time to plan," Steele answered.

"Good," Walt said. "What else." He was playing the mediator. Like a good football coach trying to press the right buttons to squeeze the most out of his players.

The room was quiet for a minute while Walt drummed his thick fingers on the desk.

Finally, Nick said, almost absently, "They're using cash."

This brought a great big grin to Walt's weathered face. "Go on."

Nick looked over at his deputy who was sitting in the back of the room, paying attention, but not seeming comfortable with a roomful of federal agents. "Luke, you've been here the longest. Go to all the local realtors. Find out who paid cash to rent a place up here five and six months ago. Only the ones who paid by cash. There won't be many. It's not like Barzani opened a checking account. After that, check the car lots. Find out about any big cash purchases within the same time frame."

Luke left the office with a smile, seeming grateful to be part of the chase.

Nick thought about Luke's level of skill with terrorists and gestured to Steele. "Jen, go with him. I don't like him out there without someone with experience. He has a tendency to react too quickly."

Steele nodded and left the room.

They sat silent for a moment. Walt pointed to Tommy. "You have any connections in Mexico?"

"Sure," Tommy said. "What are you looking for?"

"We've discovered a large tunnel under the California border. It went directly into a dirty warehouse a couple of hundred yards into the country. It's different than most tunnels we find, very sophisticated. Halogen lights, oxygen, the whole works. I need to know if there was any Kurdish involvement with this project or simply a high-end drug tunnel."

Tommy hopped to his feet, pulled out his cell phone and headed for the door.

"I'll make a call and find out," Tommy said. Then he closed the door behind him.

Chapter 8

Tommy felt the cool mountain air hit him as he stepped out of the sheriff's office and dialed a contact number on his phone. Even though he'd been in Payson less than a day, he was beginning to develop an appreciation for the small town's atmosphere. It was more open and serene. He could see himself living in a place like this where the skyline was etched with pine trees.

Back in west Baltimore the streets were teeming with possible assailants. Tommy's innate ability to detect a foreign body in the city's bloodstream had always served him well, but it had been fine-tuned from years of mingling with the crowd and creating alliances. Out here, however, it seemed much easier to spot an intruder. There were no drug dealers hanging out on the corner, or gangbangers looking to initiate new members.

So it was easy for him to spot the shadow lingering behind the steering wheel as he strode out onto the wooden deck. The figure behind the wheel seemed to track Tommy as he moved onto the gravel parking lot, paying too much attention to an ordinary man on his cell phone.

Tommy waited four rings, then heard the tone click over to voicemail. A male voice on the phone said, "Go."

"Hey, Hector, it's Tommy. Give me a call."

Tommy pushed his phone off and watched the figure in the car stare at the sheriff's office. From the parking lot Tommy could see Julie standing by a small window. The man's attention seemed to be on her.

Tommy considered getting help from inside, but was afraid the guy might bolt. He decided to be direct. Maybe the guy was simply waiting for someone, but Tommy couldn't afford to wait. From what he'd heard, this Barzani guy could be using anyone to get Nick.

Something gnawed at Tommy's gut and it took a minute for him to realize what it was. Julie. She was inside that office waiting for Nick, being the good wife. Being brave. He had to eliminate any possibility the shadow was a danger.

Tommy went to his rental car, which was parked behind the man's car. He went around the back and opened the trunk, stalling for time. Trying to figure out what to do next. From behind the opened trunk he could see the back of the car. Tommy waited for someone else to leave the office or someone to pull in, but in this one-horse town, it could be a while. He was about to dial Nick's cell phone when the guy started the engine. Tommy lost his patience and decided to do what he did best. Go head first. Be the aggressor. Take the tail by surprise.

He slammed the trunk shut and took long, strong steps toward the sedan. As he approached the passenger side of the car, he could hear the window slide down. He bent over to see who he was dealing with and saw right away his haste had cost him. The man behind the wheel held a pistol with a confidence which took years to acquire.

"Get in," the man grunted.

Tommy had one option. As he opened the door, he got a good look at the man. There was an unlit cigar in the corner of his mouth and a smug grin on his face.

Tommy dropped into the passenger seat, shut the door, then wheeled and snatched the gun from the man's hand. He aimed the gun directly at the man's chest and pulled the trigger. A sliver of a yellow flame popped out of the top of the gun. He held the gun still while the man leaned over the flame and sucked his cigar to life.

"Joey Tess," Tommy said. "Always with the toys."

Joe Tessamano held the freshly lit cigar between his left index and middle fingers and reached over to give Tommy a bear hug. "Been too long, Tommy."

Tommy patted Joe's back and pulled away to see him smiling, his bright white teeth gleaming against his tanned face. "The fuck are you doing out here?"

"I'm living down in Scottsdale now," Joe said, taking a quick drag on the cigar to keep it going. "A couple of hours' drive."

"Hey, how's Kenny doing?"

Joe rolled down his window and blew out a stream of smoke into the mountain air. He paused for a moment and Tommy braced for the bad news. Joe's son had been strung out on heroin for years. When Joe came to Tommy for help, Tommy put the word out on the street: any dealer who sold to Kenny would pay dearly. Tommy had cachet back then. He never had to say things twice.

Now Joe looked over at Tommy with a sparkle in his eye. "He's doing great."

"Really?"

"He's a veterinarian over in San Diego. Got a wife and three-year-old daughter." Joe fished around the inside of his jacket with his free hand and came out with a photo of a young girl in a pink dress holding a giant lollipop in one hand and a "Happy Birthday" balloon in the other.

Tommy grabbed the picture. "Aw, she's not spoiled at all, is she?"

Joe chuckled, taking the picture back and stuffing it into his pocket. "She's the love of my life." He looked over at Tommy with a sentimental smile. "Hey, Tommy, listen . . . uh, thanks."

"For what?"

Joe cocked his head slightly at Tommy's charade of ignorance.

Tommy waved the back of his hand at him. "Yeah, of course, Joey. I'm glad he made it. I'm happy for you."

Joe pointed his cigar at Tommy. "You know what I always liked about you? You never took an order without asking why. Cap would tell you to scare someone, or break a bone and you'd always look at him and ask why. No one ever asked Mr. C why about anything except you. And the beautiful way you'd spin it when he gave you that dark glare. 'But Mr. Capelli, should someone ask me why I'm doing something and all I do is shrug, well pretty soon they're going to fill their head with their own ideas and maybe it's not the right ones. Maybe they guess wrong about your motivation, then maybe they start talking behind your back, start making their own plans.'

"Then," Joe added, "you'd give him that classic Tommy look with your eyebrows raised and say, 'I've gotta have your back, Boss.'"

Tommy grinned. "Yeah, well, I guess I've never been very good at taking orders, have I?"

Joe's face grew somber as he puffed on his cigar, the ashes glowing orange in the afternoon shadows. He reached into his jacket again, only this time he came out with a folded manila envelope and handed it to Tommy.

Tommy opened the envelope and saw the stack of hundreds held together with a rubber band. On top of the money was a photo. Tommy pulled out the picture and held it by the window to catch a ray of sun. It was a surveillance shot, grainy because it was taken from a distance and then blown up to give a better view of the target. And Tommy knew that's exactly who this was too—a target. His mouth curled into ugly scowl as he recognized the woman in the photo. Julie Bracco.

He looked over at Joe Tess and said, "Tell me everything."

* * *

Hestin Jirdeer sat in his car across the street from the Gila County sheriff's office, pulled the binoculars down and pursed his lips. He didn't trust the assassin he'd hired to kill the FBI agent's wife and now understood why. Even from a hundred yards he could see the man hugging the FBI agent's cousin in his car. The same gangster who'd helped the FBI capture the KSF's supreme leader. They were obviously very friendly and the assassin was certainly helping the FBI himself. Jirdeer dreaded even making the call he needed to make, but decided to do it quickly, before too much time had passed. Their plans were dependent on timing. He dialed his cell phone.

"Yes," came the deep voice.

"Sarock," Jirdeer's breath became short in his chest. "They have Semir."

Barzani grumbled something Jirdeer didn't quite understand.

Jirdeer decided to go forward with all the bad news. "Also, the assassin is working with the FBI. He was a plant."

The silence was too long for Jirdeer's nerves to handle. He watched the two men exit the assassin's car and head into the sheriff's office.

"Sarock?" Jirdeer said. "It is better we know now rather than later," giving his leader a positive method of considering the information.

Temir Barzani didn't seem willing to accept the setback. Jirdeer could hear heavy breathing and that was all. He gripped his steering wheel tight, his arm muscles aching with anticipation.

Finally, Barzani barked, "Get that squad over there right now. I want that woman dead."

Jirdeer wasn't sure where he wanted the hired team of soldiers to go. The sheriff's office? Was he to order a shootout? He thought about the consequences of having the conversation linger and decided the shorter they spoke, the better for Jirdeer's standing.

"Yes, Sarock," was all he said.

* * *

Temir Barzani slammed his cell phone down on the kitchen table and shouted, "Shik poot." Two soldiers stood by windows with their automatic weapons tight to their chests. They stood more rigid now, darting their eyes around the perimeter of the cabin. Even though there were plenty of surveillance cameras, they were the last line of defense for their leader.

"Mano," Barzani called out.

A soldier peeked in from the next room. "Yes, Sarock."

Barzani pointed to the floor next to him. "Come here."

Mano Surtek scurried around the oak table and stood next to Barzani. He looked up at him with fear in his eyes.

"Mano," Barzani said, seething, "how long have we been on this mission?"

"One hundred and forty-three days?" Mano answered, seeming to grope for the correct response.

Barzani could see his security team watching from the corner of their eyes. He grabbed Mano around the throat and squeezed hard until he felt the soldier's larynx cracking between his fingers. "At what point in the plan was Semir to be captured by the FBI?"

Mano tried to answer, shaking his head and pleading with watery eyes. His mouth opened, but nothing came out.

Barzani shoved him down, driving him to his hands and knees. Mano gasped for air while rubbing his neck.

Barzani had understood the value of a small inner circle. He wasn't about to make the same mistakes his predecessor had made by spreading hundreds of soldiers throughout the United States, leaving loose ends for the FBI to capture and garner information.

Barzani leaned over and spoke softly into his soldier's ear. "Do you know how much our people are relying on us to accomplish our goals?"

Mano nodded as drool dripped from his lips onto the wood floor.

Barzani whispered, "Our people in Turkistan are being slaughtered while we make feeble attempts to rid our homeland of these American meddlers. We need them to understand the trauma our families are enduring. All we ask for is fairness. Our passion will carry us to victory. Do you understand this?"

Mano's head sunk to his knees. "Yes," he squeaked.

"Now, I have one more question," Barzani said. "Are the explosives in place?"

Mano looked up with a sense of hope in his eyes. "Yes," he said.

Barzani reached down and grabbed a handful of Mano's hair and pulled him to his feet. "Congratulations," Barzani said. "That is the first correct answer you've had today."

Chapter 9

They huddled around Nick's dual computer screens, Nick, Matt and Walt. Walt had logged into the FBI's secure antiterrorist site. He was positioning the cursor over an image of LAX airport, zooming in and out of parking lots and employee entrances with the skill of a computer programmer. Los Angeles was an hour earlier than Arizona so the setting sun was higher in the sky there.

"What kind of intel drew you to this threat?" Nick asked.

"Morris found a Kurdish snitch willing to receive leniency for information about the KSF."

"Who?"

Walt hesitated, while he moved the images on the screen larger, then smaller. He moved the images so quickly he was giving Nick a headache.

"Walt?" Nick repeated.

Walt sighed. "Baldar Nemit."

"Baldar turned?" Matt said, stunned. "Are you kidding me?"

The leader of the FBI's antiterrorist department removed his hand from the mouse and sat back in his chair. He folded his arms across his chest as he addressed his old teammates.

"You think this is a dictatorship?" Walt said bluntly. "You think I didn't tell Ken the source was suspect?"

Matt said nothing. He and Nick both knew the politics that went into Walt's job. Protect the big targets first, then worry about the small ones. They were minnows compared to LAX.

"There's only one reason I'm sitting here right now," Walt said, picking up steam as he went. "I went over Ken's head and told Sam to get the president's approval. How many lives you think I have left once I get back to the beltway? Huh?"

Matt looked down at his shoes.

Nick patted Walt on the arm. "We appreciate what you've done for us, Walt. Really we do."

"I hope so boys, because I need you two around." Walt's face softened. He wagged his finger back and forth between Nick and Matt. "If I could just download all the information in your brains..." He leaned back and rested his head on the chair. "See, the new Bureau is all about data and profiling and things which can be manipulated. An informant could be nodding his head 'Yes,' but if he says 'No' that's what'll show up in the damn file. You guys were there in the trenches. That's why I say, use your instincts. It's not the FBI's way anymore, but that doesn't mean you have to give it up."

Walt swung his legs back under the desk and replaced his hand on the mouse. He zoomed in on an image of workers filling in the Mexican tunnel. "Our two best friends in the fight against terrorism have been the Atlantic and the Pacific. But if these tunnels are becoming this sophisticated, we may as well hand out speeding tickets down there."

"What kind of tracings did you find?" Nick asked.

"Semtex," Walt said, referring to the plastic explosive which was a favorite of the KSF.

"So let me get this straight," Nick said. "Baldar, the strongest component of the KSF's American occupation, squeals on his Kurdish brethren and gives up a tunnel laced with Semtex?"

Walt said nothing.

"Then," Nick continued, "he tells us this tunnel was built to bring in explosives to detonate a bomb at LAX? Right?"

Walt kept his attention on the computer screen.

"You don't buy it either, do you?" Nick said.

Walt moved his head side to side, ever so slightly.

Nick rubbed his only free hand through his hair. "An enormous diversion," he said. He looked over at Walt and saw understanding in his eyes. Walt knew.

"So what do we do?" Matt asked.

"You mean what do *you* do?" Walt said, looking at his watch. "In another hour, I'm taking the entire Western region with me to L.A. You guys need to figure this out. The minute you have credible evidence there's something else going on, call me. I can be here in ninety minutes."

The door opened and Tommy rushed in trailed by a man with a deep tan and a black leather jacket. Tommy had a harsh expression as he came to the front of the desk.

"This here is Joe Tess. He's a friend of ours." Tommy said, while handing Nick an envelope. "He received this from a KSF member earlier tonight."

Nick looked over at Joe and nodded. He understood the reference. If Tommy introduced someone as "a friend of *his*" then it was someone outside of the Family. But a "friend of *ours*" meant Joe was a Family member. Someone Tommy trusted.

"How did they contact you?" Nick asked Joe.

Joe had his hands in his pocket and shrugged. "They called my cell."

"How did they get your number?"

"I asked," Joe said. "He wouldn't tell me."

"Nick," Tommy said. "Open the envelope."

Nick unfolded the manila envelope and saw a stack of hundred dollar bills. He immediately understood what it meant. An amount that large could only mean one thing—a payoff for a murder. Then he saw the photograph under the stack. When he realized whose picture it was, his chest tightened into a knot.

He looked up at Joe. "When do they want you to do this?"

"By tomorrow."

Nick examined the photograph. A surveillance shot. Taken from a distance to avoid detection. Julie was walking out of a local coffee shop by herself. He tried to determine when the shot had been taken, but couldn't.

"Joe's a sharp cookie," Tommy said. "He took the job even though he would never do such a thing."

Nick handed the photo to Matt and saw Walt look over his shoulder. Nick felt a sense of gratitude emerge. His wife was a target of Temir Barzani. With a shaky arm he reached out and shook Joe's hand. "Thanks."

Joe smiled a lopsided smile. "Yeah, well, Tommy's good people." Then his face turned severe. "Besides, I'm an American. These punks need to learn a lesson."

Nick turned and saw Matt watching them, waiting for his turn.

"Let's give him a book to look at," Matt said. "Maybe he can pick the guy out. My money is on Jirdeer."

Joe was looking down at the photo of Dave Tanner's body sitting on the desk. He seemed fascinated. He picked up the photo and examined it closely.

"You recognize him?" Walt asked.

Joe squinted. "No."

Everyone waited as Joe moved the picture sideways, then at arm's length, then close up again.

"Something you care to tell us?" Walt asked.

Joe dropped the photo onto the desk, then looked over at Tommy with a question on his face.

Tommy seemed to understand. He nodded to Walt. "Should Joe here offer you some information which might incriminate himself—"

"He has immunity," Nick assured him. Then he turned to Joe. "This man was an FBI agent, a friend of ours. We need all the help we can get. Anything you say will never leave this room."

Joe looked at Tommy and saw him nod.

"Well," Joe said, suddenly seeming unsure of himself. "Have you done an autopsy on the body?"

Walt looked over at Nick, then Matt. All three of them confused by the question.

"I think we know the cause of death," Walt said. "He was shot close range, two bullets to the back of the head."

Joe nodded. "Yeah, but that's not how he died."

Nick picked up the photo and scrutinized Dave's figure lying there. His body was face down with his head twisted away from the camera.

"I don't understand?" Nick said. "What are we missing?"

Joe glanced at Tommy again.

"Go ahead, Tess," Tommy said, firm. "He's my cousin. We can trust him."

Joe seemed to search for the proper words. "Well, I'm interested in these types of situations . . . I mean from a strictly curious perspective."

"Of course," Nick said, sounding sympathetic, as if they were discussing bird watching.

"And I've observed a couple of bodies which were left just this same way. The head was left twisted up and away because the killer snuck up on the victim and twisted his head almost off his body. This is exactly the same angle. The killer was left-handed and tall, you can tell by the way his chin is pulled up away from his torso."

Nick studied the photo once again and saw what Joe was talking about. "I see what you mean. Where did you see these photos?"

Joe hesitated.

Nick held up his hand. "Total immunity. I promise."

"Bolivia," Joe said. "There was a professional called in to assassinate the president. I heard rumors about this guy from Russia. Ex-KGB. He preferred to use his hands. Less noise, I guess. I don't know. They never found him."

"Anything else you remember about him?" Matt asked.

"Yeah, a couple of years later I heard about a murder in Indonesia. Same thing. In my circle I began to hear stories about the guy. He was considered the most dangerous man on the planet. No one even knows his name. They just call him The Russian. The thing is though . . ." Joe looked down at the photo. "Where did this happen?"

"Washington, D.C.," Walt said.

Joe's face seemed to twitch. "Well, supposedly he's never been to the States before." He looked around the room. "Until now."

Nick's stomach clenched as he considered the news. He shook Joe's hand and thanked him once again for all of his help. He immediately thought of Julie, though. She couldn't possibly go through another ordeal like this. His poor wife deserved to be protected from the types of maniacs who drew targets on Nick's photo. He pushed a button on the phone on his desk.

"Hey, Jule," he said into the speakerphone. "Can you come here please?"

A moment later Julie stepped into the room with an even expression.

"Tommy's going to take you home so you can grab some clothes," Nick said.

Julie's face soured, but she said nothing.

"I'm being over-protective, sweetie, that's all. We're going to have you stay in a safe house for a couple of days."

Julie nodded, but it was clear she wasn't happy. Nick quickly got to his feet and followed Julie into the outer room. The only person there was Semir sitting cross-legged on his cot.

"Listen," Nick said, touching Julie's shoulder as she turned away from him. "Look at me."

Julie spun around with slightly puffy eyes. "Yes?"

"This will be over quicker than you know," Nick said, trying to look brave with his arm sling a constant reminder to his wife exactly how dangerous his job was. "This isn't like the last time. There's less than a dozen of them. I have Matt and Tommy with me."

He was trying to push her comfort buttons. She'd always considered Matt his guardian angel and Tommy's presence gave her immense reassurance.

Then she did something which made his heart melt. Julie tucked her head into the side of Nick's face and gingerly placed her arm around his waist. He could feel her soft skin against his unshaven cheek.

"I love you," she whispered into his ear. "We'll always love you."

The baby, Nick thought. She was already making them a family, letting him know what was at stake.

Nick clutched her with his one good arm and whispered. "I'm so very blessed to have you."

Julie pecked him on the side of his face, then went for her purse on a nearby chair.

Nick turned to return to his office and noticed Semir staring at them without expression.

"What are you looking at?" Nick said.

Chapter 10

Tommy drove his rental car down the tree-lined street like he was going to a county fair. He had a pleasant smile as he observed the falling leaves through his open window. Julie knew it was Tommy's way of calming her down and it was almost working.

"I tell you, Jule," Tommy said, "I could get used to this up here."

It was a good show, but Tommy kept eyeing the rearview mirror just a little more than necessary. It was a narrow two-lane road with very little room before the trees came into play, which made Julie feel closed in even at sixty miles per hour.

Tommy's cell phone chirped. He glanced down at the display and put the phone to his ear.

"Hey, Hector, how's it going?"

He listened for a moment, then said, "Good. Hey, I have a question about that tunnel the Feds just discovered on the California border."

Tommy's face tensed up. "No, I'm not wired, Hector, jeesh. I'm just calling to ask—" Tommy pursed his lips. "Relax, will you?" He pulled the phone down to his lap and said to Julie, "The guy really needs an intervention, but everyone's too afraid of him."

Tommy replaced the phone to his ear. "Easy, Hector, you're not listening to me. You're acting all paranoid for no reason. I just want to know if you knew of any Kurdish involvement with this tunnel."

He waited.

"It's a type of people. They live in Turkey."

Tommy glanced in the rearview mirror while listening. Their car cruised along without much traffic.

"They're some kind of ethnic group," he said, gesturing with his fingers while the palm of his hand steered. "Yes, sort of like Jews, but not like . . . hey, Hector, if you don't even know who they are, don't you think that answers my question?"

Tommy shook his head while listening. "Hector, that's all I needed to know. Really. You've been a terrific help. I can't tell you how much this means to me." Tommy rolled his eyes, seemingly attempting to get off the phone as quickly as possible.

"Yeah, yeah, next time I'm down there we'll get some cervezas together, you bet."

Another few seconds, then Tommy said, "Thanks, Hector. Adios."

Tommy pushed a button, then put the phone on the console next to him. "Last time I had cerveza with Hector, a jackrabbit knocked over his glass and got ten bullets for being an animal in the desert."

Julie picked up Tommy's phone. It was glossy and black and sleeker than she'd ever seen before.

"Is this new?" she asked, looking it over.

Tommy beamed. "You like it?"

"I do," she said.

"It's the newest technology. The things I can do with that are unreal. It has a radar loaded on it. I can point it at a car and see how fast it's going."

Julie pressed the screen and scanned the icons. "That's impressive. I'm sure that comes in handy all the time." A little sarcasm leaking out.

"Yeah, well, it does a ton of other stuff too."

Julie tapped into his music player. "Let's see what we've been listening to," Julie said, scrolling down the list of artists. "Oh my. Coldplay? Tommy, you like Coldplay?"

Tommy glanced at her sideways. "I don't necessarily like Coldplay, I just like their music."

"Of course," Julie said, scrolling further. "Kaisher Chiefs, Nada Surf, Razorlight? I've never heard of half of these bands."

"That's because most of them are from the U.K. That's where all the new alternative stuff comes from, then we copy the original over here and muddle it up. Me, I like the original. By the time some copycat artist picks it up, I'm on to the next thing."

Julie looked up at Tommy and it seemed he felt her stare.

"What?" he said.

Julie smiled. "I never knew this side of you."

"What side?"

"I don't know, I guess I pegged you for the Frank Sinatra type of guy."

"Oh really?" Tommy said, mocking disappointment. "I think

that's some sort of stereotype, Mrs. Bracco."

Tommy kept his eyes on the rearview mirror for too long and Julie turned to see a black pickup truck rushing up behind them. Tommy grabbed his phone and tapped the screen. The truck was speeding so fast the front end was bobbing up and down with the contours of the asphalt. Julie's heart sped up as well.

As the vehicle closed in she could see three teenage boys with exhilarated expressions sharing the front seat. The driver ran up to within a few feet of their bumper, then swerved fiercely around them while Tommy eased over toward the shoulder to allow them to pass. As the truck flew by, the kid by the passenger window held out an open beer can as if toasting Tommy.

Tommy saluted them as if to say, "Carry on."

The truck sped on ahead of them and Julie finally caught her breath. Tommy held up his phone to show her a red blinking "95" on the screen.

"See?" Tommy said. "Pretty accurate, huh."

Julie let out a big sigh. "Weren't you worried?"

"About what?"

She waved her hand at the back of the speeding truck. "That?"

"Nah," Tommy said. "I saw them peeling out of the gas station a few miles back. I knew they were coming."

Julie looked down at her trembling hands. She wanted to know what made him so confident, so secure in his decisions. Before she could say anything, Tommy had grabbed her left hand and looked at her with a level gaze. For once there was no humor in his expression.

"Look," he said swapping his attention between Julie and the road. "I know what you meant." His voice turned harsh. "It's just that the people who are trying to hurt Nick are foreigners. And I'm sorry, but no punk from Turkey is going to come into my country and take out a Bracco. It's just not happening."

Julie nodded meekly and Tommy seemed to notice her uncertainty.

"Okay," Tommy went on, "you see that kid in the jail cell? Semir? You look into his eyes and you tell me there's any real creative intelligence going on. That guy is just smart enough to follow directions, and no more. I wouldn't trust him to pick me out a decent loaf of bread at the grocery store."

Tommy held up his index finger. "There's only one guy who

knows what he's doing and that's this Barzani guy. We get him . .
." Tommy shrugged. "Game over."

He gave Julie his best "Trust me" smile then put both hands on
the wheel.

Julie guided him into the side road which took them to her
gravel driveway, seventy-five yards of tires crunching and shock
absorbers working overtime. Tommy parked sideways in front
of the single-level cabin. It was tucked away in the woods with
a small manmade lake in the backyard. Both Nick and Julie had
loved the remoteness of the place when they bought it, but now
solitude felt closer to dangerous than peaceful seclusion. She
opened the door and immediately Tommy headed for the kitchen.

"You got anything to eat, Jule? I never had lunch today,"
Tommy said, opening up the refrigerator.

Julie slid past him and pulled out a tray of leftover lasagna.
She cut a piece for him, then put it in the microwave and set it for
ninety seconds.

"Thanks," Tommy said, then shooed her away. "Go grab some
clothes and let's get going."

There was no urgency in his voice, but she'd been down this
road before. After fifteen years as an FBI agent's wife, she knew
enough to stay one step ahead of trouble.

She went into her bedroom and began throwing shirts and
jeans on her bed. She kept opening and closing drawers searching
for matching outfits. As she made her third trip into her walk-in
closet, she checked out the stack of books on a shelf above her
shoes. There were books on marriage, self-help books, even some
autobiographies she'd enjoyed. Her friends teased her because
she'd never read any James Patterson or John Grisham thrillers,
but the truth was she'd had enough harrowing experiences in her
life. She didn't need to read about anyone else's drama.

Julie grabbed a book on finance. Maybe learn how to invest
their money better since she'd taken a year off of teaching to move
to the mountain community. She turned to go throw the book on
her bed and screamed. A man wearing black fatigues stood in her
closet doorway with a sinister grin and a pistol trained on her.

"Don't do that again or I'll have to use this," the man sneered.

A surge of blood and nerves rushed into Julie's head and
tightened into a bottleneck around her throat. "Who . . . who . . ."

"The name's Buck Martin," he said. "I work for a private
security force called Iron Mountain."

Julie's mouth dried up and her knees seemed unable to hold her up. "But, I don't underst—"

"Yeah," Buck said, standing there wearing a communication headset and seeming to understand what she wanted to ask. "I get that all the time. Aren't I too old to be playing soldier?"

Julie's breathing became erratic and she needed to sit. He must've noticed her struggling because he stepped aside and gestured to the bed.

"Go ahead, Mrs. Bracco," the man said. "Sit down."

Buck moved just enough to allow Julie to squeeze out of the closet. He gently pressed his pelvis into her tiny frame as she passed through.

Julie sat on the edge of the bed and held her stomach. Nick had trained her to be aggressive in these situations. The quicker, the better. Before the assailant could decide whether he was prepared to kill. She was ready to attack, kick him hard in the nuts and grab the gun. If she was alone she wouldn't have hesitated, but she wasn't alone. She was carrying her baby now and it made her wait. She turned into pure protective mode.

"I'll do whatever you want," Julie said, the words vibrating out of her mouth.

"I'll bet you would," he said, looking her over like a fine piece of steak. "And I could show you a thing or two around the bedroom." He grabbed his crotch with his free hand. The gun was still pointed directly at her.

Julie's stomach lurched at the man's lascivious expression. She crossed her legs and wondered about Tommy. Was he dead?

"Here's what we do," Buck said, suddenly looking businesslike. "I'm going to give you the phone and you're going to call your husband. You're going to tell him you're not feeling too well. You feel sick. See if he volunteers to come home. If he doesn't, you ask him to come home."

Julie listened, trying to remember certain phrases she could say that would tip Nick off. She was lightheaded and not thinking right. It was all happening too fast. Her baby. She felt grateful she was too early in the pregnancy to begin showing.

Buck pulled a small sheet of paper from his pocket and handed it to Julie. "Here are the exact words you are to say. Should you throw in even one extra syllable, I'll shoot you."

Julie looked at the words on the sheet. They were hard to see.

Her hands were shaking and her eyes were blurry from tears. She wiped her cheeks, took a breath and gathered herself. She knew she had to attack him. Every second she waited worked against her.

Buck looked around the room. "There's no phone in here."

"No," Julie said, irrationally hoping that caused a severe delay in his plans.

He pressed the remote device on his collar and spoke into his headset. "Travis," he barked, "bring me a house phone in here."

Buck stood there with a sly grin and gestured his gun upward. "Let's have a little peek," he said staring at her chest.

Julie pulled down her shirt, ready to go, wanting to go. Now.

Buck seemed to sense her attitude. He held the gun to her head and said, "You're not going to do anything stupid, are you? Because I'm getting paid a hundred thousand dollars to kill you, so if you get hasty — I collect sooner."

Julie tried to focus. With every move he made, she considered her assault. If she raised her shirt, maybe he'd get careless and drop his guard. He might reach for her breast and that could give her an opening. She uncrossed her legs and prepared herself.

Buck stepped back for a moment and pushed the button on his collar. "Travis, where's that phone?"

Then to Julie he added, "But I get another two hundred thousand for your husband. And that's some real incentive. So let's do this the right way and I'll make it quick."

He looked at the closed bedroom door and his face turned harsh. Into his headset, he barked, "Travis? Marshall? Will?"

His somber face told her he wasn't getting any response. Julie wondered now about Tommy. Buck never mentioned him and it gave her hope. He took a step toward the door, then thought about it. Julie didn't remember closing the door. He glanced outside through the open shades. The windows faced the front of the house. Julie couldn't see any other cars. The sun was beginning to set, throwing streaks of light through the bare fall trees. The nearest house was almost a mile away, so screaming was worthless.

Then Julie heard a sound which made her heart soar.

"I wouldn't do that if I were you," said Tommy Bracco from outside the door.

Buck grabbed a handful of Julie's hair and yanked her to her feet. He shoved her in front of him for protection and clutched her tight around the waist.

"Go ahead," Buck yelled, jamming his pistol into her neck. "Just try it and she's dead."

Buck dragged Julie to the side of the bed, all the while keeping her between him and the door. "Now listen," he said. "Crack open the door and slide your weapon toward me. If you do anything slightly wrong, I'll kill her first."

There were a few seconds of silence on the other side of the door.

"I wouldn't do that if I were you," Tommy repeated, seemingly mocking him. Buck fired his gun twice into the middle of the door. The noise rattled the bedroom and caused Julie to cower. When she didn't hear anything on the other side of the door, she worried.

Buck was jittery though. Julie could feel his indecision through his tight grip, which was leaving her with little oxygen. He was pulling tighter and tighter. This couldn't last much longer or she would collapse. She had to try something.

"Shoot him, Tommy," she yelled, hoping her voice might give him the position he needed.

"I'm not counting to three, jerkoff," Buck snapped. "I'm killing her right now. Then you."

Tommy just said, "I wouldn't do that if I were you." It sounded exactly like the first two times and it clearly baffled Buck. Julie was confused as well.

Until she heard the high-pitched clink of her bedroom window cracking and felt Buck's arms loosen their grip around her waist. Then his body slumped onto the floor behind her. His mouth was open in shock. On the side of his head was a round bullet hole with red and white liquid oozing down the side of his face and onto her beige carpet. She finally sucked in a full breath and put her hands on her knees. She looked up to see Tommy opening her bedroom window and scrambling up into her room with a silenced gun. He dropped his gun onto the bed and pulled her into his arms.

"You okay?" he said, holding her gently, like cradling a newborn.

"Yeah," she said, gathering herself. She held her belly while huffing. "Oh, Tommy, I wasn't sure there for a minute."

Tommy backed up and held her chin in his hand. "You wanted

to go after him didn't you?" He grinned. "I saw your face. You wanted a piece of him."

Julie grinned. Mostly out of relief. They both look down at the dead man.

"Who are these guys?" Julie asked.

"They're mercenaries. Soldiers for hire," Tommy said. "I guess they'll work for just about anyone as long as you pay them enough. Even a terrorist."

"You saw them coming?"

Tommy kicked the headset from the soldier's head. His lips curled into a disgusting scowl. "These assholes are so arrogant they can't even imagine someone could be smarter than them."

"But . . . how . . ." she said not quite understanding what happened.

"My new phone," Tommy said. "I can hear wireless transmissions within a hundred-yard radius. I knew exactly where they were."

Julie wanted to laugh. She nearly cried.

Once again Tommy's recorded voice came from the other side of the door. "I wouldn't do that if I were you."

Tommy walked over and opened the door. Sitting on a chair outside the door was his phone. He grabbed it and held it up with pride. "I'm telling you, Jule. I love this thing."

Chapter 11

Anton Kalinikov stood behind the wheel of the forty-foot yacht and became comfortable with the rhythm of the waves in the Chesapeake Bay. The restaurant he spied sat at the end of a long pier, out in the bay, by itself, exposed. Nightfall had blanketed the coastline and left him floating in darkness. The water was calmer than he'd anticipated, just a jostling of waves slapping at the hull as he peered through his binoculars. His eyes perked up as he spotted the target entering the restaurant.

It was Carl Rutherford's twentieth anniversary and he smiled while taking his wife's hand and sat her at their table by the window. He'd made the reservations a week ago like a good husband. Most people felt there was safety in numbers, so Rutherford didn't appear apprehensive. It helped that he'd brought along three of his FBI friends to watch over him while he enjoyed his meal. Two for the inside, one outside.

The three agents came in the same car two hours prior to the reservation. They had been efficient in their sweep of the area. They'd inspected the table, spoke with the kitchen staff and scrutinized the perimeter. Very professional. Kalinikov knew, because he'd been at the bar watching the entire time.

A professional assassin, however, must always stay unpredictable. Once you develop a pattern you become vulnerable. Kalinikov wondered now how much the FBI knew about him. He had to believe they knew he was Russian, maybe even knew he was left-handed by the first body he'd left. That was okay. He was a complete stranger to the American authorities and the FBI had no data to draw from. If they'd known anything about his history they would suspect he preferred to work close up. That helped.

Now he could see the waiter standing by the Rutherfords' table, hands behind his back, probably explaining the menu. Crab cakes were their specialty.

He heard a moan and pulled the binoculars down to address the bound and gagged man next to him. Even in the darkness Kalinikov could see the fear in the man's eyes. He sat behind the wheel on the captain's chair, obviously petrified of his fate.

"I told you I will not kill you," Kalinikov offered. "But you must remain still."

The man nodded furiously, trying to agree as much as possible. His fears were most certainly elevated by the rocket-propelled grenade launcher lying on the floor across from him.

Kalinikov scanned his surroundings first with the naked eye, then through the binoculars. Nothing seemed irregular. A few random fishing boats. A marine police boat slowly trawled the shoreline, moving away from him.

Kalinikov pushed a green button on the control panel and heard the creaking of the anchor ascending into the side of the hull. He maneuvered the boat sideways to allow the RPG's backblast to avoid the cabin. The FBI agent on the pier outside the restaurant pretended to be on his cell phone, pacing back and forth, while examining the customers as they arrived for their meal. Half the time he opened the door for them, a reason to get even a closer look.

Now the agent seemed to pick up the new movement and gained interest in Kalinikov's boat. It was time for the distraction.

Kalinikov reached into his pocket and removed the remote control. He placed it in his fingers and carefully scanned his surroundings one more time. Then he pushed the red button.

From the parking lot on the opposite side of the restaurant an explosion pierced through the still night loud enough to alert even the casual diner. It was nothing more than an abandoned car Kalinikov had left there for his diversion. The FBI agent guarding the pier immediately sprinted around the restaurant and out of view.

Kalinikov mounted the Russian-made RPG to his shoulder and steadied it on his torso. The exact Russian translation for an RPG is "handheld, anti-tank grenade launcher." It had enough power to take out the entire restaurant with one launch. The only problem with the device was its range, so Kalinikov had to risk coming to within eighty yards of the front window before he stepped out into the cool bay breeze. He'd thought about using his rifle, but the boats movement made the shot too risky even for him. This was the correct choice.

Carl Rutherford had grabbed his wife while she gathered her purse and jacket from the back of her chair. The inside agents moved quickly to usher their colleague away from danger.

That's when Kalinikov pulled the trigger.

* * *

FBI agent Mark Renton was on his knees in the restaurant parking lot tending to a burned valet driver when he'd heard the familiar sound from behind him. It was a sound he'd heard in Afghanistan many years earlier, but once you've heard it, it never leaves your brain. It was the distinct hiss of an RPG heading in his direction. Self-preservation kicked in. He instinctively ducked and covered his head. Seconds later the impact of the grenade hitting the restaurant blasted throughout the bay and a giant fireball expelled its energy into the night sky.

The heat swept over Renton as he protected the injured valet from shards of debris. Renton knew instantly it was the Russian assassin. Carl Rutherford and his wife were dead along with two other FBI agents and lots of other innocent people.

His ears were ringing as he scrambled to his feet and saw pedestrians calling 911 on their cell phones. He quickly scrambled around the side of the restaurant, his body slanted to his left as if he'd just come off an amusement park ride and couldn't gain his balance yet. His equilibrium was shot from the pounding on his eardrums. He saw a yacht going full throttle away from the shoreline, cutting through the bay in a straight line for the Atlantic.

Renton had had a bad feeling about the boat floating so close to the pier, but couldn't see inside the cabin to quantify his concerns. A police boat was in high pursuit of the fleeing yacht, its lights flashing and reflecting off the water as it gave chase.

Renton needed to get out there. His friends were just murdered and the killer couldn't get away with it. Not while he was still alive.

He saw a man by the dock apparently checking out his boat. Renton ran over and flashed his FBI shield. "You the owner?" he asked.

The man seemed unsure of Renton's motive. He looked like he was being accused of something.

"I desperately need your help," Renton said. "Can you take me out to that police boat?

The man stood there and didn't answer. Then it dawned on Renton. The man was wearing a button-down shirt and nice, creased jeans. His face turned toward the ball of flames. He must've had family inside the restaurant. He was in shock.

Renton's blood was flying through his body, his pulse pounding at his temples. He saw the yacht getting farther out into the bay and had nothing but revenge on his mind.

Renton pulled the man's shoulders to face him. "Can I use your boat? Please."

The man absently fished out a set of keys from his pocket and handed them to him.

Renton untied the ropes and jumped on board. He had nothing more than a rudimentary understanding of how to drive a boat. It was a cabin cruiser around thirty feet in length. He hunched down to get inside the cabin and found the control panel. As the engine coughed to life he pushed the throttle and headed out. From behind him he heard sirens. He looked over his shoulder and saw people gathering outside the restaurant. Some were hugging each other. Some stood in shock. The man whose boat he borrowed stood in the exact same spot and stared at the sight.

Renton felt a sense of loss, but there were professionals just minutes away and those precious minutes could allow The Russian to escape. And if he escaped, even more people would be in danger. More FBI agents. Renton couldn't allow that to happen.

The cabin cruiser had reached top speed and the boat skipped over the water like a dolphin. He found the spotlights and was able to see thirty yards ahead of him. The police boat was close to the assassin's yacht. Renton felt his phone vibrate. He pulled it from his pocket and said, "Renton."

"What the fuck's going on?" It was Lynn Harding, the assistant special agent in charge of the Baltimore field office. The ASAC was taking over while Walt Jackson was in LA. She'd been at the bureau for nearly twenty years, most of those as a field agent, so she wasn't your typical administrator. She was well respected.

"The Russian," Renton said, his hearing just coming back. "He fired an RPG at Sylvio's." Renton glanced over his shoulder, the pier now a dim shadow in the glow of the flames.

"Where are you now?" she asked.

"I'm in pursuit in the Chesapeake. We need the Coast Guard out here immediately. I don't see this guy going down easy. He's got an RPG. Who knows how much ammo he has."

"Don't get too close," Harding said. "Let's keep him in sight. I don't want you becoming another victim."

Renton heard the warning but had no intention of listening.

"Mark?"

"Yeah," Renton said.

"What about the rest of the crew?"

Renton was forced to think about his teammates. Not something he could afford to do right now. Not while he was gaining on the yacht.

"They're gone," Renton said.

The line was silent for a moment. The roar of the inboard engines was all Renton could hear.

"Mark," Harding said, "the Coast Guard is on the way. Tell me what else you need."

"I need eyes in the sky. If he's a pro, he'll have an escape plan."

"Got it," Harding said.

"Also get some shoes working the shoreline. I don't trust this guy."

"Done."

Renton finished the call, then slipped the phone into his pocket as the yacht came into view less than a hundred yards away. The police boat was alongside the yacht now; spotlights illuminated the vessel like a night baseball game. Three officers lined the deck with rifles to their shoulders. Renton was close enough to see the shadow inside the cabin. The Russian was standing behind the wheel swiveling his head around between the police boat and the water ahead of him. He waved his free hand in the air frantically, trying to show he didn't have a weapon. No, it was something else. He was shouting and waving and attempting communication, but he didn't slow the boat down.

One of the policemen used a megaphone to command him to stop. This caused The Russian to wave even more fervently, shaking his head and motioning to something inside the cabin. Something told Renton to get away from the yacht, but he pressed on, moving to the starboard side until he was exactly even with the vessel. The yacht had slowed slightly, but not much. It was still forging ahead at about thirty knots. The police boat kept veering into the yacht forcing it to turn into Renton's path. Renton was bumping hulls with the yacht which was a bit higher and had more mass. His cruiser was becoming unstable. He opened the door to his cabin and steered with his right hand while gauging the distance to the yacht. He needed to time it just right if he was going to jump.

It was a bad choice. Not something a rational human being would ever consider attempting at night. Not at thirty knots, with an assassin waiting for you in the next vessel. But Renton had just lost some close friends and the only thought running through his head was revenge.

The port side of his boat dipped low enough to take on bay water, then raised high enough to be two feet above the yacht's deck. He waited three dips before making his move. On the way up, he ran out and jumped. It was only four feet away, but it was clearly the scariest thing he'd ever done. Halfway over, the wind caught him and held him back, keeping him suspended in midair. His momentum got him as far as the railing and he slammed into the brass rails so hard he could feel his ribs cave in. He hung onto the railing, and tried to breathe. His eyes watered from the wind and lack of oxygen. The Russian didn't move however. He remained behind the wheel yelling something to the police about a tong. A tong? Renton felt like he was losing consciousness. A tong?

He was able to get his knee onto the deck and remove the pressure from his rib cage. He finally took a long breath and gained a better grasp of the railing. The Russian was still yelling at the same time the police ordered him to stop.

A tong? Then it occurred to Renton what The Russian was saying. A bomb.

Renton needed to act. He swung his foot over the rail and pulled himself onto the deck. The Russian paid no attention to him. He was beginning to wonder why the assassin stayed behind the wheel, oblivious to Renton's presence. He acted as if he was still going to outrun the police. Renton could see a helicopter approaching, nose down, spotlighting the choppy bay water.

Renton scrambled to his feet and pulled out his gun. The Russian had his back to him yelling at the police, one hand on the wheel. Renton entered the cabin with his gun out. The police spotlights illuminated the cabin and he could see a man handcuffed to the wheel. He seemed to sense Renton and turned to face him. The man was older than he'd suspected. Maybe sixty-five. He wore a Hawaiian tee shirt, jeans and sandals.

"Stay still," Renton ordered.

A policeman hopped onto the port deck and entered the cabin with his rifle out front and looked Renton over.

"FBI," Renton exclaimed, pulling out his shield for the man to examine.

The officer nodded.

Once Renton put away his shield, he reached for the throttle. That's when the man handcuffed to the wheel screamed, "No!"

Renton froze. "What's the matter?"

"You don't understand," the man said exasperated. "There's a bomb on board. It will explode if this boat goes under twenty knots. We have to keep up our speed."

"Why do you say that?" Renton said.

"That's what the man told me."

"What man?"

"The man who blew up Sylvio's."

Renton looked around the cabin. "Where is he?"

"He's long gone," the man's voice now urgent, lifting his handcuffed hand. "Can you please release me? We need to get out of here."

Renton looked the man over. He had a southern accent. He wasn't The Russian, that was for sure.

"Is this your yacht?" Renton asked.

"Yes."

"How long was he on the boat?"

"Maybe an hour before he blew up the place."

Renton put his gun away. "Where's this bomb?"

The man pointed to a plastic container below the front windshield, just out of his reach. There were no wires coming from the container.

He looked at the man. "How long did he work on attaching the bomb?"

"A couple of minutes," the man said, his eyes darting from Renton then to the bomb.

The police officer said, "Let's get out of here and call the bomb squad."

Renton looked at the man's face, scarred from fear. Renton knew a little about boats. He knew a lot more about bombs however. He pulled the plastic container from the wall. It was attached with double adhesive tape.

The man yelled, "No, don't!"

Renton yanked open the small container. As he suspected, it was empty. He showed it to the old man.

"You've been watching too many movies," Renton said.

"But . . ." the man seemed incredulous. It was no act. The assassin had him completely convinced. Especially after firing an RPG at Sylvio's. The man was simply a decoy to give him time to escape.

Renton looked back toward the shore. The flames from the restaurant were down to embers. He could see four or five Coast Guard vessels speeding toward them, while a helicopter hovered overhead. Suddenly it dawned on him. The pieces fit together perfectly. The Russian had seen Renton watching the yacht. He used a remote to detonate the car bomb in the parking lot to draw attention away from him. He must've leapt off the boat immediately after the restaurant explosion.

Renton knew they were going to scour the shoreline for hours and he also knew they weren't going to find a thing. The Russian had a thirty-minute head start. He was long gone.

Chapter 12

President Merrick was reading *Goodnight Moon* to his daughter Emily when her bedroom door opened and his wife's face came into view. Her blank expression told him everything. Whenever she didn't have her patented smile, something was wrong. She approached the bed and took the book from Merrick. The smile made a forced return.

"I'd like to finish reading this if I could," his wife said to Emily.

"Aw." Emily pouted as her dad lifted himself from the edge of her bed and gave her a gentle kiss on the forehead.

"But daddy never gets to read to me anymore," the young girl cried.

"Now, Sweetie," Merrick said. "I'll be reading that same book to you tomorrow night. I promise."

Merrick closed the bedroom door and found a male aide anxiously waiting for him, holding out a cell phone.

"There's been an explosion, sir," the aide said.

Merrick put the phone to his ear.

"We need to talk," Samuel Fisk said.

* * *

The FBI's Baltimore field office held the most extensive antiterrorist war room in the nation. It was fifty feet below the building and required an iris scan and an elevator to get there. The room was lined with slim computer monitors ranging from forty to ninety inches long. Each screen displayed a satellite image from different parts of the globe and was monitored twenty-four hours a day by thirty-five information technicians. These technicians sat behind a long narrow tabletop which extended continuously throughout the entire perimeter of the rectangle room. Each technician had their own laptop computer and moved around the room constantly searching for answers to data received from different field agents.

These technicians worked long hours and sometimes got so lost in their assignments, they would lose track of time and even become disoriented. That's why the war room was designed to emulate the outdoors. The ceiling displayed a real-time image of the sky, piped in from a camera on the roof. When it was raining, the employees saw the rain coming down, when it was sunny out, it was sunny inside the war room. Now it was nighttime and there were stars up above, with a few scattered clouds.

In the center of the room was a round mahogany table with over twenty leather chairs available. Right now the tension in the room had escalated to a new level. Sitting around the table were FBI Director Louis Dutton, CIA Director Kenneth Morris, Defense Secretary Martin Riggs, Secretary of State Samuel Fisk and ASAC Lynn Harding.

Lynn Harding had just finished her brief on the bombing of Sylvio's. Most people around the table had been in the war room since breakfast so the conversations were becoming more spirited as fatigue set in and patience wore down.

"So tell me what you know about The Russian?" FBI Director Louis Dutton asked the ASAC.

Harding crossed her legs, her pant suit was solemn black and her demeanor even darker. She fished through some notes she'd scribbled down while getting briefed from a European colleague with the MI6 in London.

"His name is Anton Kalinikov," she said, scanning her chicken-scratch shorthand. "He's ex-KGB. Tall. Left-handed." She looked up. "He's very capable. No one has ever taken a surveillance image of him while he operated. His last known photo was taken almost twenty years ago."

"That's it?" Defense Secretary Martin Riggs asked. "That's all you have on the guy?"

Harding understood Riggs's frustration. He was an ex-marine and saw most things as black and white. She looked down at her notepad. "That's all we know for sure. Everything else is conjecture."

Harding looked over at CIA Director Ken Morris. The FBI dealt mostly with domestic terrorism while the CIA handled much of the collection of global information. Morris pulled down on his tie and unbuttoned his first shirt button.

"Shit," Morris said. "I'm still not sure how we came up with The Russian for this stuff. My sources tell me he's still in the Ukraine."

Morris looked back to Harding, lobbing the question of shared information into Harding's lap.

Harding was fine with the volley. Her boss, Walt Jackson, had given her the name without providing a source, which was code for, "Don't ask me questions you don't want the answers to."

She took in Morris with an even expression. "Your intelligence is quality-challenged."

Morris seemed ready to enter attack mode when the chime announcing the elevator's arrival rang. The doors opened and two secret service agents with navy-blue suits entered the room and separated to allow President Merrick to pass between them. He was followed by his press secretary, Fredrick Himes.

Everyone at the table stood up while Merrick immediately waved them down. Himes found a seat on the far end of the table, while Merrick took the chair between Lynn Harding and Louis Dutton. He was the ultimate diplomat, knowing all too well the acrimony between the FBI and CIA when it came to domestic terrorism. The FBI was the leading agency, yet the CIA had most of the overseas resources which could and should anticipate some of the events.

Merrick had his white shirt rolled to his elbows. He placed his hands on the table and looked around at his department heads. His gaze landed on Dutton.

"Well?" Merrick said. "Tell me what we know."

The FBI Director told him. Hitting on the facts while not including any subjective opinions. Harding was impressed with the report. She couldn't have done it better herself and she was the one who'd briefed Dutton.

Merrick glanced around, seemingly searching for something. "Where's Walt?"

"Payson, Arizona, sir," Dutton replied.

Merrick first nodded, then shook his head. He pointed to the dome-shaped speaker in the center of the table. "Get him on the phone."

Dutton twisted his head and gestured to a nearby agent who waited for just such requests.

Merrick tapped Harding on the leg as he stood up. "You want some coffee?"

Harding grinned. "That would be great. Just black and a couple of sugars."

Merrick disappeared into a nearby alcove where the refreshments were kept. He returned a few minutes later with two mugs and handed one to Harding.

"Thanks," she said. "What are you drinking?"

"It's a combination of crystal meth and herbal tea." He smiled. "Except we're out of crystal meth right now."

"I know," Harding said. "I used the last of it this afternoon."

Walt Jackson's voice came over the speakerphone and Merrick rubbed his hands together and said, "Now we can proceed."

It made Harding feel good knowing President Merrick had so much respect for her boss.

"Walt," Dutton said, "Who's there with you?"

"Nick and Matt."

"Evening, gentlemen," President Merrick said.

"Evening, sir" came the two voices.

"Walt, this is Lynn," Harding said. "You've been briefed on Carl?"

"Yes," Walt said. "What about Mel?"

"It was just confirmed to be ricin poisoning," Lynn said somberly. "He won't make it through the night."

"Shit," someone said over the speakerphone, but Harding couldn't tell whom.

"This is all The Russian?" Merrick asked.

"Yes," Walt said. "But Barzani's paying the bill. The KSF has deep pockets.

They can offer obscene amounts of money to get people to do the work for them. It's the reason that Iron Mountain squad was compelled to make an attempt on Nick's wife."

President Merrick frowned. "How is she, Nick?"

"She's fine, sir."

"She's coming to L.A. with me," Walt said.

Defense Secretary Riggs said, "We're examining our Iron Mountain contracts. They won't be operating in the U.S. again. We've already brought their overseas teams in for debriefing."

Merrick raised his eyebrows at Riggs. "When this is all over I want a serious discussion about the future of outsourcing the military."

Riggs just nodded.

Merrick looked at Samuel Fisk. The Secretary of State sat with a stoic expression.

"How come you're so quiet?" Merrick asked Fisk.

Fisk shrugged. "I'm waiting for someone to ask the right question."

"Which is?"

"If the majority of the KSF is in L.A., why is Walt taking Nick's wife there?"

Merrick looked around the table at closed mouths and averting eyes.

"Guys?" Merrick raised his voice. "What are you not telling me?"

Silence.

"Nick?" Merrick said.

Silence.

"Our nation's security is at risk here, boys and girls," Merrick said. "So you better not be allowing me deniability, because that takes me out of the loop. I need to know everything or I could make a poor decision."

Merrick turned to Lynn Harding. She felt the weight of his authority as he kept staring at her.

"Mr. President," she said with a low, reluctant tone. "There's been conflicting opinions about the credibility of the LAX threat."

Merrick leaned back in his chair and crossed his arms. "Walt?"

"We found traces of Semtex in the border tunnels," Walt said.

Merrick seemed to be losing his patience. "Go on."

"Then a KSF member turned on his squad for leniency. He told us the KSF used the tunnels to bring Semtex into the country to bomb LAX."

Merrick waited.

"Then," Walt said, "a reporter for the L.A. Times received an anonymous tip about the LAX threat."

Walt stopped. Merrick squinted in apparent confusion. He looked at Harding. "What's the catch?"

Harding was about to speak when Nick Bracco took her off the hook.

"It's too easy, sir," Nick said over the speakerphone. "It's like they're dropping bread crumbs on the floor for us to follow."

"It's good intelligence," Ken Morris said with a tight face. "Why are we questioning good, hard work?"

"Nick?" Merrick said.

"Too easy," Nick repeated. "I know these guys. It feels contrived."

Morris shook his head in disgust. "Feelings? That's what you're going with?"

Merrick leaned forward and rested his elbows on the table. "Nick?" he asked. "What do you think is going on?"

"I haven't figured it out yet, Mr. President. But I will."

Merrick grinned. "I know you will."

"In the meantime, they need resources here in Payson," Walt said.

"And that's the argument?" Merrick asked.

"Pretty much," Harding said.

"Nick," Merrick said. "What do you need over there?"

"Not much, sir. One good investigator is worth more than fifty Marines. We just need a few good eyes and ears."

Merrick looked at Dutton.

"I can send some people up from Phoenix," Dutton said unenthusiastically.

"That help, Nick?" Merrick asked.

"Yes, sir," Nick said. "How are the diplomatic channels going, sir?"

"Good question." Merrick stared at his mug and twisted it between his fingers while in deep thought. He looked up at his press secretary. "Freddy, contact the Turkish Prime Minister and tell him we need a face-to-face meeting, at the White House."

"But—"

Merrick held up his hand. "I know, he'll want to speak with me on the phone. But I won't. I've already sent him signals I might withdraw our troops from Turkey. This has him concerned I'm sure."

"But, sir," Himes said, "he'll want to know if your threat is serious."

"Which is exactly why I won't speak with him over the phone. He'll ask me that exact question and I don't want to lie to him. I know Hakim, he's a worrier. If he can't get me on the phone, he'll fly here to see me in person." Merrick pointed to Fisk. "Remember the Environmental Conference in Brussels when his gift basket was smaller than Israel's? He spent the entire weekend asking everyone what they'd received when they arrived. He's neurotic."

Merrick looked down at the speaker on the table. "Then, Nick, we can use his unexpected visit to Washington as a bargaining tool with the KSF. Let them know we're beginning a conversation with the Prime Minister to resolve the conflict in Turkey." He looked up at Himes. "Maybe we can leak something to the press about a possible withdrawal."

"That's a good tactic, sir" Nick said. "Maybe buy us some time."

Merrick smiled, seemingly proud of his diplomatic acumen.

"There's one other thing we need to consider, sir," Harding said. "The Russian. If he's truly in D.C., then we can't overlook the fact you might become a target."

Merrick nodded, somber. "Okay. Let's be careful."

"Suggestion, sir," Himes said. "We've been meaning to update the White House's website. Let's take it down for a few days and leave a message it's being overhauled . . . no . . . improved. This way we can eliminate posting your daily schedule without its absence being conspicuous."

"Good." Merrick slapped his hands on the table and stood. "I have a budget meeting to attend so we can pay for some of these things." He looked directly at Harding when he said, "Keep me informed."

Chapter 13

Jennifer Steele pulled over the Sheriff's cruiser in front of the last house on their list. Luke hopped out of the car and stretched his arms over his head with a big yawn.

"You tired?" Steele asked.

"A little," Luke said, looking up at the twilight. Stars were beginning to peek through the atmosphere as the sun made its exit.

The cruiser was parked thirty yards from the large cabin in the gravel street right next to the mailbox. The road was completely secluded without a neighbor in sight. Across the street from the cabin was nothing but thick pines and a sharp drop-off.

Luke stepped toward the house, crunching his way up the drive while Steele stayed with the car and examined the realtor's information sheet about the place. It was an investment property which was rented by an out-of-state owner for passive income. Not uncommon in these parts of Arizona. The renter had prepaid for an entire year with cash. That wasn't so common. Why part ways with your money unless you have a reason? Like not wanting to pay with cash each month and becoming conspicuous. Luke found his way to the side of the house and stuck his face up against a garage window.

"One car," he said in a low voice.

Steele finished examining the rental info, and stuck the sheet on the passenger's seat, and closed the door. She continued up the gravel driveway and examined the grounds. Mostly pines with decorated rocks around the exterior. A few clumps of weeds seemed ready to sprout, but with winter coming, their growth would be seriously threatened. She was halfway up the driveway when she heard something behind her. It was a mechanical sound, out of place in this serene setting.

Steele walked back down the driveway toward the woods opposite the cabin. She didn't hear the noise again until she moved left to get around the car. She stopped. The noise stopped. She moved right to go around the front of the car and the noise began again. She stopped. The noise stopped.

Steele's instincts told her to leave.

"Luke," she said over her shoulder.

There was no response.

She moved to the back of the car and zoned in on the noise this time. It was a tiny camera, perched atop one of the pine trees. It was following her movement and being a bit noisy about it. Probably a drop of oil might've taken care of it, but now it had her attention.

Having a security system was one thing, but a roving camera was excessive even for a federal building. Something deep down inside made her step away from the woods.

"Luke," Steele called out in a low voice. The deputy was nowhere to be seen.

"Luke," she said, a little louder now.

Nothing.

The house appeared deserted. What was a peaceful cabin now seemed creepy.

"Damn you, Luke," she muttered under her breath. "Stay in my line of sight."

She found herself tracing the exterior of the car with her hand, while staring at the home searching for clues. She was deciding what to do next when she heard a noise. A manmade noise. She was ducking behind the car when the first shot was fired. It whizzed past her ear and startled her to the ground.

"Shit," Steele cried. Frantically, she pulled her gun out and poked her head up to see through the windows. A barrage of gunshots rang out pelting the side of the car and shattering the windows. She crouched below the window line and grabbed her phone to hit the send button. A moment later she heard Matt's voice. With gunshots ringing out into the wilderness, all she could think to say was, "You busy?"

* * *

Matt was finishing up a strategy session with Nick and Walt when he felt his phone vibrate in his pocket. He looked to see it was Jennifer.

"What's up?" he said, but immediately heard the familiar sound of gunfire and shouted, "Jennifer?"

"You busy?" she asked, panic in her voice.

"Where are you?" Matt said. Nick and Walt stopped their

conversations and surrounded Matt; Nick put his ear close to Matt's receiver.

"385 Willow," she yelled. "They've got Luke."

"Are you near the car? Can you get out?" Matt said.

"Yes."

"Get the fuck out of there Jennifer," Matt shouted.

"But, Luke—"

"Luke is dead," Matt said, breaking into a trot out through the outer office where Tommy and Julie were talking. "Get out, now," Matt yelled again to Steele.

* * *

Barzani watched the deputy get taped to a chair in the kitchen while his security team pelted the female FBI agent with round after round of rifle and pistol shots from the upstairs windows. It was getting dark outside, but he could still see the agent crouched behind the car. Barzani knew they had to kill her quickly before backup came.

Mano Surtek was playing with a plastic remote while watching the activity outside.

One of Barzani's personal security guards tugged on his arm. "We need to get you out of here, Sarock," the man said.

Barzani shook off the guard. He was too captivated to leave. The woman FBI agent was cornered and he was willing to wait a few moments to enjoy the kill.

"Tell them to hold their fire," Barzani said.

The security guard ran around out of the kitchen and up the stairs. A few moments later the shots ceased.

As expected the female FBI agent took the opportunity to open the driver's side door and sneak into the car. The woman was good, he could barely see her head sticking up as she stepped on the gas and spun dirt with her tires.

Barzani Martin Riggsplaced a hand on Mano's shoulder while staring intently on the road in front of the car.

"Ready?' Barzani asked.

"Yes, Sarock," Mano said, hovering his thumb over a button on the remote control detonator. As the Sheriff's car fishtailed down the unpaved street, Mano timed the vehicle's forward motion perfectly.

He pushed the button.

The car jumped up in a ball of flame as the explosion catapulted the vehicle five feet in the air. It tilted the car sideways and the charred shell skidded to a stop just before hitting a large pine. The blast echoed throughout the woods and Barzani couldn't keep the smile from his face as debris from the car littered down over a stand of trees.

"Now," Barzani said, nodding with satisfaction. "Now we can go."

* * *

Matt raced down the gravel road and drove furiously until he saw the devastating sight. Jennifer's car sat on its side, smoke drifting from its carcass.

Nick, Matt and Walt jumped out of the car and ran to the disfigured vehicle. Heat still steamed off the metal in shimmery waves.

Matt ran up to look inside the shell and saw nothing. He turned around in a circle searching for clues, then looked at the cabin and saw the upstairs windows open. He pulled out his Glock and said, "The house."

Nick and Walt took attack positions around the perimeter of the cabin. Matt tried to catch his breath. Nick was already at the front door and gestured for him to take the back.

Matt's heart pounded in desperation as he crept along the back wall of the house. He peeked up into a window and saw nothing unusual, but nightfall was making it difficult. His mind wandered dangerously to the fate of the only one he'd ever loved. Jennifer needed to be safe. Breathe, he thought. As he approached the back door, his hand trembled while reaching for the knob.

"Are you looking for me?" a female voice said behind him.

He whirled around to see Jennifer Steele smiling with leaves clinging to her jacket and dirt covering her face.

Matt grabbed her and squeezed her until she squealed, "I'm okay."

Relief flooded his system. His vision blurred and he wiped his eyes to clear it.

"Hey," Steele said, "you're not getting moist on me, are you?"

"What the . . . why didn't you call me?"

"Sorry, I dropped my phone in the car as I rolled out."

"Rolled out?"

"Well," she said, "you always taught me to watch for booby traps with these guys. I saw a bump in the road which looked like an IED, so I jammed a rock on the accelerator and rolled out and down that incline."

"Are they gone?"

She nodded. "I couldn't raise my head to see what they were driving, Matt. Sorry."

He gathered her in his arms again. "It's okay."

The back door opened and Walt said, "You better get in here."

Before they even reached the kitchen Matt could smell death in the air. Luke sat in a chair, his arms hanging limp, his head slumped down. When Matt circled around the deputy, he could see the long slice mark across his neck. The blood had drained out and left nothing to hope for.

Nick leaned over and kissed Luke on the forehead, then turned and put his hand over his mouth as he paced a small oval.

On Luke's chest was a piece of paper jammed into his torso with a boning knife. The note read, "You're next."

"Shit," Matt said.

Nick's pace quickened as he simply shook his head and murmured obscenities.

Walt looked at Steele. "You okay?"

She nodded.

"You see them leave?"

"No," she said, with a tinge of shame on her face. "I had to take cover."

They seemed to stay quiet while Nick worked things out in his head. Finally, he turned to Steele and pointed. "Call the State Police and get roadblocks up on 60 and 260. Maybe fifty miles out. Did you get the color of the vehicle?

"It was a white SUV. Maybe a Suburban?"

"Give them what you know. Tell them it's a long shot, but prepare them."

Steele fished her hand into Matt's pocket and pulled out his phone, then went outside for the call.

Nick pointed to Walt. "You need to get to L.A."

Walt cocked his head in apparent confusion.

"Because," Nick said, "if I'm wrong about LAX, they'll crucify you. And right now I can't afford to have anyone else I care about get hurt."

Walt didn't argue. He had a family to feed as well.

"Besides," Nick added, "if you go over there and cause a big ruckus, it might give Barzani a false sense of security. Like we've lost their scent."

Sirens blared nearby.

Nick adjusted his arm sling. He looked down at Luke with a tight chin. "Walt," he said, "before you go, get Stevie Gilpin on the red eye. Have him bring his bag of toys with him."

Walt crossed his arms. "Aren't you forgetting something?"

Nick squinted.

"You're the Sheriff of Gila County, Arizona. I can't exactly be giving you access to all this confidential FBI stuff."

Nick's eyes roamed around the room as if searching for something. "Then reinstate me," he said.

From his inside jacket pocket, Walt pulled out a worn leather badge case. He handed it to Nick with a sad smile. "I thought you'd never ask."

Chapter 14

Julie Bracco packed the last of her things and dropped her bag on the living room floor. She looked at Matt and Jennifer Steele cuddled up on the couch watching the evening news.

"Anything else on?" she said, pulling her hair back into a tight bun. A local Payson reporter stood a distance away from the abandoned KSF safe house. The news crew had illuminated the scene for the viewers and offered Nick's written statement announcing the terrorists' escape, the death of Deputy Luke Fletcher, and the possibility of Kurdish militants still operating in the vicinity. Nick had given the news media the FBI's hotline number to report any suspicious behavior. Meanwhile, he had the Baltimore Field Office email over pictures of Temir Barzani and a couple of his known soldiers.

Matt sat with his hand on his forehead seemingly in complete disgust with the report, as if being forced to relive the day was too much for him. He pushed the remote and found a college basketball game on ESPN.

Steele yawned. "Well, I'm about ready for bed." She looked at Matt with raised eyebrows and held out her hand.

"You need real sleep," Walt called from the kitchen with his paternal voice. He was scraping up the remains of a salad Julie had made for dinner.

Matt grinned mischievously and took her hand. He looked at Walt and said, "Yes, Dad." Then he followed Steele into the guest bedroom.

Julie frowned. Even though her house had bloodstains and a bullet hole through her bedroom window, she was sad to leave. The front door opened and Nick came in with shoulders slumped. He'd just met with Luke Fletcher's family.

Nick came over and brushed a loose hair from Julie's face.

"I'm going to miss you," he said.

"You take your meds, understand? Dr. Morgan said you can regress if you miss any dosages. I have them all laid out on the bathroom counter," she said. "And I already have the coffee machine set to go at six. Make sure you—"

Nick placed his index finger on her lips. "Shh. I know that's your way of telling me you love me."

Julie looked surprised. "You've been reading that book I gave you, haven't you?"

"Every word."

"Then you know how important it is to listen to your wife when she's giving you instructions."

Nick leaned over and kissed her on the tip of her nose. "I love you."

"Love you, too," she said.

Walt washed his salad plate in the kitchen sink, then took a circuitous route to the front door and lingered there, obviously waiting for Julie.

"I really need to leave?' she asked.

Nick nodded. "I just don't have enough people to keep you safe, sweetie. I had to beg for a couple of deputies from Globe to watch the office while we figured out what to do with Semir."

She wrapped her arms around her husband and whispered, "Please be careful, baby."

"Don't worry," he said. "I've got it under control."

She pulled back, looked at his bandaged shoulder and almost said something.

Tommy's voice came over a radio sitting on the counter between the kitchen and living room. "We have visitors."

Nick and Walt immediately pulled out their pistols as Matt flew out of the bedroom, shirt off, gun ready.

"Relax," Tommy said. "They're friendly."

It was Tommy's turn to watch the perimeter of the house. A chorus of engines could be heard coming up the driveway. Walt opened the door and smiled.

"You'll want to see this," he said.

Nick and Julie walked over to the doorway. Idling in the semicircle gravel driveway were three camouflage Humvees. Their headlights pierced through the night with intimidation as dust from their tires floated over their beams. A thin, wiry soldier jumped from the passenger seat, pulled off his cap and saluted the trio in the doorway.

"Major Flynn, Special Forces, Fort Benson, Arizona," he said, dropping his hand after the salute. "I'm looking for Nick Bracco."

Nick walked out onto the porch and stepped down the two

steps to shake the major's hand. "I'm Nick," he said.

The three Humvees sat motionless, their engines simmering with power, like a herd of rhinos waiting to charge.

"Mr. Bracco, sir," Major Flynn said. "I have orders from the Commander-in-Chief to make our squadron available to you for any duty necessary."

Nick turned to Julie and smiled. "Well, honey, it looks like you'll be staying."

* * *

It was almost midnight when Ed Tolliver finally rolled into bed. After getting the news about Carl and Katherine Rutherford, he'd had a hard time getting to sleep. Even with a team of agents protecting his home, he still felt uneasy. He'd been briefed about the Russian assassin and knew how dangerous the man could be, but he refused to go to a safe house across town, so they brought the protection to him. His cell phone chirped in the kitchen and he peeked over at his wife to make certain she didn't wake. He hopped out of bed and scrambled down the hallway to get to the phone before it woke the kids.

FBI agent Rolley Chandler was already standing at the counter with Ed's phone in his hand. Chandler studied the display for a moment, then frowned and handed it to Tolliver.

"Private caller," Chandler said, looking disappointed.

Tolliver took the phone and headed into the guest bedroom on the opposite side of the house from his family's bedrooms. He didn't mind his fellow agents protecting him, but he didn't like certain areas of his life intruded upon. Under any circumstance.

"This is Ed," Tolliver said in a near whisper.

"Hi," came the female voice.

Tolliver froze. He immediately glanced out into the hallway, then closed the bedroom door and sat on the guest bed.

"What are you doing?" he said in a hushed tone.

Vicki Peters sounded nervous. "I uh . . . needed to talk."

"Are you crazy?" he said. "Don't you know what time it is?"

"Yes, I know."

Tolliver's head began to pound. He rubbed his temple. "Listen," he said, "now's not the time for this. Don't ever do this to me again."

There was a pause, then, "It's over, Ed," she said. Her voice was shaky and seemed genuinely upset.

"What?" Tolliver's voice pitched an octave higher than normal. "What do you mean? I thought we agreed," he said, groping for the right words. "The twins are gone in two months. That's just sixty days. You mean you can't wait sixty days?"

"No, Ed, I can't wait sixty minutes," she said with a little ugliness to her tone.

Tolliver couldn't believe this was happening. He moved even farther away from the door and placed a pillow to his cheek covering up his phone and drowning out his voice from eavesdroppers. "C'mon now, Vicki, what's going on? Why now?"

"Because," she said, "I've met someone else."

Now Tolliver's heart began to thump irregularly. "What? Are you kidding? When?"

"A few weeks ago," she said. "I just can't wait any longer, Ed. I've done it for too long."

"But . . . but," Tolliver didn't know what to say. He had been completely blindsided. "Let's talk about this, okay?"

"Sorry," she said, "when you say let's talk about it, you mean next week or tomorrow. My tomorrows are going to belong to someone else. Someone who deserves my tomorrows."

"Oh, come on, you sound like you've been reading a Maya Angelou novel." Tolliver glanced at the door. He was pretty sure agent Chandler would have his back if the wife suddenly woke up. "Let's get together for lunch and—"

"No," she said. "No more. I'm going to go now."

"Wait." Tolliver stood up and ran a hand through his hair. "Wait, baby, please. I'll meet you . . ." he noticed the clock on the nightstand. It was 11:47. "I'll be there in thirty minutes."

"In thirty-one minutes you'll be too late."

Tolliver put the phone down from his ear and stood there in the dark. His life was falling apart. Someone wanted him dead and his lover wanted to leave him. His foot tapped involuntarily; he was thinking about how to work it out.

* * *

Vicki Peters pushed the end button, then handed her phone to the man next to her. She was trembling. The man had already sliced open her beagle, Josie, leaving her on the dining room table with her guts heaped in a pile next to her. The man had forced her to look at Josie during the entire phone conversation. Blood had begun to spread across the table and drip over the side onto the tile floor. Vicki had already vomited twice and was about to purge again. She gripped her stomach in agony.

"Good girl," the man said. "You did exactly as I asked you."

"Please," she begged, her eyes filling with tears. "Please let me go now. You promised."

He looked down with a serious expression, as if considering his options. When his head came up, the knife came with it. She didn't even have time to scream.

Chapter 15

Nick woke to a jab in his side. He moved and grimaced from the sudden pain in his shoulder. He looked up to a familiar shadow over him.

"Let's go," Matt said.

Nick wiped his eyes, then saw the time. 5:19 AM.

Matt left, leaving the door open and the living room light beaming into the bedroom. Nick forced his weight forward and pushed off with his good arm. When his legs were planted on the floor, he glanced over to check on Julie. She was still in a deep sleep. He threw on a pair of sweatpants and tee shirt before heading into the other room, quietly closing the door behind him.

Matt waited for him in the living room, standing in front of the television.

"Look at this shit," Matt said with his arms folded and nodding at the television.

A local male news reporter stood in front of the charred remnants of a house. Smoke drifted over the embers while a firefighter's hose maintained a steady stream of water. The only thing left standing was the rock chimney. It was still an hour before sunrise so tiny flickers of flame stood out in the dark.

The man was scanning his notes on a sheet of paper while reporting the facts of the story.

"At 4:05 this morning there was an explosion here at twelve fifteen Fallen Rock Road, the home of Maggie and Devon Grabowski."

Nick felt his throat tighten as a picture of an elderly couple filled the screen. The reporter spoke over the image. "We don't have any confirmation yet, but all indications are that the Grabowski's were inside their home when the explosion occurred. Firefighters said they were able to maintain the integrity of the tree line around the building and prevent the spread of a forest fire."

Matt grumbled something.

Nick said, "They were the first couple to welcome us to Payson when we bought this place," as bile pushed its way up into his esophagus.

"Apparently a neighbor heard the blast," the reporter said, "and ran outside to see what had happened." The reporter came into view again as a small woman with a pink sweatshirt came into the picture, still appearing startled.

The reporter stuck the microphone in front of the woman and said, "Can you tell us what you saw?"

"Well," the woman said, "I heard the explosion and it was so close I thought it was our house that got hit. When I went outside, I saw the Grabowski's place in flames." She looked up. "They were up over the tops of those trees," she said. "It's a miracle the whole street didn't catch fire."

"And did you see anyone or hear anything when you first came outside?"

"No, I didn't see a thing. Just . . ." the woman seemed to realize what had just occurred and she appeared to be struggling to gather herself. Of course the reporter went in for the kill.

"Did you know the Grabowskis very well?"

The woman put her hand over her mouth and looked back at the crumbled ruins behind them. "Yes," her voice cracked through her fingers.

The reporter must've realized the line he'd just crossed and looked genuinely concerned. He gazed back at the camera as a cue to phase out the grieving woman.

"Well, there's certainly a lot of pain being felt by the community here in Payson." The reporter's face now filled the screen. "Authorities are hesitant to say the exact . . ."

The report went on but Nick's stomach wasn't up for it. He reached down to get the remote and Matt grabbed his hand.

"No," he said. "You have to see this."

Now the reporter's head was down again looking at the sheet of paper. "The Kurdish Security Force has taken responsibility for the brutal attack on this sleepy mountainside community. Temir Barzani is a high-ranking member of the terrorist organization. In a statement sent exclusively to Channel 5 news, Barzani claims to have made this attack because Gila County Sheriff, Nick Bracco, failed to abide by the constitutional rules which govern the United States, thereby causing the deaths of innocent civilians. He goes on to say that a new family will die each night until Bracco turns himself over to the KSF to pay for his crimes."

The reporter looked up at the camera. "So far, no word from

the Sheriff about this demand. Back to you in the studio, Mary."

Julie came into the room wearing a tan robe, yawning and playing with her hair. "What are you guys doing up so early?" she asked, walking around them to the kitchen.

Nick shut off the TV. "The Grabowskis have been murdered." He got it out quick, as if pulling a Band-Aid off in one motion.

Julie stopped. She looked back and forth between Matt and Nick. "Barzani?"

Nick nodded. "They bombed their house."

First Julie appeared in deep thought, then Nick could see her backing up. She leaned against the counter between the kitchen and living room. "It's the same thing Kharrazi did," she said in a stupor. "He blew up all those homes to get the President to remove troops from Turkey. Now this Barzani is starting it all over again."

Nick stepped toward his wife, careful as he approached. "It's not the same," he said.

She looked up. "No?"

"No," he said. "The KSF doesn't have the manpower anymore, so Barzani is just attacking homes in Payson."

"And what does he want?"

"Me."

"I don't understand." Her voice cracked.

"He wants me to turn myself in to the KSF or he's threatening to destroy a home each night I don't."

Julie gazed at her feet and cupped a hand over her eyes.

Nick was closer now, bending forward to see her face. "Honey?"

Julie didn't move.

"Jule?" Nick said. "I'm going to find him."

Julie looked up. "Then what?"

"Then we're done," he said. "There are no reinforcements. Once we get Barzani, it's over."

Julie held her stomach, her eyes pleading with him. "But what about . . . us? We'll still be targets."

Nick didn't have an answer for that. He couldn't guarantee someone new wouldn't come after him, even if he did believe it. Which he didn't. He wanted to say, "One thing at a time, please," but she deserved hope.

"We won't." Matt stepped in.

Nick glanced at him with an expectant expression.

Matt approached Julie and put a hand on her shoulder. He looked at her with compassion. "We know how the KSF operates. They don't have anyone approaching Barzani's political acumen. He and Kharrazi both had Political Science degrees from Georgetown. They were the two great hopes of the KSF. Once Barzani's gone, there is no one else."

Julie seemed to take it in. She nodded absently. "How are you going to get him?"

"We have a plan," Matt said. Nick hoped Julie didn't call him on it.

Maybe because she believed him, or maybe because she wanted so desperately to believe him, she didn't challenge the statement.

Nick was grateful to see a faint smile come across her face.

There was a tap on the front porch.

He pulled open the door and saw a weary-eyed man carrying a large green duffle bag over his shoulder. A soldier stood behind him as an escort.

Nick smiled. "Stevie Gilpin," he said. "Just who I was hoping to see."

The two men shook hands.

The soldier saw the exchange and left to return to his position.

"Been flying and driving all night," Stevie said. He wore khaki pants and a blue long sleeve shirt, creased and expensive looking. His eyes were framed with lightweight glasses which were completely transparent from any angle.

As he stepped into the cabin, Matt bumped fists with the high tech analyst.

"Still stylin' I see," Matt said.

Julie pulled her robe closed and waved. "Hi, Stevie." Then she scampered back to the bedroom.

Stevie dropped his bag with a grunt. "Man, I could use a cup of coffee."

"It's already made," Julie said from the bedroom.

Nick went and poured Stevie a cup of coffee, then placed the cream and sugar on the counter next to the cup with a spoon. As Stevie prepared his drink, Nick looked at the duffle bag.

"Is that everything?" Nick asked.

"No, I've got another case out on the porch." He took a sip of the coffee and sighed. "So, tell me what you need."

"We've located Barzani's safe house," Nick said. "He left in a hurry, so I need you to go over there and inspect every centimeter of that place. He's shrewd, but he left clues behind, I'm sure of it. We just need to figure out which ones matter."

Stevie glanced at the clock on the wall. "I'm ready anytime."

"Okay," Nick said. "I'll go wake up Tommy and have him take you there."

"Tommy, as in your cousin?" Stevie asked.

"Yeah," Nick said. "That okay?"

"No," Stevie said with a tired smile. "That's better than okay. I need the entertainment."

Chapter 16

President Merrick sat slumped back in a chair in Press Secretary Fredrick Himes's office. He was reading the *Washington Post* with his legs crossed while Himes worked on notes for Merrick's upcoming press conference from behind his desk. Himes's office was a small, white room with the American flag prominently displayed behind the desk.

"Isn't that a little old fashioned?" Samuel Fisk said from the doorway, pointing to the newspaper in Merrick's hands.

Merrick didn't turn his head. "I hear you've been searching the White House for me."

"I have," Fisk said, leaning against the door jam and folding his arms. "They've just increased the terrorist threat level again. That's twice in five days."

"I know. I've already read the reports." Merrick squeezed his eyelids shut, then reopened them. "That backlit screen is just too harsh. Sometimes I just need good old-fashioned paper and print."

"Is your statement finished?"

Merrick lowered the newspaper and looked at Himes. "Freddy?"

"Just about," Himes said, his face glued to the computer monitor.

"What's the main theme?"

"We don't negotiate with terrorists," Himes said flatly. "Should they want a serious conversation, we'll have one. If they just want to threaten, we can do that as well."

"I see," Fisk said. "By the way, John, have you been playing online poker again?"

Merrick turned a page. "Is there something you want to tell me, Sam?"

"Well, apparently your little bluff with Hakim has worked."

Merrick shut the newspaper so fast, it almost ripped. "And?"

"He's on his way to the airport as we speak."

Merrick slapped his hands together. "Yes." He turned to Himes. "Get this news out to Nick in Arizona. Maybe he can do something with it."

"Can I ask you something?" Fisk said.

"Sure."

"What exactly are you going to tell him when he asks you about your withdrawal strategy?"

Merrick folded the newspaper and placed it on Himes's desk. "Well, to be honest, I never thought it would get this far."

"I know," Fisk said. "That's why I asked."

Merrick leaned back in the chair. "You know, Sam, you can be a real pessimist sometimes. I just bought us another twenty-four hours. Maybe I just saved some lives out in Payson. Maybe Barzani sees this as a positive sign and gives us enough time."

"Enough time for what?" Fisk asked.

"Enough time for Nick and Matt to catch the bastard," Merrick said, putting some mustard on that last word.

Fisk shook his head. "You put a lot of pressure on those two. How many bullets do you think they can dodge?"

"I don't know," Merrick said, looking outside the double window at the South Lawn. Thunderstorm clouds threatened to the east. "I guess I'm always banking on their experience to pull us through."

"Did you notice Barzani didn't mention LAX once in his message to the television station?"

"I noticed."

"Any idea what that means?"

"I wish I knew," Merrick said as lightening lit up the eastern sky. "I wish I knew."

* * *

Nick entered his office right at 8 AM, and shook hands with the deputy behind the receptionist's desk. He held a rifle in his left hand.

"Good to see you again, Hank," Nick said with a grin. He pointed to Semir, lying on the cot behind bars. "You have any trouble overnight?"

"None," the deputy said.

Just then the door to Nick's inner office opened and another deputy came over and shook Nick's hand.

"I want to thank you guys for filling in," Nick said. "I can take over from here."

Outside, a Humvee came into view and half a dozen soldiers

came jumping out to set up a perimeter around the building.

Hank gestured outside. "Looks like you got some serious protection."

Nick pulled up on his arm sling. "Yeah, well I've earned it."

The two deputies gathered their stuff, leaving Nick alone with Semir. Nick pushed the keypad on a metal cabinet which hung on a wall behind the desk. When the door opened, he took out a key from the cabinet and walked over to Semir's holding cell.

Semir sat up and carefully watched as Nick unlocked the door. He seemed startled when the Sheriff entered the cell and took a seat on the opposite side of his cot.

Nick noticed Semir glimpse at the open cell door. "Don't even think about it," Nick said. "There's a platoon of soldiers out there just dying to shoot someone."

Semir slumped back against the wall.

Nick gestured to the bandages on his face. "You okay?"

Semir gently nodded.

"I want to apologize for what happened out there," Nick said. "That old guy was a jerk."

When Semir remained quiet, Nick added, "He's dead now. My cousin Tommy shot him."

Semir gave nothing away.

Nick looked down and picked at a fingernail. "I wonder what would've happened to you if Matt hadn't stepped in?"

Nick let the concept sink in before he continued.

"I don't believe we should have troops in Turkey right now," Nick said. "I think it's a mistake. The only reason we're there is because Turkey is part of NATO. They're an ally and we need to show support to our allies."

Nick was a professional interrogator. Unlike most of his colleagues, he understood the difference between law enforcement interrogation and intelligence interrogation. Nick wasn't there for a confession. In fact a confession could actually hurt him because it would only reinforce the fact that Nick and Semir were opponents.

Now, he sat next to Semir, on the same cot, behind the same bars. For that moment, they were no longer enemies. Nick rubbed his fingers across his forehead and said, "I'm going to tell you something I haven't told anyone. Not my boss, or my partner. No one."

Nick waited a second for Semir to give him his full attention.

"My wife, Julie, is pregnant."

Semir's eyes rose.

"That's right," Nick said. "She doesn't want anyone to know until she's three months along. Apparently, that's when the baby has a better chance of going to term."

Finally, Semir said, "Why are you telling me this?"

"Because I felt like sharing. I feel it's part of communicating. Maybe there's more common ground between us than you think."

Semir looked down. Nick could tell he was thinking about the comment.

Nick adjusted his arm sling, momentarily grimacing until he found the right spot.

"Either Barzani or I have to die, Semir. I think you understand that."

Semir nodded.

Nick waited again before saying, "Who would you have your money on, if you were a betting man?"

There was no arrogance on his face when Semir said, "Barzani."

"I see," Nick said. "What makes you believe that?"

"Because, I know something you don't."

"Ah." Nick wagged a finger at Semir. "Now you're sharing. That's good. What exactly is it you know that you think I don't?"

Semir looked genuinely sad. His expression had so much compassion, Nick's eyelid twitched. "He's going to send someone after you, which you will not be able to survive."

Nick didn't want to hear it, but his professional side had to know. "Who?"

"I don't know his name," Semir said. "But he will not fail."

Okay, Nick thought, that was a big concession for the young man.

"Thank you, Semir," Nick said. "I appreciate your honesty."

Nick checked the time on his cell phone. He pointed the remote at the TV and CNN sprang to life. It was the top of the hour and Nick didn't have to guess what the lead story would be. He'd received word from President Merrick's press secretary an hour earlier which story was the lead that morning.

"I think you may enjoy this news update," Nick said.

On the screen, a female reporter sat stoically behind an oval news desk and said, "Good Morning, here are the top stories.

Turkish Prime Minister Hakim Budarry is making an unscheduled visit to the White House later today. Reports are he's meeting the President about the possible withdrawal of U.S. troops from Turkey. Budarry has been steadfast in his opposition on the occupation of the KSF in Turkistan. It is possible the President is attempting to help negotiate peace talks between the KSF and Turkish officials. President Merrick has announced a press conference at 8 PM Eastern Standard Time."

Semir couldn't hide the faint smile growing on the corner of his mouth. He looked at Nick and wordlessly made eye contact. The report seemed to lighten the mood in the cell. Just two men understanding their roles in the political power play they were in.

Nick was about to click off the TV when the reporter said, "And in Baltimore this morning two FBI agents were found dead outside an eastside apartment complex. Agents Rolley Chandler and Ed Tolliver were shot by a sniper at 12:40 AM. Neighbors claim to have heard the gunshots, but no word on any witnesses. There was also a women murdered in the very same complex at around the same time. Officials say there appears to be a connection between the three killings. No word yet on the identity of the woman."

Nick turned off the TV and dropped the remote on the cot. He stared at the dark monitor while the blood drained from his face and left him lightheaded. He felt as if he'd jumped from a tall cliff and desperately wanted to go back. Julie thought the move to the mountains would solve their problems. Now Nick understood, his family had no future as long as Barzani was alive.

As his mind raced with ideas and maneuvers and wishful fantasies of a terrorist-free world, he heard a voice next to him.

"Back home we have a saying," Semir said with a dour expression. "Don't go buying any green bananas, Agent Bracco."

Chapter 17

Matt watched Stevie Gilpin take fingerprints, examine the contents of the refrigerator and extract DNA samples from the toilet. But it wasn't until Tommy walked into the kitchen from the backyard that they finally got their first break.

"I think I got something here," Tommy said, holding up a cigarette butt.

At first Stevie didn't appear impressed. He grabbed a pair of forceps from his duffle bag and clenched it around the cigarette butt Tommy was holding. "Let's see."

He held up a magnifying glass to the butt and smiled. "Ah," Stevie said. "This is good."

"What is it?" Matt asked.

"Well," Stevie said squinting through the magnifying glass with one eye shut. "This particular cigarette is Turkish. A very rare brand."

Stevie put the magnifying glass down and looked at Matt. "How long did you say these guys were here?"

"At least six months," Matt said.

"That's great," Stevie said.

"Why?"

"Because chances are they had to purchase them here. How many places sell Turkish cigarettes in Payson, Arizona?"

Matt finally understood the significance. He smiled. "Only one."

* * *

President Merrick stood in the kitchen and leaned over a plate of leaf-wrapped finger food.

He held up one of the wrapped pieces and asked, "What's this called?"

The chef, who was on the opposite side of the stainless steel table, said, "It's called dolma. It's stuffed with a rice and meat mixture."

Merrick took a bite of one of the pieces. "Mmm. This is delicious." Then the spices kicked in and he flipped his fingers at the chef.

The chef grabbed a bottle of water from the massive refrigerator and handed it to him. Merrick guzzled down half the bottle before coming up for air.

"Geez," Merrick said. "You trying to kill me, Jason?"

"No sir," the middle-aged chef said, concern on his face.

Merrick dropped the rest of his dolma into the chef's open hand and patted the man on the back. "It's okay," he said, coughing. "As long as the Prime Minister likes it, that's all that matters."

"He's just left the Map Room," a voice said.

Fisk entered the kitchen and headed for the plate of dolma. Merrick grabbed him. "Don't do it, Sam. It's lethal."

Fisk took a bite of one, then smiled. "What's the problem?"

Merrick folded his arms across his chest. "Just wait."

Almost a minute passed and Fisk took another bite to finish off the Turkish delicacy. He pulled a paper towel from a stainless steel wall dispenser and wiped his mouth, then threw the paper into the trash.

"C'mon, you wimp," he said, leading Merrick into the hallway toward the Oval Office.

As they walked down the corridor, Fisk grabbed the bottle of water from Merrick's hand and took a swig, then handed it back and burped.

Merrick grinned. "Is there any food you can't eat?"

As they approached the Oval Office, a tub containing half a dozen cell phones sat on the table outside the room. There were no cell phones allowed in the Oval Office during official meetings. Fisk handed his phone to a secret service agent standing against the wall. Merrick simply set his on vibrate. He was the only exception to the rule.

Hakim Budarry was dressed in a grey business suit and introduced his two assistants, while Merrick introduced Fisk. Press Secretary Himes and Chief of Staff Paul Dexter were already situated near the couches across from the President's desk.

Merrick waved everyone down into their seats. Budarry sat in the tall guest chair directly across from Merrick who found his seat.

"Well, Mr. Prime Minister, it's a pleasure to have you here at the White House," Merrick said with a genuine smile.

Budarry nodded. "Yes, Mr. President. It's a true honor to be here."

Merrick pointed to the table behind Budarry and said, "Would you care for something to drink?"

"No, thank you, Mr. President," Budarry said. "I would like to discuss our relationship, if you don't mind."

"Our relationship?"

"Yes," Budarry said. "I understand there have been some rumors that you are considering removing U.S. troops from my country. Is this a misunderstanding?"

Merrick sighed. Even though he knew this would be the first words from Budarry's mouth, he still wanted more time.

"Mr. Prime Minister," Merrick said. "You do understand the turmoil in Turkey is spilling over into our country now. Yes?"

"Yes, I do."

"And you do realize we have to protect our citizens any way we can, right?"

"Yes, of course. These KSF terrorists are brutal scoundrels who will stop at nothing to—"

"Stop." Merrick held up his hand. "Please, don't start this conversation. I know who the KSF is and what they want. Their tactics are primitive and severe, but their demands are nothing more than a place to live in peace."

"Oh, Mr. President, you have no idea the type of war mongering criminals these Kurds can be. Temir Barzani is a madman."

"Yes, I know," Merrick said.

"Then you will not be removing your troops from my country?"

Merrick looked straight at Budarry. "I can assure you—"

From behind the Prime Minister, Samuel Fisk got to his feet and nodded toward Merrick's private office. His face burned with tension.

Merrick stood and said, "Pardon me for just one moment, Mr. Prime Minister. I need to tend to one item very briefly."

Fisk opened the side door to Merrick's office and held it for him as he entered the room. At the same time, a secret service agent who was sitting in a guest chair sprang to his feet. The second the door was shut, Fisk walked to the far window and waved Merrick over.

"What are you doing?" Fisk asked.

"What do you mean?"

"I mean, didn't you remember my brief on this guy? I told you not to look him in the eyes. It's a sign of sincerity."

"But I'm being sincere."

Fisk took a breath and folded his arms. "Boy, for a valedictorian from Yale, you can be one dumb son of a bitch."

"Sam, make your point."

"He came all the way from Turkey to assure his security from us and you're about to let him off the hook."

"I'm not going to lie to him, Sam."

Even though they were in a soundproof room, Fisk leaned his head forward and whispered. "You don't have to. If you're going to tell him we will not be reducing our troops in Turkey, make damn sure you're not looking him in the eyes when you tell him. He'll take that as a sign of insincerity and not trust you."

Fisk raised his eyebrows. Merrick finally understood. If the Prime Minister believed Merrick wouldn't pull out of Turkey, he wouldn't be motivated to work with the KSF. But if he didn't trust Merrick, he might be forced to negotiate more aggressively. Or do something even more drastic. Without U.S. support Turkey could easily be overrun by the Kurdish faction of their population, and Budarry could not afford to see that happen.

Merrick punched Fisk in the shoulder. "Good job."

When they returned, Merrick's absence only added to the tension in the room, which worked to the president's favor. He returned to his seat and picked up a picture of his family from his desk. While examining the photo, he said, "Mr. Prime Minister, I can assure you the United States will not be removing troops from Turkey any time soon."

From the corner of his eye, Merrick could see Budarry grip the arms of his chair as if it were moving.

They spoke for another twenty minutes, then agreed to meet in the Map Room for a photo opportunity where the president would show deference to the Prime Minister's visit. Their meeting was cordial and tidy, but contained very little eye contact.

When Budarry left the Oval Office, he could be seen whispering harshly with his aide. He was clearly upset about something.

Merrick looked over at Fisk and received a well-deserved wink.

Chapter 18

Nick sat at his desk and pecked at his keyboard, searching the FBI databank for something, anything which could get him closer to Barzani. Every few minutes he'd turn on the tiny TV on his desk and watch the local news. Payson citizens were reacting predictably. A heavy flow of people were causing a traffic jam leaving town for the safety of Phoenix. The remaining citizens were creating community block watch programs at a rapid pace. Nick wanted to reassure the residents of Gila County they were safe, but he couldn't.

His cell phone chirped and he picked it up from his desk. He froze when he saw the name on the screen. Luke Fletcher. Nick had expected this call ever since they'd discovered Luke's cell phone missing from his corpse.

Nick touched his cell and put it to his ear. "Yes."

"You seem a little worried," said the baritone voice.

Nick abruptly stood. He looked around for someone to help trace the call, but of course it was futile. He was alone. "What do you want, Barzani?"

"I was wondering what it felt like to be hunted like an animal."

"I don't know," Nick said. "I was just asking Semir the same question about you."

"Semir is a dunce. You will learn nothing from him."

"He's a good soldier who would take a bullet for you," Nick said. "He's just misguided is all."

Silence. As if Barzani didn't expect the comment.

"Have you seen the news," Nick said. "Prime Minister Budarry is at the White House right now visiting with the president."

"Yes."

"He's there to discuss the possibility of reserving a portion of Kurdistan for the

Kurdish people. Your fight here may now be pointless."

There was a pause while Nick waited for a response. His knees buckled unexpectedly and he needed to sit down again. The pain in his chest reminded him of the medication he'd forgotten to take that morning.

"I see the president has scheduled a press conference for tomorrow tonight," Barzani said.

"Yes," Nick said, scrambling through the drawer on his desk for a vial of pills. His stitched up shoulder pinched as he stretched his left hand from the arm sling to grab the bottle.

"Then, he will be announcing the withdrawal of troops from Turkey?"

Nick pulled up the cap from the vial and slid a couple of tablets onto his desk, his face growing numb with anxiety.

"Did you hear me?" Barzani asked in a menacing tone.

Nick was slowly dissolving into a Post-Traumatic Stress Disorder attack. Dr. Morgan tried to warn him of the possibility, but he'd been symptom free for six months.

"I hear you," Nick managed to say as he threw the two anti-anxiety pills into his mouth and chewed. "I'm just not in the habit of lying. Not even to you, Barzani. I don't know what will come of this meeting for certain, but the president would hope for a reprieve until his press conference."

There was another long pause while Nick watched his left hand develop a tremor.

"That is only one day," Barzani said. "We will wait. But if there is no announcement . . . well, let us say, Arizona could look very different the next morning."

Nick had a question on his mind, but his anxiety-filled brain struggled to get it out. "And me?"

"Unfortunately, Agent Bracco, your fate is sealed. You will not be allowed to survive under any circumstance."

Nick forced his hand into a fist, then unclenched it, trying desperately to control the adrenalin coursing through his bloodstream.

"You know, Barzani, I *will* find you."

"I'm certain you will."

"Then you know I'm close."

"Oh yes."

"Then why not come in and we'll talk. Maybe we can find some common ground."

A slow chuckle came from the receiver, bellowing into a full out laugh. "Tell me Agent Bracco, are you suggesting we become friendly?"

"No," Nick said. "I'm suggesting you accomplish the goal you were sent here for and you have a better chance of succeeding with my help."

"I see," Barzani said. "And how is your wife?"

Nick slammed his fist onto his desk and immediately writhed from the piercing jolt of pain in his shoulder.

"Don't you ever try to hurt her again, or I swear, I'll go to Turkey myself and find every one of your family members and have them tortured. Do you understand me?"

The silence seemed to go on for a couple of minutes. Finally, Barzani left Nick with the most frightening words he'd ever heard.

"Tell me, Agent Bracco . . . how good is your Russian?"

* * *

Anton Kalinikov sat back in his seat on the Amtrak train and enjoyed the scenery passing by. Trees and open fields were interrupted by the occasional railroad crossing where several cars lined up to wait out the passing train. He'd always preferred public transportation to rental cars. Probably a European thing he supposed. The train was headed to Pittsburgh where he would fly out to Edmonton, Canada. These were very soft target airports with little scrutiny from the authorities. Once in Canada he would be free to fly home and pack his gear. His dream house was waiting to be built in South Bimini in the Bahamas. It's where Earnest Hemingway lived back in the 1930's. Kalinikov had bought property on the beach almost a decade ago in preparation for his retirement. The time had finally come for him to relax and relish the fruits of his labor. He was imagining the sand between his toes when his phone chirped. He checked the number. Not surprisingly, it was blocked.

"Yes," Kalinikov said.

"You have one more job before you leave," said a man with a thick Turkish accent.

Kalinikov was almost expecting the call so he knew precisely how to answer. "No, thank you. I am done here."

"But you have not heard the offer?"

Kalinikov had to sigh. This was always the tough part for him. He knew this day would come when money would be offered and he would have to refuse. He'd come from a very poor upbringing, so turning down money had always been a weakness.

"I am sorry," Kalinikov said. "You will just have to find another person for the job."

"I have two million reasons why you're just the right person."

Kalinikov actually glanced around the train to see if anyone could possibly have heard what he'd just heard. "Two million?"

Kalinikov's beach house had just gotten bigger. Even his fantasies were becoming obsolete.

"Yes," the voice said. "Two million."

Kalinikov took a breath. He tried to find a loophole, anything to convince himself it wasn't worth it. "American dollars?" he asked.

"Yes."

Kalinikov finally leaned back and closed his eyes. Although he'd already known the answer, he asked, "Where am I going?"

"Payson, Arizona."

Chapter 19

Nick slowed his car on the unpaved road as it led him to the back of a brick building where four Harley Davidson motorcycles and three worn pickup trucks sat in a dirt lot. He parked between a couple of the trucks, took his gun from his holster and placed it in the glove box.

He went up a set of brick steps where a large plaque on the wall said, "Loyal Order of the Moose."

Nick approached the wooden door and knocked. Cobwebs hung from the overhang above him. The sound system inside was loud enough for The Allman Brothers Band to bleed through the door. Duane Allman was ripping his slide guitar during one of their live performances. Nick couldn't recall the song. "In Memory of Elizabeth Reed?"

A sliding peephole opened and a pair of eyes examined him. It was late afternoon, but there was enough light to make Nick completely visible.

"I was hoping to speak with Sarge, if that was convenient for him."

The peephole scraped closed and Nick waited.

A minute later the door opened. He stepped inside and held up his right arm, while his slinged arm stayed by his side. A scraggly middle-aged man with a "Hog Heaven," t-shirt patted him down, then nodded him in.

The place looked like an old cowboy bar you'd see in the movies. Round wooden tables were spread unevenly across the uneven floor. A long bar took up the back wall with a ceiling to floor mirror behind it. A bartender wiped glasses with a brownish towel. There were a dozen men wearing jeans and a variety of tee and flannel shirts. The two men playing pool stopped to stare at Nick. As a matter of fact, every eye in the place was now on him. The Allman Brothers were still cooking on the jukebox, but nothing else in the room made a sound.

Nick found Sarge sitting at a round table playing poker with a few of the boys, his back against the wall. One by one the poker players dropped their hands on the table and slowly stood up, leaving the table for Nick.

Sarge had a big belly, a long beard and hair that hung well past his shoulders. He had a cigarette in his mouth and was shuffling the cards as if he didn't have a care in the world. Nick wasn't halfway to the table before the smell hit him and he realized the cigarette was marijuana.

"How's it going, Sheriff?" Sarge said while flipping the cards between his stubby fingers with the skill only years of practice could provide.

"May I sit?" he asked.

Sarge put the deck of cards down, then took a huge drag on the joint and blew it out just above Nick's head.

Nick worked hard to control himself. He took his seat across from the large man.

"What can I do for you, Sheriff?"

Nick looked around at the roomful of eyes taking in the scene, then looked back across the table.

"Sarge," he said in a low voice. "I realize this is a private club, but I came here and showed you the ultimate respect. I asked for permission for a sit down. I allowed a pat down. I even asked permission for a seat." Nick nodded to the joint in Sarge's hand. "I think the least you could do is allow me the dignity of not smoking that in front of me."

Sarge gave him a steely glare. He took a long drag, then blew the smoke out the side of his mouth. With a yellow-toothed smile he snuffed out the joint into a half-full metal ashtray.

Sarge lowered his head, then said, "I'm listening."

Nick's heart paced a little quicker than he'd hoped. Composure was a key when dealing with the Harley Mafia. They were mostly ex-soldiers, patriots who'd found a home transporting marijuana across the Arizona border and running a gambling racket. A bunch of misfits who would normally have trouble working in an office, but found the freedom of self employment.

Nick cleared his throat. "All the months I've been Sheriff I've never once paid you a visit or even spoken with anyone in your club."

"What club would that be?" Sarge said with an antagonizing tone. "The Order of the Moose?"

Nick rubbed his temple, then took a breath. "The reason I let it go is because it's mostly harmless stuff in my world. I'm a big picture kind of guy. Marijuana should probably be legal. I don't care about it. You book football, basketball . . . I don't give a crap. Shit, I've been known to throw down a dime or two on a game myself."

The bearded man sat still and waited.

"What I need to know is what's that sticker doing in the back window of your pickup truck?"

Sarge looked baffled. His eyes roamed in thought. "The only thing I got on my back window is an American flag."

Nick pointed his index finger. "Exactly. Why would you do something like that?"

Sarge's face lightened up. He seemed amused now. "Because I'm a fucking patriot," he bellowed, causing a few chuckles from men at the nearby tables.

"I was hoping you'd say that," Nick said. "Because my next subject concerns your patriotism."

Sarge leaned back in his chair and placed his chubby hands on his belly.

"I've spoken with Clark over at Nelson's," Nick said, "and he told me about a delivery of cigarettes which were stolen from a van outside of Payson about three months ago. It was an insignificant robbery as far as I was concerned. Cigarettes are bad for your health anyway."

Sarge didn't appear pleased about the subject.

Nick continued. "Someone with your connections would know who'd done this job. I mean this is your turf. I can't imagine someone would be allowed to work in your own backyard without permission."

"Sheriff, if you think—"

Nick held up his hand. "Please. Wait."

Sarge glanced down at his joint, as if he considered lighting it up again.

"I'm sure you know there's a terrorist cell in the area. These are people who hate patriots like yourself. I track these people for a living. Or at least I did. But now I've discovered a cabin here in Payson where they've been holding up, and low and behold we discover a Turkish cigarette butt. The same brand cigarette which was stolen just a few weeks back. Sarge, if you really are a true patriot, then tell me where I can find the bastards who're trying to kill Americans. People like Devon Grabowski, whose house was bombed by this group. Devon was in the Navy during the—"

"I knew Devon," Sarge said, his jaw tense now as he leaned forward onto the table. "You're certain the KSF killed the Grabowskis?"

Nick nodded.

Sarge sat upright and began pulling on his scraggly beard while mulling things over. Nick understood Sarge wasn't exactly a friend of the law, so this was a tough spot for him. He couldn't afford to look as if he were assisting the authorities.

Nick leaned over and spoke in a whisper. "Should you feel the need to talk, I'll instruct the dispatch at the Sheriff's office to put you through to my cell phone anytime, twenty-four hours a day."

Nick pushed away from the table and stood. He raised his eyebrows and received a subtle nod in agreement.

As he walked to the door, Nick heard Sarge call him.

Nick turned.

"Tell your cousin Tommy to stop by and have a drink with me," Sarge said. "On the house."

Nick smiled. Was there a place on the planet where Tommy wasn't welcome?

* * *

Nick stood on the front porch of the sheriff's office staring through the stand of trees to the main road. He was there for five minutes before a car went by. A couple of minutes later, a green Humvee slowly drove by, patrolling the area. Soldiers casually showed their assault rifles as they examined their surroundings. Payson was down to twenty-five percent occupancy.

A white van came speeding up the gravel entrance and stopped short in front of Nick. A large man with a blue cap and blue uniform hopped from the vehicle and pulled open the back door. He yanked a giant cardboard box from the back of the truck and carried it toward Nick.

"Looking for Steven Gilpin," he said, holding the box on his knee for a rest.

"Stevie," Nick called through the open door.

A moment later, Stevie came out and smiled. "Great," he said, signing the invoice and grabbing the box. He hauled it up the steps into the open door and plopped it down on the vacant receptionist's desk.

"What is it?" Nick asked, following him in.

"It's a Keating 7600," Stevie beamed like a proud parent. When Nick didn't say anything, Stevie looked at him and said, "It's an analytical chemistry analyzer. Before you sent Semir down to the Phoenix Field Office I took samples from his shoes and fingernails. I thought I might be able to find out where he's been lately."

Nick slapped him on the shoulder and said, "That's why I asked for you, Stevie. You're always a step ahead of me."

Stevie smiled, then began tearing open the cardboard box.

Nick returned to the porch and tried to clear his mind. The silence of the normally busy road gave him a creepy feeling. "What are you up to, Barzani?"

"He's making you crazy," Matt said from behind him, stepping out onto the deck. "That's what he's doing."

"He told me on the phone, 'Arizona will be a very different place,'" Nick said. "Not Payson will be a very different place, not America will be a very different place. Arizona."

"Maybe he wanted to spread you out so you don't focus on just Payson."

"Maybe."

"Or maybe it's a mistake."

Nick turned to face Matt. "See, it's my job to know that. To be able to read him and know the difference. But I'm coming up empty."

"So, we do what we do best," Matt reminded him. "Start with what we know."

"And what do we know?" Nick said.

"We know Barzani is a bomb-loving fiend."

"And he's had six months to plant a bomb somewhere in Arizona," Nick said. "If you were trying to create the most destruction, what would you bomb?"

"Palo Verde?" Matt asked.

"That's what I was thinking," Nick said. "A nuclear power plant. But with a group his size? What's he got, ten, twelve soldiers?"

"A Sun's game?"

"Maybe," Nick said. "I keep leaning toward a soft target. Something not so conspicuous."

Nick's phone chirped. He looked at the screen. "Hey Walt," he said. "How's L.A.?"

"I'm done here," Walt said. "We had dogs sniffing everything but the pilot's butt crack and there's no Semtex to be found anywhere near LAX."

"You sure about this?"

"Positive."

Nick smiled. "Good, because I could really use some help."

"I'm bringing a team over there with me," Walt said.

"Hey, Matt and I are thinking Palo Verde might be a target. Can you get some—"

"Done," Walt interrupted.

"Okay, good," Nick said. "Why the change of heart?"

"Because I just got off the phone with the president and he told me to get my ass over to Payson and get you whatever help you need."

"So maybe going over Ken's head wasn't such a bad move after all," Nick said with a grin.

"As long as I stay out of D.C. I might have to run for sheriff of Payson."

A roar of multiple engines began to grow in the distance. It sounded eerily incongruous with the serene setting around them. As the engines approached, a trio of men riding Harley Davidson motorcycles slowed and turned into the gravel drive of the sheriff's office. A couple of American soldiers standing guard in the drive looked at Nick for instruction.

"What's that?" Walt asked.

"I've got to go," Nick said. "I'll see you in a couple of hours."

He shut his phone and waved the group in. The soldiers spread apart to allow the approaching riders to make their way to Nick.

Nick nudged Matt. "Why don't you head inside, check your emails."

"You sure?"

"I'm sure."

All three Harley riders shut their engines and dismounted. The silence was palpable. They all wore jeans, tee shirts, bandannas and sunglasses. The rider in the middle pulled off a pair of riding gloves as he approached.

Nick stepped down from the porch.

"Sheriff," the man said with a nod of reverence.

Nick nodded back.

"Sarge wanted you to know he appreciated your visit . . . I

mean the way you handled yourself. He said to tell you he's sorry he mistook your motive. It wasn't until you were gone that he fully understood your intentions."

Nick shrugged. "It's understandable."

The leader looked around before he spoke again. His wing men stood with their hands behind their backs.

"The fact is," the leader said, "Sarge is as American as apple pie."

"You'll get no argument from me."

This put a smile on the man's face. "So, he wanted you to know the Harley Mafia had nothing to do with any cigarette heist you two had spoken about."

Nick waited.

"But he did a little research and discovered a coincidence in his gambling books. A little while back, a local resident came by to pay up his debt. This was someone who'd owed Sarge over three thousand dollars for most of the past two years. Sarge has a soft heart, so he let this guy run a tab longer than most. The guy's a compulsive gambler and Sarge feels a little guilty taking his money, like he's an enabler."

Nick let that one go. What else would you call a bookie except an enabler?

"So," the man continued, holding his gloves in both hands, "Sarge checked his dates correctly to be sure and discovered that the day this man paid off his debt was precisely one day after the cigarette robbery came down."

Now the man smiled hard, as if he'd just offered Nick the key to the city.

"I see," Nick said. "Has the man come back since then to place more bets?"

"Yes. He's down over a thousand dollars already and six hundred of it is sitting on the books awaiting payment."

Nick nodded. "That's valuable," he said. "Care to offer the man's name?"

"Sarge told me to get a read on you, to decide whether you could be trusted to keep his name away from the connection." He stared through his sunglasses at Nick as if he were trying to search Nick's soul. After a few seconds, he said, "I trust you."

"You should."

The man began to put on his gloves. "Eddie Lister," the man

said. "They call him Fast Eddie. Mostly because he loses his shirt so quickly."

Nick reached out and shook the man's hand. "Tell Sarge, America owes him."

The man mounted his bike along with his two friends. As they sat back in their seats about to push the start button, the man smiled from behind the sunglasses and said, "I'll have him put it on the tab."

Chapter 20

Anton Kalinikov sat by the small window and watched the horizon darken as the plane headed west. His final job, he thought. He'd never allowed himself the luxury of thinking past his next assignment, it was too dangerous. But ever since he'd heard the staggering amount he was getting paid, his retirement plans became an irresistible reality.

"You traveling for business?" the voice next to him said. Kalinikov turned to see a middle-aged man with a pot belly and a bookmarked copy of "The Iliad," on his lap.

Kalinikov smiled amiably and spoke with a tremendous Midwestern accent, "Yes, I am," Kalinikov said. "How about you?"

The man grinned. "Just coming back from a sales trip to Philadelphia. I've lived in Phoenix for almost forty years, so I'm practically a native."

Kalinikov extended his hand. "Norm Jennings," Kalinikov said.

The man shook his hand. "Marv Sinter."

"What kind of sales?" Kalinikov asked.

"Medical supplies. You?"

"Insurance." The word alone always put a damper on any conversation, so it was no surprise when he spent the next ten minutes reading the airplane magazine. He'd achieved the desired effect.

The plane began to descend and the airline attendant made all of the necessary announcements. As Kalinikov was moving his seat into an upright position, Marv nudged him and gestured out the window.

"Look," Marv said, pointing to a long line of headlights below them. The row of cars were at a virtual standstill and seemed to continue on for eternity. They were all going in the same direction away from the mountains and toward the desert.

"What is that?" Kalinikov asked.

"That's the road out of Payson," Marv said. "My brother is in one of those cars with his family. They're all heading to Phoenix."

"How long of a drive is it?"

"An hour and a half if you step on it. But the way that looks, it'll be four or five hours."

Kalinikov noticed no traffic going the opposite direction toward Payson.

"They really think this terrorist is going to destroy the town?" Kalinikov asked.

Marv shrugged. "After what happened a few months back, I wouldn't blame them if they never returned. That Sheriff up there is just inviting trouble."

"Why do you say that?"

"Because he's a target, that's why. If he left town, the place would be safe again."

Kalinikov grinned. "Is that what you would do? Run away? You would spend your entire life chasing bad guys, then one of them threatens you and your community and you'd run? Is that the kind of sheriff you would be?"

Marv grinned back at him. "You bet your ass. Especially if I had kids. I'd run like a little girl."

Kalnikov stared down at the huge traffic jam below them. "Does he have children?"

"I don't think so," Marv said. "That's probably part of the problem right there. Give a guy kids and their entire philosophy on life changes."

"Really? Tell me about it."

"You don't have kids?"

Kalinikov shook his head as the plane bounced on clear air turbulence. "I have two nephews however. Does that count?"

"Sorry," Marv said. "I can't let you into the club unless you have one of your own."

"I see," Kalinikov turned to face his new friend. "And this Sheriff doesn't have any children, so that's the main problem?"

"Yes," Marv said with a grin threatening to break out. "That's the issue. He's got too much testosterone. Give him some young ones and he'd soften up a little."

"Let the terrorist do what he wants with the city as long as his kids are safe, right?"

Marv looked over at Kalinikov incredulously. "You're actually having fun with this, aren't you?"

Kalinikov smiled. "Of course."

"What about you, tough guy?" Marv asked. "What would you do?"

Kalinikov gave it some thought. "Me? I'd probably track the terrorist down and kill him."

Marv appraised Kalinikov as if seeing him for the first time. "You've got some years on you, Norm, but I'll bet you could kick some butt when you wanted."

Kalinikov gave him a paternal smile. "You have the wrong guy, Marv." He gazed back out the window toward the tail of the spiraling line of cars. Toward Payson.

"I don't even like watching hockey on TV," Kalinikov added. "Too much violence."

* * *

Lynn Harding was sleep deprived and she knew it. Three straight days without more than a two-hour nap. As the ASAC of the Baltimore Field Office, she'd just lost four of her fellow FBI agents to a Russian assassin hired by Temir Barzani. All of this led to a nervous stomach and bags under her eyes.

She sat in a booth along the side of the War Room, fifty feet below ground and tried to catch her breath. There were three separate booths along the perimeter of the room set up for officials to make and take calls without interrupting the flow of conversation around the table in the middle of the room. The booth looked very much like an old fashioned telephone booth with a much more comfortable seat and a soundproof glass door which allowed private conversations.

Her hand trembled from both physical and mental anguish as she pushed the button on her cell phone.

"Hey, Lynn," Nick Bracco said in her receiver.

Just hearing his voice calmed her nerves. "Nick, how's it going?"

"I'm still breathing, so I've got that going for me."

Harding gazed out the booth window at the circle of men hunched over the round table with varying degrees of ugly expressions. Most hadn't left the building in days and their ties were dangling from the back of their chairs while their shirts were opened to the third button or more.

"Nick," Harding said, "it's getting rough down here."

"What's going on?"

"Ken is pissed that Walt went over his head to the President."

"Of course."

"Well, now Ken has intelligence from Switzerland that a half a million dollars has been wired from Kharrazi Construction Company in Istanbul to a Swiss bank account."

"Sure, payment for the murders of our team," Nick said bluntly, putting it together quicker than even she'd expected.

"Yes, however that's not how Ken is spinning this. He's suggesting this is payment for an assassination on President Merrick. He suggests we focus our attention on the D.C area and find this Russian before he gets to Merrick. He wants everyone to return back home to track him down."

"Oh, so now all of a sudden he believes the Russian is in America?"

"Yes."

"And if he's wrong about this, he can say he was just protecting the president."

"Uh huh."

There was silence while Nick seemed to think it over.

"He doesn't like Walt sending support my way, does he?" Nick said.

"No. Once this LAX thing blew up, he wanted everyone back here."

"Boy." Nick breathed out a long breath. "I knew the guy hated me for bagging Kharrazi, I just never knew how much."

Harding said nothing. She waited to hear something she could use. Information was the most potent currency an intelligence agency could traffic. Those with it had the leverage. The average civilian had no idea how much the FBI and CIA used this leverage to maintain their status. Each one fighting for their own budget survival.

"I've got hunches, Lynn," Nick said, "that's all."

Lynn glimpsed out the window and saw CIA Director Ken Morris glaring at her as if she'd just poured sour milk in his coffee.

"I'll take it," Lynn said, desperate for something to use against the CIA director's power play.

"Well, Barzani's still here for sure," Nick said. "He called to threaten me, maybe hoping to rattle me, I don't know. But he said if the president didn't announce a reduction in troops in Turkey at his press conference tomorrow night, Arizona was going to look very different. Not America. Arizona. I think he's planning something big here. He's had months to prepare."

"What have you come up with?"

Silence.

"Nick?"

"Nothing. I've got a weak lead from a Turkish cigarette left behind at Barzani's safe house, but otherwise . . . nothing."

"What about tonight? Has Barzani got something planned?"

"I don't think so. He knew about the Prime Minister's visit to the White House. He seemed to allow a reprieve until the President's speech."

Harding closed her eyes and took long, deep breaths. She could almost feel Morris staring at her from the table. They had just twenty-four hours before the President's speech.

"Nick," she said, "your best guess. What's going to happen tomorrow night?"

"The President isn't removing troops, is he?"

"No."

She could hear Nick breathing, but nothing else.

Harding twisted her back, which was stiffening from all the sitting. "Nick, I don't want Walt's job."

"I know that, Lynn." Nick snapped. "This is bigger than our careers."

"So why don't you give me something I can run with?"

After a few moments of silence, with a reluctant tone, Nick finally said, "Palo Verde is the country's largest nuclear power plant."

Harding smiled with relief.

"Is that enough to keep Walt safe?" Nick asked.

"I don't know," she said. "But it might be enough to save the country. I'll take your instincts over Ken's any day."

Chapter 21

Tommy sat at the bar and picked at the stale peanuts while nursing down his beer. Special Forces, FBI and National Guard were scouring the town for this Lister guy while Tommy was stationed at the Sonoran Brewhouse. A local pub where Eddie Lister was known to hang out.

The place was a dingy pub with wood columns along the ceiling and booths along each side of the main room. At least it was quiet, making it easier for Tommy to inspect each individual as they entered. He watched a west coast college football game on the TV while keeping an eye on the door.

A little after 10 PM a man came in and stood inside the doorway allowing his eyes time to adjust to the darkness of the dreary tavern. Tommy watched through the mirror behind the bar as the man headed his way. He was tall and athletic looking, maybe early fifties. Sitting a couple of stools down from Tommy, he ordered a draft beer. He wore a button down shirt and blue jeans. Too fancy to be a local. Since they were the only two people sitting at the bar, the man took notice of Tommy and raised his glass in a mock toast. Tommy returned the gesture.

It was the fourth quarter of the football game and UCLA was beating Oregon State by three touchdowns. Tommy was losing his patience waiting for this guy to show up, especially since he didn't have any action on the game.

"You're not from around here," the man next to him said.

Tommy turned in his seat to face him. "You pick that up with just my clothes?"

"Naw," the man said. He seemed to have a Midwestern accent. "I'm good at reading people. Sort of a hobby of mine."

Tommy placed his elbow on the bar and rested his head in his hand. "Really?"

"Sure," the man said, picking up a peanut from the wood bowl and popping it in his mouth.

"Okay," Tommy said. "Where am I from?"

Now the man swiveled to face him. He appraised Tommy with a pair of intense eyes. "From your attire, to your demeanor, to your accent . . . I'd have to say somewhere around the east coast, maybe Washington D.C. area."

Tommy smiled. "You're good," he said extending his hand. "I'm Tommy Bracco. Baltimore."

The man shook his hand with a firm grip. "Norm Jennings. West Lafayette, Indiana."

Tommy snapped his fingers. "I had you pegged for the Midwest," he said. "West Lafayette. The home of the Purdue Boilermakers."

"That's the place," Jennings said.

"How's the basketball team doing this year?"

"Lousy." Jennings said, then took a sip of his beer. "Just one and four so far."

"I see," Tommy said. He drank his beer, then returned his attention to the game. He pulled his phone out and checked the Purdue Boilermakers record, just for something to do. One and four, just like the guy said.

"Bracco?" Jennings said. "Any relation to the sheriff?"

Tommy nodded. "My cousin."

"Really?" Jennings seemed to perk up. "You two must be close."

"Very," Tommy said. "Pretty much grew up together."

"So are you in law enforcement as well?"

Tommy chuckled. "Hardly. I just came by for a visit after one of these terrorists took a shot at him. "

"That's right," Jennings said, swirling his finger around in the bowl of peanuts until he found the one he wanted. "I read about that. Is he okay?"

"He'll be fine," Tommy said. "He'll be even finer once we catch the rat bastard."

"I see. So you're helping him track this guy down?"

"Something like that," Tommy said, suddenly realizing he'd been answering a lot of questions. "How about you? What brings you into a war zone like Payson?"

"My mom lives up here and refuses to leave. I thought I'd better keep an eye on her if she's going to stay."

"So you're staying with her?"

"Yes, how about you? Are you staying with your cousin?"

"I am," Tommy said, checking out the new arrivals as they entered the bar. Two girls and one guy. The guy fit the description.

He watched the trio slide into a booth. The guy, maybe Eddie Lister, opened up the plastic menu from between the salt and pepper shakers and looked it over.

"People you know?" Jennings asked, following Tommy's gaze.

"Maybe," Tommy said. He returned to his beer trying to figure out the best way to handle the situation. A little patience might help him, but Tommy wasn't so good with patience.

"Is there something I could do?" Jennings asked.

"Excuse me?"

"I mean with this terrorist," Jennings added. "Is there anything I could help you with?"

"Sure," Tommy said. "Just tell me where he is and I can go home."

"Hmm," Jennings said. "That's a good question. Where would you hide if you were trying to outrun the authorities? In plain sight, or tucked away in a cabin somewhere?"

"Me, I'd hide out. But then, I'm not into killing innocent Americans."

"Why do you think there's such a spike in violence recently?" Jennings asked solemnly, like a schoolteacher searching for the correct answer.

"Beats the crap outta me," Tommy said.

"Do you know what I think? I think there's too much violence on TV. Kids can turn on any channel twenty-four hours a day and see explosions in the Middle East, or movies with special effects so real, who can tell the difference anymore? First time I saw the towers going down on September 11th, it felt like I was watching a movie."

Tommy nodded. "I know what you mean, you get desensitized to the pictures you're seeing."

Tommy noticed Jennings was sipping his beer even slower than he was.

"Listen," Tommy said. "You wanna give me a hand here?"

Jennings looked interested. "What do you need?" he asked, placing his beer down and wiping the foam from his lips with the back of his hand.

"Just make sure no one blindsides me, okay?"

"Blindside? What do you intend to do?" Jennings asked.

"I don't know yet. Maybe nothing," Tommy said. He looked at the man who was already twisting in his bar stool and facing the room behind them. "You with me, Norm?"

Jennings gave a small and decisive nod. "I have your back."

Somehow the way he said it, Tommy believed him.

The bartender paused in front of them as he was going past. "You two still okay?"

They both held up their hands.

"Hey, wait a second," Tommy said. "Could you get me a small bag of ice?"

The bartender had a questioning look on his face.

Tommy flexed his hand and twisted his wrist. "I messed up my hand at work," he said. "I just need to get the swelling down."

The bartender nodded. Before he could leave entirely, Tommy added, "And a clean bar towel."

The bartender waved his acknowledgment as he left.

Tommy returned to his beer.

"You okay?" Jennings asked.

"Huh?'

"Your hand," Jennings said.

"Oh, yeah, I'm fine. I'm just thinking ahead."

A minute later the bartender returned with a small plastic bag with ice and a semi-clean bar towel. When he left, Tommy stood and handed the items to Jennings.

"Hold onto this," Tommy said. "I'll let you know if I need them."

Jennings shrugged.

Tommy walked over to the booth where the three young people sat. The young man sat by himself while the two girls shared their side of the booth. The kid was early twenties, dark complexion with a few days stubble which the women seemed to like these days.

"Hey, Eddie," Tommy said.

"Yeah," the kid said, looking a bit confused.

"Eddie Lister, right?" Tommy smiled like he was an old friend.

"Yeah, that's right. Do I know you?"

Tommy rested his palms on the table and smiled at the two girls. "Ladies," he said.

All three looked at him waiting for an explanation.

"Listen, Eddie," Tommy said. "Can I get a word with you alone?"

Eddie's face grew dark. "About what?"

Tommy looked around the room, trying to be discreet. He noticed Jennings paying close attention at the nearby stool.

"Eddie," Tommy said, "you don't know me, but I'm a nice guy. I just need a word with you so we can all go back to our dreary little lives."

Eddie looked bewildered. He seemed to feed off the apprehension on the girls' faces. "I don't think so."

Tommy sighed. "We don't need to do this dance, Eddie."

"What dance we talking about?" Eddie said, fishing around under the table, then coming up with a pistol. It was dark in the room, but Tommy figured it to be a single action Ruger. Popular out west for some reason.

The girls squealed while leaning back in their side of the booth. Eddie held the pistol low so no one else could see it very easily.

"You gonna shoot me, tough guy?" Tommy said, feeling the blood running hard through his veins.

"If you don't get out of here in five seconds, I'm going to end this," Eddie said with a convincing expression.

Tommy noticed Jennings watching the event with an intense stare. He didn't seem the least bit intimidated by the event. The bartender was too busy stocking liquor at the end of the bar.

Tommy looked at Eddie with disdain. "This isn't the movies, kid. You don't need to count. Either you're gonna to shoot me, or you're not."

Eddie did what most people did in situations like this when they weren't prepared to act. He screwed his face into a tight, angry expression and held the gun out closer to Tommy, as if the shorter distance would add to the threat.

Tommy placed his hand on the back of his neck and shook his head. "You want we should count together, or is this like one Mississippi, two Mississippi and we count in our heads?"

"I'm dead serious," Eddie scowled.

Tommy jumped sideways, then pulled the gun from Eddie's hand and cold-cocked the kid in the nose. One hard punch was all he needed and the kid's head lurched back, then forward. Both of his hands immediately covered his nose. Blood seeped between his fingers as the girls shrieked and scurried out of the booth.

The front door opened and closed as the girls left and the room became quiet. Tommy slid into the booth next to Eddie and tucked the gun between his legs. He pulled a bunch of paper napkins from the dispenser at the end of the table and handed them to Eddie.

"Here," Tommy said.

Eddie took the napkins and pressed them against his nose. His eyes were glossy and he anxiously watched Tommy's every move.

"I got your attention?" Tommy asked.

The kid nodded ardently.

Tommy gestured to Jennings and the guy came over with the bag of ice and towel, then returned to his seat at the bar.

The few people in the room seemed to miss the action, but were paying close attention now. The minimal staff was too busy to notice.

Tommy handed the towel to Eddie and said, "Here, put your head back and hold this."

"You didn't need to do that." Eddie sobbed openly. "It wasn't even loaded."

Tommy took the bag of ice and covered the knuckles on his right hand, pressing it down on just the correct spot.

"Let me ask you something," Tommy said. "You ever shoot a gun before?"

"Uh uh," Eddie mumbled through the towel, his head back now.

"See, that's your problem," Tommy said, wincing as an ice cube found the tender part of his hand. "You're a beginner pretending to be a professional. Anyone with experience sees you're a virgin. That's a single action revolver you got there. You gotta have the hammer back to shoot the damn thing."

"Aw, shit," Eddie said, feeling his nose with his free hand. "I think it's broken."

"Of course it's broken, you idiot." Tommy lifted the kid's chin. "Keep your head back," he said.

Large tears trickled from the corner of Eddie's eyes and meandered down the side of his face while his torso shuddered.

Tommy rubbed the kid's back. "It's okay, Killer. I need you to breathe."

Eddie tried to take a full breath and coughed into the towel.

"You know, Eddie, there's Payson tough and then there's West Baltimore tough. I'm sure you're a real handful in Payson, though. Maybe you could steal some milk money tomorrow and get right back on the saddle, huh?"

Eddie's eyes were wide and frightened. "What do you want from me?"

Tommy removed the bag of ice from his knuckles and flexed his hand. "Apparently you came into some cash not long ago and there's an ample amount of evidence to suggest you may have found some easy money."

There was nothing but fear on the kid's face.

"And," Tommy continued, "at this very same time a delivery of Turkish cigarettes were stolen from a delivery truck outside of town." He raised his eyebrows. "You putting it together yet?"

Eddie's entire body shook, which made him appear to be nodding.

Tommy got closer to him and lowered his voice. "I need to know some information about the heist."

"A . . . a . . . are you the law?"

Tommy put his hand on his forehead. "Good grief, Eddie, you think I look like the law?"

"N . . . n . . . no."

Tommy shook his head. "I'm not. I need this info so I can track down some bad people. People who are much worse than me even. And that's hard to do."

"But I don't know anything," Eddie pleaded. "Please, just let me go. I won't ever steal anything ever again."

"Here's the problem," Tommy said. "The people you did the job for are terrorists. You've been watching the news, right? The KSF? That's who you're dealing with."

A flicker of recognition crossed Eddie's face.

"It's all making sense now, isn't it?" Tommy said.

Eddie pulled the towel down and examined the large red spot. "Look at me, Eddie."

The kid turned with glossy eyes and a mangled nose.

"Here's how it works," Tommy said. "We'll bring you to the Sheriff's Office and take a statement. He'll announce it to the press that they've discovered the cigarette thief and have found valuable information about the KSF from this thief."

"N . . . No," Eddie stammered. "You can't. I thought you weren't the law?"

"I'm not, but my cousin is the Sheriff, and he'll make sure the KSF knows about your little visit with him. Then he'll release you." Tommy raised his eyebrows. "How long before these terrorists come by to pay you a visit? Only with guns which have bullets. And I promise there won't be any counting when it happens. I'd give you good odds you don't live to eat lunch."

"You would do that?"

Tommy rolled his eyes. "Eddie, I just broke your nose. You don't think I'd give you up to these terrorists? Shit, I'd give them your home address and sleep like a baby."

Eddie's eyes roamed around the bar searching for something, maybe thinking of a way out. Tommy wasn't about to spoon feed him the answer. It was always better if it was the mark's own idea.

"What if I can help the Sheriff find these guys?" Eddie blurted, his nose beginning to leak again.

Tommy took the kid's hand with the towel and placed it up to the leaky nose.

"That something you can do?" Tommy asked while applying pressure to Eddie's nose.

"Uh huh," Eddie murmured through the towel, excited about seeing a positive ending to his dilemma.

"Okay," Tommy said. "Let's see what you got."

Tommy grabbed Eddie and pulled him from the booth. As he headed toward the door, he noticed Norm Jennings was no longer sitting at the bar. He looked around but didn't find him. A loose thought entered his mind. It wasn't something he wanted to think about.

Chapter 22

Nick lay in bed next to Julie and wondered if she was asleep. He glanced over at the digital clock on the nightstand. It was only a minute later than the last time he looked. She was turned away from him. He reached over and touched the small of her back.

"Will you find him?" Julie's voice came out of the dark.

Since she didn't know about The Russian, he knew she was talking about Barzani. "Yes," he said.

She took a long breath. "I believe you, Sweetie."

A few seconds passed while Nick's mind raced with dire thoughts. He needed to keep Julie safe, physically and mentally.

"Do you think they'll be more after he's gone?" Julie asked.

"No. His crew is the last cell they have here."

"But what about others from Turkey?"

"It would take years to develop enough soldiers to infiltrate the states."

"But . . ."

He knew where she was going. It only took one maniacal terrorist to destroy her world and take the father of her baby away from her.

"It's a long shot, Honey," he said. "There's a better chance I'll get hit by lightning." Or killed by a Russian assassin, he thought.

His words seemed to hit the proper note, however, because he could sense her breathing slow down.

"You need to sleep," Julie said.

"I have lots of needs," he said.

Julie turned to face him. Even in the dark he could see her teeth smiling back at him. "Oh, really. Care to name one?"

"Yes. I have the insatiable need to feel your belly."

This made her eyes twinkle as she pulled up her sleeping shirt.

Nick placed his hand low on her stomach. She was soft and warm. "I feel something moving."

"That's the chicken quesadilla," she said. "I'm too early to be able to feel the baby."

"Still," he said. "A guy could dream can't he?"

He felt her fingernails caress the inside of his thigh. He tried to turn, but his damaged shoulder kept him on his back.

"I'm a little immobile at the moment," he said.

"The better for me to take advantage of you," Julie said as she sat up and pulled off her shirt. A slice of moonlight cut across her naked body and exposed her smooth, shiny skin.

She straddled him, then leaned forward, her lips brushing against his ear. "You just stay right there, sailor," she whispered. "I'll do all the heavy lifting."

* * *

"Who were those girls you were with?" Tommy asked Eddie as he drove the Sheriff's car down an empty two-lane road. Eddie was in the passenger seat pushing buttons on his phone with his thumbs.

"My sisters. I'm sending them a text right now," he said. His bloody towel sat on his lap and occasionally he would place a clean spot to his nose to check for any new blood. The kid seemed to calm down once he was put in the Sheriff's car. As if it gave Tommy some legitimacy.

Tommy had only been driving a few minutes when a pair of distant headlights popped into his rear view mirror. The roads were extremely quiet, yet the car behind him didn't seem to gain on him.

"I want you to do me a favor, Eddie," Tommy said. "I want you to promise me you'll throw that gun away."

"Okay," Eddie agreed too easily.

"Eddie," Tommy said firmly. "I'm serious. Don't tell me what I wanna hear. Carrying a gun will get you killed. Especially an unloaded one. You understand?"

Tommy glanced over at the kid. Eddie was nodding, as if to himself.

"Yeah," Eddie said. "I understand."

"Good. You're not a bad kid. You're just watching too many action movies. Start watching comedies, then go around impressing the girls with your wit instead of your unloaded weapons."

"Okay," Eddie said, then glanced down at a text message.

Tommy pulled out his phone and pushed a contact button.

After a couple of rings a breathless voice said, "Yeah."

Tommy looked at the clock on his dashboard. 10:45 PM.

"Nicky?" Tommy grinned. "You working out?"

"Very funny," Nick rasped. "What's up?"

"Well, I found Eddie Lister," Tommy said. "He's with me now."

"That's great. Does he know something?"

"I think so."

"Bring him right over."

Tommy checked his rear view again and saw the headlights keeping its distance. "Yeah, well, let's meet at your office instead."

"Something wrong?"

"Probably not. Just being careful. Go back to your workout and I'll meet you there."

Tommy ended the call, then pushed a couple of buttons and handed the phone to Eddie.

"Here," Tommy said. "See the red beam?"

Eddie looked confused. He aimed the beam at his feet. "What is this?"

"It's a radar detector. I want you to turn around and aim it at the car behind us."

Eddie twisted in his seat. "I don't see any car."

"I know, he's back there a ways. Keep your eye out for him."

Tommy took his foot off the gas and the car slowed.

"Who is it?" Eddie asked.

"I have an idea."

The road was tree-lined and had gentle twists. A few seconds later, a pair of headlights popped out around a distant curve.

"Okay, Eddie, point and read me the display."

Eddie was on his knees, completely turned, arms outstretched.

"Sixty-five," Eddie said.

Tommy let the Sheriff's car slow to a gentle roll.

"Keep reading," Tommy said.

"Fifty-nine," Eddie said. "Fifty-three . . . forty-four."

"Shit," Tommy muttered.

"Thirty-one," Eddie diligently read the display. "Twenty–three."

"That's enough," Tommy said, stepping on the gas. "Turn around and put your seat belt on."

The kid listened. His voice got excited. "Are you going to outrun him?"

"Don't be such a thrill seeker."

Tommy got the car up to cruising speed again and scanned the shoulder for a place to park. Someplace he could get some quick cover. The headlights temporarily disappeared behind him.

"Hey, you like Coldplay?" Eddie said, browsing through Tommy's phone.

Tommy snatched the phone from the kid. "Will you pay attention here? I'm trying to keep us alive."

Eddie's face turned cold. "You think the terrorists are in that car?"

Tommy frowned at the thought. "I'm not sure. I have an idea, but it's not fun to think about."

The Sheriff's car needed some suspension work because the chassis kept bouncing over the winding road like a boat over choppy water. As they swerved from side to side, the headlights came into view again.

"Hang on," Tommy said, as he tapped the brakes and turned into a narrow gravel driveway. The path was lined with trees and Tommy just cleared a pine as he dashed down the driveway twenty yards before turning off the lights and skidding the car to a stop. He pulled out his gun and turned to Eddie.

"Keep your head down and stay still," Tommy ordered.

He jumped out of the car and ran back up the path to the side of the road. There was very little moon out so Tommy was practically invisible as he crept between the pines, gun by his side. He was only a few feet from the road and tucked behind a large trunk. Even in the cool night air, he felt a trickle of sweat wander down his temple. He forced himself to take deep breaths and waited. And waited.

No headlights.

As he stood there contemplating his moves, he realized he wasn't going to track this guy down by himself. Not in foreign territory. Maybe back home he could make a couple of calls and get some lookouts, but not here. Tommy slumped against the tree and shook his head. The guy was a pro, no doubt.

He waited for almost three minutes when a terrible thought entered his mind. He was dealing with a professional. Norm Jennings had appeared harmless because he had that Midwestern, fair-haired look. Pale skin. Blue eyes. A Midwestern look, but also a European look.

Maybe even Russian.

Chapter 23

"Where's Walt?" Matt asked while driving his SUV seventy down the crooked back road. Nick sat in the passenger seat and gripped the door handle tight. Jennifer and Stevie were in the back seat checking their phones while swaying back and forth.

"He's at Palo Verde securing the site," Nick said.

Nick glanced behind them and noticed the lead Humvee falling behind.

"You're losing our soldiers," Nick said.

"They know where the office is," Matt said, staring intently on the road as far as the headlights would take him.

Stevie's face was screwed up into a knot while squeezing his thumbs over his phone's keypad.

"What are you doing back there, Stevie?" Nick asked.

"I'm trying to find out why I found traces of chloride in Semir's shoe," Stevie said, not looking up.

"Isn't that a common mineral around here?"

"Chloride itself is not a mineral per se, it's a negatively charged ion and must be paired with a positive ion."

"Okay," Nick said. "I'll take your word on that."

Matt finally cruised the final mile before the Sheriff's Office, then swiveled his head around as he pulled into the parking lot.

"Where is he?" Matt said.

"Good question," Nick answered, remembering Tommy's reluctance to meet at the house. He pulled out his cell phone, then stopped when he saw the Sheriff's car come charging into the parking lot to park beside them. There was only minimal security lighting, so both drivers left their headlights on.

"Where've you been?" Nick asked as they got out of the car.

Tommy looked disgusted as he slammed his door shut. "I picked up a tail on the way over here."

Nick and Matt exchanged glances.

Tommy motioned them away from the cars. Nick and Matt followed. "Listen," Tommy said, "I have a bad feeling about this guy I met at the bar. It seemed like a chance meeting, but the more I think about it, the less I like it."

"What'd he look like?' Matt asked.

Tommy met his cousin's eyes. "He looked and sounded Midwestern. But he tailed me like a pro. I don't like it."

"You get a name?" Nick asked.

"Norm Jennings from West Lafayette, Indiana," Tommy said. "But I doubt that'll mean anything."

Nick rubbed a hand through his hair. "Great," he said.

"Hey, I don't like it any more than you do," Tommy said.

"Did you tell him anything?" Nick said.

"What?" Tommy squinted. "Did you really ask me that?"

Nick covered his eyes and sighed. "Sorry. I'm a little frazzled right now."

Matt looked over at the car where the kid sat in the passenger seat. "What's he know?"

All three of them stared at Eddie who was talking on his cell phone.

"He says he knows where these KSF guys are," Tommy said.

Matt headed for the Sheriff's car. "Well let's get going then."

Tommy raced around Matt and pulled the twenty-something kid from the passenger seat. He had three-day-old facial stubble and a red rag in his hand.

As they got closer, Nick could see the kid's nose appeared broken. He shot Tommy a look.

"This here is Eddie Lister," Tommy said.

Eddie nodded, carefully.

Nick pointed to his face. "You okay."

"The cigarette thief," Matt said flatly.

"Hey, easy," Tommy said. "He's a good kid. He just made a bad choice, that's all."

The two Humvees filled with soldiers came rolling into the lot and Nick waved for them to stay put until they've figured out a plan. The lead driver flashed his lights for confirmation.

"So, how did you come to discover the safe house?" Nick asked.

"The what?" Eddie said.

"The place where the bad guys are hiding out," Tommy translated.

"Oh, yeah, well," the kid glanced around the parking lot. "Should I be calling my lawyer or something?

"Oh, for crying out loud," Tommy cried. "There's four FBI

agents and a freakin' platoon of soldiers here. You think they got out of bed to arrest some kid heisting cigarettes?"

Eddie looked at Nick, who groped one-handed into his pocket to pull out his credentials. Matt did the same. Nick motioned to Jennifer and Stevie in the back of the SUV. "They're agents as well," he said.

Eddie had a wary expression on his face.

"We don't care about the robbery," Nick said. "But if you can help us track down these terrorists, it would mean a great deal to the United States. You'd be considered a hero."

Eddie seemed to like the sound of that. His face brightened. "So then I can tell you what happened and I won't get into trouble? You promise?"

Nick had to move his arm sling a little to cross his heart. "I promise."

Eddie nodded. "Okay, well, this guy asked me–"

"Whoa, stop," Nick said. "What guy? How did he contact you?"

"I didn't know the guy. He would come in the store every Thursday and buy us out of the carton of cigarettes he liked. Finally, one day he comes in and asks if he could order a couple of cases instead of buying them one carton at a time. When I looked into it, we couldn't. It was coming from Turkey and there was some sort of allocation going on so we were only allowed one carton a week."

The sound of an engine approaching stopped the conversation. A red convertible cruised by, all four of them thinking the same bad thought as it passed.

Nick looked at Tommy who shook his head.

"Anyway," Eddie continued, "one day he comes in with this wad of hundred dollar bills and explains how the truck which delivers the cigarettes goes down to Phoenix to drop off the rest of its load. He says there's at least five cases of cigarettes on the truck and I can keep the money if I find a way to steal the cigarettes for him. . . . so I stole them off the truck when the driver was making a delivery in Pinetop. No one was hurt or nothing."

Eddie looked around at the group as if looking for an understanding face.

"Of course," Matt finally said. "A completely harmless crime. We'd all do the same thing if it was us."

Eddie raised his eyebrows, as if they were one big happy family of

thieves. "Really?"

"No," Matt said. "That's okay though. Things happen."

"So how did you discover where they stayed?" Nick asked.

"Well, they asked me to drop the cigarettes off in this dumpster behind the Native New Yorker. So I did what I was told and went into the restaurant to get a sandwich. After I'm done, I'm going to my car and I see this guy going through the dumpster and tossing the cigarettes into the back of a pickup truck . . . and well I was curious, so I followed the truck back to their cabin."

"Get outta here." Tommy laughed and clapped his hands. "You and your bulletless gun followed a group of international terrorists back to their hideout? Are you kidding me?"

"Well, I didn't know who they were," Eddie said defensively. He touched his contorted nose. "Not until you came up to me in the bar tonight."

"Hey, I'm sorry, okay?" Tommy said.

"You know the address?" Nick asked.

"No, but I could take you there."

Nick placed his hand on the kid's shoulder. "Good work, Eddie. You did the right thing by coming clean."

Eddie smiled like he'd just saved a baby from a burning building.

* * *

The first thing Temir Barzani did when he'd taken over the American operation, was plant a miniature video camera up in a tree across the street from the Sheriff's substation. It was far enough away to escape detection, yet could zoom in to determine faces and license plates. He wanted to know exactly who came and went to determine his timetable.

Now he sat at the kitchen table of their safe house and examined the video screen on his tablet and grunted with disappointment. In the darkness, two cars had just sped into the Sheriff's parking lot, followed by two large army vehicles. He knew they were coming. He could feel it.

Whether it was Semir, or another loose end, Barzani had no choice but to close the circle of information. He couldn't afford to have any more of his men taken prisoner. There was too much risk involved. His mission required absolute secrecy. He would create a disaster which would exceed any destruction ever produced on American soil. His name would become synonymous with this event. A slaughter of such magnitude, his cunning would be renounced for decades.

A scratchy voice came over the radio on the kitchen counter. "Jemin and Tzardif are returning. They just pulled into the driveway."

Barzani nodded and a member of his security team acknowledged the message by picking up the radio and saying, "Understood."

A few moments later two members of his crew came in through the garage door and approached Barzani.

"Yes?" Barzani said.

Jemin Hester approached Barzani with a look of satisfaction on his face. "The bombs are all set, Sarock," he said. "The detonator is in the cave where you instructed. The code is one-two-two-four."

"Very good." Barzani stood and patted them both on the back. "Jemin, I am in the mood for one of your cigarettes. It is a time of great celebration."

Jemin smiled, drew a pack of cigarettes from his pocket and handed them to his leader.

Barzani held a cigarette between his fingers and held up the pack with his other hand. "May I keep these?"

"Of course, Sarock. It would be my honor."

Barzani barely had the cigarette in his mouth when a lit match was waiting for him. He inhaled the burning tobacco and let out a breath full of smoke. He smiled at his squad of devout soldiers which was now forming a semicircle around him.

"It is time to prepare for battle." He gestured to one of his security team. "Tell our two scouts to return inside. I want everyone out of harm's way. Let us make certain we are ready for this confrontation."

The command made sense and his crew responded appropriately. He watched them attend to their chores with perfect loyalty. Men who'd chosen to leave their homeland for months at a time to accomplish their goal. For a moment, he actually felt a pang of guilt for what he was about to do. Just a moment.

He took another puff on the cigarette and casually said, "Memu, you will drive me to the cave so I can prepare for the great holocaust."

"But Sarock," Jemin said. "We have just come from the cave. There is no reason for you to risk such a move."

Barzani gave Jemin one of his most ferocious glares, which put the young man on his heels. "You do not yet have the privilege to question my authority, Jemin. There are duties I must tend to which require my attention. Only I am capable of securing these duties. Do you understand?"

Jemin nodded silently even though he couldn't possibly know which duties Barzani could have been speaking about. One of the great advantages to autonomous rule was the ability to proceed without true scrutiny.

There was a sense of anticipation in the room as his squad gathered around Barzani and awaited their instructions.

Barzani pointed his finger and raised his voice like a fierce soccer coach, "When we left Kurdistan over a year ago, we came here with great ambitions. Ambitions which are now just hours away from completion. This will be the final twenty-four hours of our journey. Tomorrow night either the American president will be removing troops from our homeland, or his country will suffer the most colossal destruction they have ever faced. Ever. This next day will bring us closer to our main objective—a sovereign state for all Kurds. Our families will rejoice in our accomplishments. We will return home to the greatest of celebrations."

The handful of men began a low grunt in agreement, like wild animals showing their excitement as their leader took in each and every face.

"This undertaking will live on as the defining moment in Kurdish history. No one will ever doubt our resolve again." Barzani pumped his fist in the air. "We are warriors!"

The squad began to jump in unison, a rhythm of ecstasy as they chanted, "Kurds, Kurds, Kurds, Kurds."

Barzani puffed on his cigarette and smiled and waved his hands as the men jumped and chanted and grunted.

"We . . . will . . . not . . . fail!" Barzani screamed over the exuberant pack of soldiers. He could feel the floor move beneath him, gyrating to the pulse of the surrounding militia.

Barzani let the celebration continue for several minutes before raising his hands for quiet. The room immediately became still. Nine pairs of eyes intently watched their leader as Barzani walked over and dropped his cigarette in the sink. He returned to address his team for one final time.

"I will arrive back here in less than two hours. By then I will expect to see every weapon sparkling, every soldier will be at their designated station. No one shall leave this dwelling until I return. Should a conflict occur, fight to the death if that's what it takes to secure our base.

"Yes, Sarock," came the unanimous chant.

Barzani looked at Memu and found his chief of security already holding the keys to their vehicle. As he left through the garage door entrance, he saw his crew already focusing on their tasks. Barzani could not be any prouder of their loyalty. They did not deserve their fate. But Barzani would not let anything or anyone jeopardize his plan for success.

Not even his own flesh and blood.

Chapter 24

They were driving down a residential street where thick rows of pines lined the road, making everything appear similar. The cabins were all set back into the darkness, barely visible, but for an occasional porch light. Many of the residents were already gone, heeding Temir Barzani's threats to destroy homes until he'd achieved his goal. Matt crawled barely over walking speed. Eddie Lister was in the back seat between Stevie and Jennifer, craning his neck for something familiar. Tommy was stuck in the far back row of the SUV.

"Anything?" Nick said from the passenger seat.

Eddie moved side to side, his head on a swivel. "It's hard to say. Everything looks different at night."

They were quiet while Eddie continued his search.

"I think it's a block over," Eddie said.

Matt took a long, disgusted breath. "Are you sure you know where this place is?" he asked.

"Yeah, yeah," Eddie said. "I know. Maybe we could come back during the day?"

"That's a good idea," Tommy said. "Let's call it a night and go get some ice cream."

Nick scrutinized each cabin, searching for something, anything he could consider suspicious. The Humvees remained in a holding pattern, idling in a vacant cul-de-sac, waiting for Nick to give them the signal. They'd been joined by a caravan of FBI SWAT agents from Phoenix who were sitting with the soldiers awaiting their turn as well. Nick wanted to scout the area and give them a quality target before the fireworks started.

"Stevie," Nick said. "You bring the parabolic with you?"

Stevie reached down into a duffle bag at his feet and pulled out a metal, cone-shaped dish about a foot in diameter. He handed the dish to Nick along with a pair of headphones. Nick put the headphones on, opened up his window and stuck the parabolic out the window. He pointed it at the first home they passed on the right and found nothing but static and some lonely crickets.

Jennifer Steele leaned over, pulling a pair of night vision

glasses and a flashlight out of the bag.

"I'm going to go on foot," she said, opening the door.

"No," Matt barked, but Steele had already closed the door behind her and stuck her head back in the open window.

"Relax," she said. "I'm staying within viewing distance."

Matt kept rolling down the street. He turned his lights off to aid Steele with her infrared canvass of the neighborhood.

"Keep an eye on her, will you, Tommy?" Matt called out over his shoulder.

"You kidding? I'm already fogging up the window back here," Tommy said.

Nick caught Matt staring in his rear view mirror. "Stay focused," he said.

Matt glanced over at him and frowned, but said nothing.

Methodically they moved through the neighborhood with the windows down, eyes and ears wide open. They were all beginning to lose their patience.

"Eddie?" Nick said. They hadn't heard a word from the kid in several minutes.

"I think we passed it," he said. "I don't recognize this."

"Stop," Tommy said.

Matt hit the brakes.

"I see Jennifer back there waving her arms," Tommy said.

They all turned to see exactly what Tommy was talking about. Once Jennifer saw the SUV stop, she lowered her arms and headed toward the car in a sprint, glancing over her shoulder at the house as she ran.

By the time she reached Nick's window she was out of breath, panting while holding something in her hand. Nick had to wait for her to shine the flashlight on it before he knew what it was. A cigarette butt.

Nick's heart raced as he realized the significance. He handed the butt and flashlight to Stevie.

"There's a bunch of them under this tree," Jennifer said, catching her breath. "It looked like a perfect spot for a lookout."

They waited while Stevie inspected the butt, smelling it, then rolling it in his hand. Finally he looked through a magnifying glass for confirmation.

After a minute, Stevie looked up at Nick with a smile. "It's the same one," he said. "No doubt about it."

"Okay." Nick jammed a thumb over his shoulder. "Get in, Jen."

Steele hopped in the car.

"Get to the end of the block and turn the corner," Nick instructed Matt. He got his cell and called the SWAT team. He sensed adrenalin surge through his veins with a massive force. He hadn't slept more than an hour in days, yet he felt as if he could run a marathon.

Matt pulled over and everyone got out and waited. Even in the chill of the fall night, Nick pulled off his jacket and tossed it in the front seat. Less than two minutes later, the posse rolled in from a different direction as instructed. They parked all in a row and immediately flowed from their vehicles to circle Nick.

Between the SWAT team, FBI agents and Special Forces, there were more than thirty of them. Everyone was already black-faced, but Tommy and Jennifer who used the SUV's side view mirrors to rub on the black wax.

"Okay," Nick said in a low voice. "Let's be careful here. I don't want to take any chances. These guys are notorious for leaving booby traps, so be careful. If it takes an extra few minutes to get where you want to be—take the time. This probably won't turn into a fleeing situation. They'll dig in and fight until their last bullet has been used."

Nick looked directly at the soldiers now. "Anyone with some IED training?"

One of the young men in the back raised his hand. "I do, sir."

"Good," Nick said. He pointed to Stevie. "Take him with you and examine the perimeter. I don't want any surprises."

"Done," the soldier said, while watching Stevie unload his duffle bag from the SUV.

Nick handed the parabolic to Stevie. "And make sure you take the metal detector as well."

"Got it," Stevie said, then headed toward the KSF safe house with the soldier. Nick pointed to the leader of the FBI's SWAT team and held up three fingers in the dark. Moments later, three SWAT agents fell in behind Stevie and the soldier.

Nick's face dripped with sweat. His body was betraying him while he resisted the urge to hand the lead over to Matt. The PTSD was kicking in as he fought to hold it together.

Matt already had his sniper rifle out and strapped over his

shoulder. Nick pointed to him. "You have a shot at Barzani, you take him out, whether or not I've given the signal yet. Okay?"

Matt patted his weapon. He was ready.

Nick looked at Tommy. "Stay here with Eddie and make sure no one enters this street."

Tommy gave his cousin a thumbs-up.

"Okay," Nick said addressing the group, "Unless they've hired some new personnel, I suspect we're looking at a number less than ten. Their scouts have already taken cover, which means they know we're here. They will have explosives waiting for us. I don't know where, or when."

Nick pointed to Steele. "Call an ambulance. Have them come without emergency signals and tell them to wait outside the community entrance."

Steele left the circle with her phone out.

Nick looked in the direction of the safe house and pulled his pistol out from his holster. The cabins on either side were dark and unoccupied. "I want this area contained," he said. "I don't want anyone escaping that house."

He looked at Matt and the crew around him. Everyone seemed prepared to run through a wall for him. It made his heart pump even harder.

* * *

Barzani saw it all. He sat in the back seat of the Jeep Grand Cherokee and watched it on his tablet as Memu kept guard from behind the wheel. They parked in a nearby condominium complex, a place where most of the units were used by renters and a new arrival in the parking lot caused no attention. Besides, none of the authorities were looking for him anyway. They presumed he was inside the safe house.

"Sarock," Memu said from the front seat, "what exactly are we waiting for?"

Barzani had the perimeter of the complex rigged with tiny digital security cameras so they could spy their surroundings. What his crew didn't know was that he'd programmed his tablet to accept the signal from a remote location.

"Sarock?" Memu repeated.

"Yes," Barzani said, "I hear you. We are simply making sure we have no one following us. Patience, Memu. We are so close to our goal, we dare not take a wrong step now."

The security guard seemed to be satisfied with the answer. Since they were backed into their parking spot, he folded his arms and kept his focus out the front window.

"Yes, Sarock," he said.

Barzani slowly removed the metal cylinder from his pocket and kept it out of view from the front seat. At the top of the cylinder was a digital keypad with the numbers 1-4 displayed. They created a slight beam and Barzani had to cover the light with his hand to avoid Memu's attention.

On his computer, he could see the authorities closing in on the cabin. They were in the shadows and although he could not identify each person, he knew Nick Bracco and his partner were there. He also knew his men were watching the same image on their monitors inside the cabin. It was only a matter of time before they began firing. His heart swelled with pride. Their dedication went beyond anything he could have ever hoped for.

His soldiers were about to make the ultimate sacrifice. Barzani wished to take as many American lawmen with them.

* * *

While Steele took the SWAT team around back, Nick and Matt watched the operation unfold from across the street. Matt was flat on his stomach, his rifle resting on the tripod, with his eye steady in his sight.

Nick was next to him on one knee, viewing the cabin through his binoculars. There were no lights on inside the house, so he kept switching between night vision and regular lenses.

"What are they waiting for?" Matt asked.

"They could be asking themselves the same question about us," Nick said.

Darkness swallowed the approaching team, while Nick controlled the offensive through his wireless headset.

Nick tapped the headset. "Stevie, you heard male voices through the parabolic?"

"For sure," Stevie said. "I caught fractions of different conversation, but I definitely heard the word Sarock several times. It's them."

"Good work," Nick said.

Nick tugged on his arm sling, his shoulder began to throb

from overuse. He'd stayed off the pain killers since the other meds didn't seem to mix well with them.

"Team A, you in position?" Nick said into the headset.

"Roger."

"B?"

"Roger."

"C?"

"Giddyup."

Nick licked his lips. He didn't want any mistakes. Barzani was finally going to be put to rest.

Nick touched his headset. "Is the gas ready?"

"Ready," came the voice.

Nick had to be definitive. He had to shake off any residual effects of the medication which kept his PTSD in check. But there was a nagging thought running through his mind, he was missing something. Like someone leaving for the airport and sensing they'd forgotten to lock the front door.

"You okay," Matt said without ever leaving his sight.

"Fine," Nick lied.

"You going to give the order, or should we wait for them to make a mistake?"

Nick took a deep breath. "I don't like it."

Matt turned to face him. "What?"

"Something's wrong," he said. "No booby traps. No snipers. It's too easy."

Mat sat up and twisted to look behind them. "You think they've doubled back behind us?"

"No," Nick said. "We have that covered. There's something else and I can't get to it in my mind."

Matt grabbed Nick's good shoulder and stared straight at him. "Look, you've taken every precaution. Sometimes you just have to take the chance. It's risk versus reward, and Nick, right about now the reward is quite appealing."

Nick nodded. Since he couldn't qualify his fears, he had no reason the hold up the attack. "You're right," he said. "It's time."

Nick tapped his headset and addressed the entire team. "They'll have gas masks and night vision, but they can't use both and still fire their weapons. So we gas them, then attack. Understood?"

He received three affirmative responses.

Nick looked down at Matt. "If they turn on the lights, our guys could be sitting ducks. Make sure you pick off as many as you can."

"I'm on it," Matt said, back into his sight, steady as a rock. His cheeks didn't even move as he spoke.

"Okay," Nick said into the headset. "Fire the canisters."

A couple of loud popping sounds echoed throughout the treetops followed by glass shattering. A moment later a muted blast came from inside the house. It only took a few seconds before the smoke began to drift out of the cabin windows, up and away from the approaching soldiers and SWAT team.

From their position, Nick and Matt could see Team A rush the front door. Two soldiers, one on each side of a battering ram, swung the large metal pipe and bashed in the wooden door like it was Styrofoam. The door crashed down in one piece separating from the hinges and slamming hard against the floor. The team of eight charged in the cabin single file, organized and skillful, like it was choreographed for a film.

Nick got to his feet, too antsy to stay back. He wanted to get inside as soon as possible.

"Stay put," Matt barked.

Nick tucked himself behind a large tree and shifted his weight back and forth, waiting for gunfire. Waiting for the offensive to take hold. Waiting for Barzani's body to be carried out on a stretcher.

Instead, there was a flash of bright light, which for a split second, didn't quite register to Nick's eye. Not until it was followed by a thunderous explosion. A wall of intense pressure punched the air out of the cabin at a rate of three hundred yards per second. Nick was thrown back into a thick bush and lost his breath. He swallowed gulps of oxygen like a swimmer who'd just surfaced from a long dive. The flash of the explosion overwhelmed his eyes and took out his sight. He could hear the crackling of flames and feel the heat generated from the blast. Screams pierced the night. Men's screams. Soldiers who'd run straight into the arms of danger.

Next to him, below him, he could hear Matt calling his name.

"You okay?" Matt's voice was muted, but he could tell he was probably screaming.

Nick had to wait before he could respond. His entire body

trembled while he struggled to breathe.

He felt a pair of hands on him while the floaters in front of his face began to give way to the night sky. He could see some tree limbs.

"I'm okay," he gasped.

Now Matt's voice was above him, while his shoulder was being tucked into his arm sling properly. He could finally make out Matt's face. He looked to be stunned, as if in shock.

"Are you okay?" Nick said, then coughed.

"Yeah, I was down against the ground already."

Nick forced himself up to see remnants of the cabin which stood there in front of him just moments earlier. Sirens were blaring from different directions. Flames began to lick the nearby treetops, threatening to turn into a forest fire.

Matt pulled Nick to his feet.

"C'mon," Matt said, his expression changed. He seemed to suddenly remember something. A trace of distress showed in his eyes. "We have to find Jennifer and Stevie."

Matt raced across the street while Nick stumbled behind him, trying to keep up. He passed a soldier on the ground, writhing in pain, holding his stomach. When he bent down to help, the soldier waved him off.

"Go. Help the others," the soldier said. "I'll be fine."

Nick was strong enough to break into a gallop around the west side of the cabin. He saw a SWAT team member carrying a soldier away from the flames, but no Steele, or Stevie.

Flashing lights illuminated the forest while Nick maneuvered around debris scattered across the ground; chunks of wood and drywall mixed with shoes and furniture. He stepped over a stainless steel sink and landed on a human arm. Burning embers floated all around him like black snow.

While his vision blurred from the smoke, Nick heard his name, but couldn't find the source. He saw Matt to his right, behind the cabin already, searching frantically for survivors.

"Nick," a voice called to his left.

Tommy was in the woods, kneeling over a body. A female body.

Nick ran over and saw it was Jennifer Steele flat on the ground. Tommy had his hand on her shoulder, but there weren't any obvious wounds.

"I'm fine," Jennifer yelled and fought to get up, but Tommy kept her pinned to the ground.

"Not a chance," Tommy said. "I saw you flying like a bird. You're staying flat on your back until the medics get here with a stretcher.

"Where's Stevie?" Nick asked.

Tommy pointed over his left shoulder. In the darkness, Stevie sat up against a tree taking deep breaths. A mixture of flashing lights and flickering flames danced over his torso.

Stevie held up a hand. "I'm okay," he said.

Matt found them and rushed next to Steele. He inspected her body while she took his hand.

She glanced at Tommy and said, "He's forcing me to stay still."

Matt looked at Tommy with a question on his face.

"She's hurt," Tommy said. "She's trying to be tough like the rest of the boys, but she's hurting and I'm not going to let her make it worse by trying to shake it off like it's nothing."

"But it is nothing," Steele uttered.

Matt brought her hand to his lips and kissed it. "Tommy's right. You stay put."

Sid Coleman, head of the FBI's SWAT team, ran up to Nick and pushed him to the ground.

"You said these weren't suicide terrorists!" Coleman blasted. He kicked Nick in the legs while he tried to get up with one good arm. "I lost good men in there." Coleman continued his assault until Matt jumped up and grabbed the agent and pulled him away.

Spittle came flying out of Coleman's mouth as he went on, "This was supposed to be a combat mission, not suicide. That's why I sent my men in there!"

Matt was bigger than the man, but adrenalin kept Coleman from being completely contained. A nearby soldier came over and helped Matt keep the man under control.

"It wasn't suicide," Nick said, finally getting to his feet. They're not religious zealots."

Coleman pointed to the ruins next to them. "Then what the fuck is that?"

"They didn't do it," Matt yelled at Coleman. He looked over at Nick and seemed to have it figured out already.

"Then who?" demanded the SWAT team leader.

It took Nick a moment to clear it up, his head full of grief and pills. "Barzani," he finally said, then saw Matt nodding back at him.

"Barzani?" Coleman said. "But I thought . . . What are you saying? He committed suicide and took his men with him?"

Nick shook his head. "I don't know how, but he knew we were coming and left his men behind. He's the one who detonated the bomb."

"So all this for nothing," Coleman spat at him. He waved his hand out in a half-circle. "Barzani is still out there?"

Then Nick felt the vibration in his pants pocket and knew his answers were a button away. He walked into the nearby woods, passing Steele being placed on a stretcher. Once he'd gotten twenty feet into the trees, he braved a look at his phone display. "Luke Fletcher."

Nick's hand trembled as his thumb hovered over the "Talk," button.

He pushed the button and placed the phone to his ear.

"You really did not think I was dead, did you?" came the low growling voice.

Nick said nothing.

"There's less than eighteen hours before your president's speech. I hope for your sake there's a troop removal."

"And I hope for your sake, I don't find you before then." Nick seethed. He realized he was trembling out of fury rather than fear. His grip tightened around the phone. "Because when I get you I'm going to split your gut open and slice up your liver to feed the neighborhood cats."

There was levity in Barzani's tone now. "Agent Bracco, really, is that necessary. We are all professionals here."

"Professional what? Murderer? Those men you killed were loyal followers of your corrupted schemes. They had brothers and sisters and wives and children back home."

"You know nothing about my home or you would have convinced the President to back out of Kurdistan already. We would have secured a place for our people to call their own by now. Instead your meddling government has decided to play the watchdog for the world's troubles. It is not your planet to control, Agent Bracco, so do not question my tactics when it comes to the security of my homeland."

"Fuck you, Barzani. I don't give a crap about your homeland

or your pathetic struggles with the Turkish government. The first sign of a dispute, you pick up a gun. That's your answer to everything. All I care about is my homeland. So get the fuck out of my backyard or I'll rip that gun from your hand and shove it down your throat."

There was silence for a moment, then Barzani said in a low, controlled voice. "It's not a gun I have in my hand. It's a detonator."

Nick felt a sense of helplessness come over him. He had no leverage at all with Barzani and although spewing empty threats might lower his blood pressure, it would do nothing to help save the country from disaster. In fact, it might even accelerate it.

He was about to say something when Barzani said, "Good luck, Agent Bracco."

Nick put the phone away and watched his world glow with flames, flashing lights and fire hoses. He had eighteen hours to capture a terrorist who had six months to prepare for this moment. And he had a Russian assassin zeroing in on him as well. He wanted to go home to hug his wife and tell her everything was going to be okay, but for the first time in his life—he didn't think he'd live long enough to tell her that lie.

Chapter 25

President Merrick started his morning as he did most, sitting on the couch in the Oval Office with his tablet computer in his lap. He'd just cleared up his email messages, when the door opened without a knock.

"Hey, Tiger," Merrick said with a grin.

Samuel Fisk sat on the couch across from Merrick and began pouring his coffee while making a plate out of the fruit and miniature muffins sitting on the coffee table between them.

Merrick scrolled across his CIA briefing without finding anything of consequence.

"Any word from the War Room yet?" Fisk asked, while stirring his coffee.

"Not yet."

"You get any sleep last night?"

"Nope. I spoke with four new widows and a life partner. I'm getting tired of apologizing."

Fisk seemed to want to say something, then stopped. He slid the *Washington Post* on the table toward him and examined the headlines.

"It happened too late to make the paper," Merrick said while watching video of an overnight bombing campaign in southern Zimbabwe.

While still scanning the newspaper, Fisk asked, "Is the final draft done?"

"Somewhat. I'm having the group in the basement look it over for any language issues."

"Can I see it?" Fisk said.

Merrick nodded, then pushed the print button on his screen. He pointed to the printer behind him as the hum of the machine purred to life. "It's coming up right now."

Fisk went over to the printer and pulled a few pages from the unit.

There was a knock on the door and Press Secretary Fredrick Himes poked his head inside.

"Sir?" Himes said. "The Prime Minister will be able to join you for an early lunch before he leaves. Around ten thirty."

"That's fine," Merrick said, shaking his head as the door closed. "It's all Turkey, all of the time around here," Merrick added to no one but Fisk.

The Secretary of State returned to the couch and took a sip of coffee while reading a copy of Merrick's speech for that evening.

"Well?" Merrick said.

Fisk didn't look up. "So far, so good."

"Stop, you're going to make me blush."

Fisk put the papers down on his lap and looked out the window. "I don't know how we're going to stop this disaster from happening, John."

Merrick placed his tablet on the coffee table and leaned forward. "Walt has me convinced it's not the nuclear power plant, so they're fortifying Hoover Dam."

"Did you hear, they ran all the data through the computer last night," Fisk said. "Everything. Barzani's history, his men's experience, their past missions, their tendencies."

"And?"

"The computer came up with Hoover Dam as well," Fisk said.

"What does Nick think?"

"He's on board. Stevie Gilpin, their techie, came up with chlorine in some of the terrorists' shoes, so they think it's from moisture near the dam."

A female voice came over the round speakerphone built into the coffee table. "The War Room is ready for you, Sir."

"Put them through, Rose," Merrick said.

A moment later, the speakerphone came to life with a series of background noises, mostly low voices and key taps from computer terminals.

"Mr. President," came the voice of CIA Director Ken Morris, "we're ready."

"Good," Merrick said. "Can anybody explain to me what happened last night in Payson?"

Two voices battled for the response, one male, one female.

"Lynn?" Merrick said. "Is that you?"

"It's me," Lynn Harding answered.

"Will you answer my question please?"

"Of course. First of all, Barzani is still alive. Apparently our team found their safe house and the moment we forced our way in, the detonation device went off. At first there was some confusion as to how and why, but Nick and Matt figured out pretty quick that Barzani was the one who destroyed the place."

"Do they know why?"

"The feeling is, Barzani knew his crew was overmatched and he decided to make sure there was no one around to give up his plans."

"Which are?"

There was an awkward silence as Merrick imagined different department heads pointing to each other.

Finally, Harding admitted, "We don't know."

"So we're guessing Hoover Dam?" Merrick said, disgusted.

"Yes, Sir."

"Are there any other targets we should be pursuing?" Merrick asked.

"Very little. That part of the country is spread out so without a nuclear device, it's hard to mount any major population fatalities."

"And you're certain they do not have a nuclear device?"

"Yes, Sir. That much we are certain of, they do not have a nuclear device."

Merrick sat back in his seat and folded his arms across his chest. He was relieved and infuriated all at once. "What about the profilers? What do they have to say?"

Harding hesitated. "Well, Sir, they're suggesting Barzani has a chip on his shoulder. They feel he wants revenge for what happened to Kemel Kharrazi and he won't stop until he gets it."

Fisk sat there with his coffee in his left hand and scribbling notes with his right. When there was a lull in the conversation, he glanced at his notes and said, "Tell me about overnight troop movement in Turkey."

Now there was no hesitation. The CIA was the lead department of the overseas activities, so it was CIA Director Ken Morris who spoke up.

"There's been troop movement away from Kurdistan," Morris said. "The government troops seem to be moving out and securing the perimeter."

"And what does that mean?" Merrick asked out loud, but looked at Fisk.

His Secretary of State seemed satisfied to let the team in the War Room answer.

"It means one of two things," Morris said. "Either Prime Minister Budarry is offering you an olive branch while he's your guest at the White House . . . "

"Or?"

"Or, the ground troops could be leaving Kurdistan to prepare for major air strikes and they want to be out of harm's way."

"Boy," Merrick muttered. "It just gets better, doesn't it?"

Fisk said, "The NSA tells me the Prime Minister has been on the phone to Ankara all morning. He's planning something, it's just hard to say what."

Merrick leaned his head back and stared up at the white domed ceiling. So much information, yet so little answers.

"What else?" Merrick barked.

Lynn Harding's voice returned. "We're sending every available soldier, National Guard, and policeman to Payson and the Hoover Dam. We've considered evacuating the towns below the dam, Bullhead City and Lake Havasu, but feel it's too risky."

"Too risky?"

"It's too close to the deadline and it would cause a stampede which would create an unsettling amount of casualties. We're better off finding the source and securing the dam."

Merrick stayed back and closed his eyes. He imagined the consequences of a bomb destroying a large section of the population in Arizona and for the first time actually felt removing troops from Turkey wasn't a bad idea.

"Anything else?" Merrick said.

"Isn't that enough?" Fisk asked.

"That's all we have so far, Sir," Harding added.

"Okay," Merrick said, sitting up and placing his index finger on a button on the speakerphone. "Keep me updated," he said, then pushed a button to end the conversation.

Merrick gazed over at Fisk. "Well?"

Fisk finished scribbling notes, then looked up. "Why don't we meet with Budarry and find out exactly what he's up to."

* * *

Kalinikov had to maintain patience. When he arrived in Payson last night,

he'd had the good fortune of spotting the Sheriff's car parked in front of a bar and decided to tag it with one of his GPS devices.

Then he went inside the bar to have a drink. There was no reason not to. He was a completely unknown figure. Besides, he might have met the Sheriff himself and garner valuable information. Instead, he'd met the Sheriff's cousin whom he liked. The guy was genuine, nothing phony about him. He was too sharp to give up any information though.

Now, Kalinikov sat in the parking lot of a large shopping center and sipped cold coffee from a fancy cardboard cup. The GPS screen on his laptop showed the Sheriff's car still stationary at the Sheriff's Office. He needed to wait and see where this led him. It was becoming more complicated, however. More Humvees kept rolling by and soldiers could be seen at every public place, asking people questions and surveying the landscape.

Kalinikov was almost too prepared. He'd been ready for a confrontation ever since he'd landed on American soil and he felt like the student who knew all the answers and couldn't wait to be called upon.

Kalinikov thought about home and decided to dial a number on his phone.

"You were supposed to be home by now," the soft female voice answered.

"I know. I've been delayed. Just one more meeting and I will be done."

"And how long should this meeting take?" she asked, with some humor in her voice. He smiled and the thought of the two of them smiling together made the distance seem to dwindle.

"Tomorrow at the latest," he said. "Are you finished packing yet?"

"What do you think?"

Now his smile broadened. She was late for everything and had he been the type who thrived on structure at home, it could have been a source of contention between them. But since his job required so much structure, he enjoyed the sloppy schedule once he was home.

"Soon, Love," he said.

"Ta ta," she said, then hung up.

Kalinikov put his phone away, then checked his computer screen. Someone was about to make a mistake. And he was going to take advantage.

Chapter 26

President Merrick wiped his mouth with the White House napkin, then pushed back on his chair and crossed his legs. He sat at a round table in the State Dining Room just below a large portrait of Abraham Lincoln. He engaged Prime Minister Budarry with an authentic smile. Two of Budarry's aides and Samuel Fisk were the only other guests at the table.

Fisk seemed to sense the impending conversation so he asked one of the aides a personal question about their function while overseas and both aides chimed in on the discussion.

Merrick took the opportunity to gain Budarry's attention.

"So, Mr. Prime Minister," Merrick said, "is the United States offering enough support to satisfy the Turkish people?"

Budarry appeared pleasantly surprised to hear Merrick's comment. Up until then, he'd been sitting rigid and avoiding any conversation regarding politics.

Although they were the only occupants, Budarry eyed the room carefully, then turned his head to speak with Merrick. "Mr. President, we are very grateful for your support. You have been an incredible source of perseverance."

Merrick smiled and kept a peaceful demeanor. "May I be direct, Mr. Prime Minister?"

"Of course."

Merrick tilted his head and measured his words. "May I ask how you intend to help alleviate our problems with Barzani and the KSF here in America?"

Budarry leaned toward the president with a gentle smile. "There is an old Turkish proverb which says, 'A wise man remembers his friends at all times; a fool, only when he has need of them.'"

Merrick glanced at the grandfather clock against the far wall. He had less than five hours before his speech. And possibly a disaster which he might have the ability to stop. Budarry seemed to sense his concern and touched his arm.

"Mr. President, let me assure you what I'm about to have done will prove that Turkey is one of your greatest allies."

Merrick raised his eyebrows. "Which means?"

"Which means, I have taken measures, a very risky one in particular, which may cause my nation great vulnerability. But I do it with the promise of continued support from the United States."

Merrick sipped some of his iced tea and placed his glass down. Did Budarry think removing Turkish troops from Kurdistan was cause for great vulnerability? It was hard to read the Prime Minister and he didn't want to make any mistakes. He nodded, then turned back to Budarry. "You have no more to offer than those words?"

"I need to be careful of what I speak because it may cause you to be culpable should my military tactic be unsuccessful."

Merrick was no closer to understanding Budarry's double talk, but knew prying any further wasn't going to get it done. He took another sip of iced tea and watched the Prime Minister drop his napkin on the table and stand. His two aides followed his lead. Merrick immediately got to his feet.

Budarry reached out his hand and Merrick gave him a firm handshake.

"I want to thank you for your hospitality," Budarry said. "And please, Mr. President, just be sure to recall this conversation during your speech tonight. You should know by then what all of my mysterious words mean."

As Merrick watched the Prime Minister leave, he sensed Fisk next to him.

"Well?" Fisk asked.

"He gave me nothing but his assurance Turkey is doing something to support us."

"Shit," Fisk muttered. "That and four bucks will get you a Frappuccino at Starbucks."

Merrick stood there thinking of the weight of his decision to stand tall and act tough. Knowing he could be causing unnecessary deaths.

"Look at me," Fisk said.

Merrick faced his childhood friend.

Fisk glared at him. "Whatever you think might happen after your speech tonight, it's nothing compared to what'll happen if you announce a troop reduction in Turkey. Terrorists around the globe will be picking up American tourists and holding them hostage until you agree to negotiate their safe return."

Fisk must've seen Merrick's eyes fade out into the imaginary world of what-ifs and he grabbed him by the shoulders and got up in his face.

"Don't even think about opening up that can of worms, John. Not while I'm still breathing."

Merrick frowned. "I wish I had your conscience, Sam. I'd sleep a lot better at night."

"I'll lend it to you anytime you'd like. Just make sure you have it with you during the speech."

Merrick nodded absently. At that very moment he was still not certain what he was going to say to the nation in a few hours. He patted Fisk's hand and smiled, "Don't worry, Sam. I'll make the right move when it's necessary."

* * *

Nick sat behind his desk with a large map of Arizona stretched out in front of him. Walt Jackson sat next to him viewing satellite images on his computer screen. They'd been there since before sunrise. Matt was still at the hospital with Jennifer Steele.

Walt looked down to check a text message on his phone, then said, "The dogs just picked up Semtex near Hoover Dam. That make you happy or sad?"

Nick's eyes were getting blurry from lack of sleep and staring too long at the map. "Normally I don't like finding what I'm looking for, exactly where I'm looking for it, but I'm neutral on this one."

They were alone in his inner office, but just outside the door were two armed military police guarding the door, plus a dozen soldiers fielding calls along with FBI agents and Stevie Gilpin working his magic with his high-tech equipment. Arizona was now completely saturated with National Guard, government agents and police. The manhunt for Barzani was in full force and Nick's office was the nerve center for the operation.

Nick looked up at the clock. "Four hours," he said.

"Uh huh," Walt replied. He pointed a finger at the computer screen, "You see that?"

"What?"

"There's a path just east of the dam with recent off-road activity."

"Could be anything."

Walt shoved the mouse away and leaned back in the chair. He rubbed his eyes and yawned. "I don't know, Nick. I'm thinking it's the dam."

Nick pushed a button on his office phone. "Stevie," he said. "Get in here."

A moment later the door opened and Stevie Gilpen came bustling in.

"What's up?" he asked.

Nick tapped his pen on the desk. "Stevie, tell me exactly how much moisture you found and how significant it was compared to someone who walked in a mud puddle."

The tech specialist seemed to understand the question. "Okay, well, Semir's shoes had significant amounts of chlorine and moisture. When I say moisture I mean saturated $H2O$. This type of fresh water is found primarily around lakes, rivers and streams. There's very little chance this concentration of moisture was the result of recent rainfall. The molecular structure just doesn't match up."

Nick and Walt were sitting back now, hands in their laps, like they were listening to a good bedtime story.

"And the two guys you scraped from the cabin last night?" Nick asked.

"The same," Stevie said. "The samples I took from their shoes were identical to Semir's. Wherever Semir was, they were within the past seventy-two hours."

"And you found this on only two of the men's shoes?" Walt asked.

"Yes. And one other thing. I sent samples to Phoenix just to verify my results and they came back with even more detail. They've also found traces of copper in all three of their shoes."

"Copper?" Nick said.

"Yes."

Nick looked to his right and caught Walt's shrug.

"Not sure what that means," Walt said.

"There's some copper mines in the area," Nick said. "Maybe that's where they've kept the Semtex."

"It's possible," Walt said. "What's the name of the power company which handles the dams in the area?"

"Salt River Project," Nick said, then considered the question. "I like where you're going." He looked at Stevie. "Get a high end

SRP engineer over here as soon as possible. Tell them it's a matter of national security."

"Got it," Stevie said, then shut the door behind him.

Nick stood up and smoothed out the paper map with his one good hand. He'd had every federal building protected, every national park. "No matter how much I look at this map, I just can't find anything which could cause significant damage with a large amount of Semtex. A building, yes. A park, sure. But there are no sporting events or large concerts scheduled for today. Everything points to Palo Verde or Hoover Dam."

Walt nodded. "Agreed. That's why I'm taking the helicopter up to the dam."

"Then, I'm going with you," Nick said.

"No," Walt held up his hand. "I need you right here controlling things. As information comes in, I need you here to analyze it and react."

"But—"

"No!" Walt bellowed. He stood and tugged up on his pants. He reached down to pick up his laptop, then returned his gaze on Nick. His face softened. "I need you to use your instincts, okay? All this technology just gives us charts and graphs and spreadsheets, but I need you here to decipher what all of it means."

Nick looked down at the map. "I don't know, Walt. My instincts got five good men killed last night."

Walt pointed a long, thick, index finger at him. "Don't you dare," he growled. "Barzani is an animal, but to anticipate he'd sacrifice his entire team of loyal soldiers is insane. You did exactly what any—"

There was a quick knock, then the door opened. A field agent from Phoenix stuck his head in. "Someone just found a dead body in some bushes outside of a condominium complex about three miles from here. It doesn't fit Barzani's description."

"Send Tompkins," Nick said. "And have him take a couple of people with him to canvass the area."

The door shut. Nick and Walt looked at each other. There wasn't much more to say. They both wanted the same thing and neither one had any more insight than the other.

"I'm leaving," Walt said. As he headed toward the door, he pointed to his temple. "Use it," he said.

* * *

President Merrick drummed his fingers on the Oval Office desk and listened to the discussion going on in the War Room via speakerphone. With him were Fisk, Himes, Vice President Gregory Hearns and his main speechwriter, Chester Grant.

Grant was scribbling notes on a legal pad while everyone else was engaged in the ongoing flow of communications with the basement full of intelligence officers.

Lynn Harding was just finishing the latest update on the security of Palo Verde Nuclear Power Plant and Hoover Dam in Arizona.

"So there's no chance of a nuclear incident, correct?" Merrick asked.

A delay always seemed to occur whenever the president wanted definite answers.

"Sir," FBI Director Louis Dutton said over the speakerphone. "We can't deal in absolutes here, but if you're asking if Palo Verde is secure, the answer is yes."

Merrick shook his head. "Come on, Louis, give me something I can grab on to. What are the chances of an incident occurring there tonight?"

"With everything we know about Barzani's manpower, or lack of manpower, plus the amount of security being applied, I would say you would have a better chance of getting hit by lightening."

Fisk let out a nasty chuckle.

Merrick placed his hands over his eyes and moaned. "Thanks for the analogy, Louis, however, I've already been hit by lightning before."

"Not tonight you haven't." Dutton recovered quickly.

Merrick stood and looked out the window, his hands clasped behind his back. The room was quiet, while muted conversations drifted over the speakerphone. A tone of excitement bubbled up from the periphery of the conversations. The words, "Fighter jets," became audible.

Merrick turned and leaned over the dome-shaped speaker on his desk. "What about fighters?" he asked.

CIA Director Ken Morris spoke. "Sir, Turkey has just deployed a squad of fighter jets over western Kurdistan. They're currently in a surveillance formation, but that's how most of their missions begin."

"What does this mean?"

"We don't know, Sir. Not yet anyway. We'll continue to monitor."

Merrick returned to the window. His back to the room. "Any thoughts?" he said to his assembly.

"Sounds like Budarry might be ready to bomb Kurdistan," Vice President Hearns said.

"Not a chance," Fisk said and left it there.

"Why not, Sam?" Merrick asked over his shoulder.

"Because you're about to offer your unilateral support for the Turkish people and a killing campaign wouldn't exactly make him look like a team player. He's neurotic, but he's not stupid."

Merrick nodded.

"Sir," Morris said, over the speaker, "now there's a small unit of Turkish soldiers heading down a road toward Karliova. This is the city where the KSF headquarters is located, it's also Temir Barzani's hometown. It's where his family still resides."

"Small unit?" Merrick asked.

"One tank, followed by one truck. The truck is a large transport vehicle covered with a canvas top. Many times used to move troops. However, it is large enough to carry a short-range missile."

"Shit," Merrick said, rubbing his chin. "What is he doing?"

"It could be his way of warning Barzani not to implement a terrorist attack on American soil," Morris said. "He might've sent a threat directly to the KSF. The fighters could be there to pave the way for their attack."

"Would he do that?" Merrick asked. "Would that work? Would that stop Barzani from detonating a bomb?"

Silence.

"We're not sure, Sir," came a voice Merrick couldn't distinguish.

"I'll bet I know who could answer that," Fisk said.

Merrick looked at Fisk and immediately knew who he was referring to. He bent over and pushed a button on the phone. "Rose," he said. "Get me Nick Bracco."

Chapter 27

Nick was circling various parts of the map with different colored pens designating the quantity of troops sent to each region. He was making sure he didn't miss anything. Tommy had just arrived with sandwiches and sat across from him with his feet on the desk, waiting for instructions.

Tommy pointed to the sandwich still sitting on Nick's desk. "You need to eat something," he said. "You need some protein to keep you going."

Nick absently unwrapped the sandwich and took a bite. His cell phone vibrated and he took the call. "Yes," he said, while chomping his food.

"It's Memu," FBI agent Tompkins reported. "Barzani's personal security guard. He's been strangled to death."

"Great," Nick said. "Barzani has now officially killed every member of his crew."

"Maybe he's done us a favor," Tompkins said.

"Doubtful," Nick said. "He's just crazy with revenge and he's not going to leave any loose ends."

"No one's seen anything. You want me to continue to canvass the area?"

"Yeah," Nick said. "Give it another hour. You don't come up with anything, head back."

"Got it."

Nick put his phone on the desk and took another bite of his sandwich.

"You gonna find this guy?" Tommy said, slurping soda from a straw.

"I don't have a choice," Nick said, and meant it. He pulled open the top drawer of his desk and grabbed a vial of pills. He opened the amber bottle and dropped half the pills on the map, then picked the correct ones and put the rest away.

"How many times a day you have to take that stuff, Nicky?"

"Right now, three times a day," he said, then popped the pills in his mouth and swallowed.

"You need to get off that crap. It's doing more damage than good."

"Why do you say that?"

"Because I know you. One minute you're all jittery, the next you look like you're falling asleep."

"Maybe it's because I haven't slept in two nights?"

Tommy grinned. "Don't start using facts to mess up my diagnosis."

"Sorry, Dr. Bracco."

The door opened and Matt came in looking like he'd just run a marathon. He lumbered over to Tommy and dropped into the chair next to him. There were large bags under his eyes. He leaned back and stretched his legs up onto the desk beside Tommy's.

"Well," Tommy said. "How's our girl?"

Matt seemed to consider the question, as if it was complicated. "Well, she went in for X-rays at one and by three thirty this morning she was in surgery."

"You're kidding," Nick said. "Why didn't you call?"

Matt gave him a look. "Like you don't have enough on your plate?"

"How is she?" Tommy asked.

Matt turned and looked at Tommy with a deadpan expression. "Her neck is fractured. The doctor said her spine was so jumbled, if she tried to get up, she could've easily become a quadriplegic, or worse." Matt reached a tired hand over and gently grabbed Tommy's arm. "You might have saved her life."

Tommy put his sandwich down on his lap and frowned. "Don't get all dramatic on me now. I saw her flying around like a ragdoll. Anyone else would've done the same thing."

"No, you're wrong," Matt said. "No one else would've thought to keep her down like that. Anyone else would have gotten her help or offered their jacket . . . but you knew exactly the right thing to do at the right moment."

Tommy took a big bite of his sandwich and with a mouthful of bread and meat said, "Okay, you're on to me. I'm a jack of all trades. I know a little bit about everything. Even spinal cord injuries."

"Well, I want to say something," Matt said. "I owe you a big apology."

"Why?"

"Because from the moment you came to Payson, I've been riding your ass and you've done nothing to deserve it."

Tommy swallowed a large chunk of his sandwich in one gulp,

then slurped down some of his drink and wiped his mouth with the back of his hand. He pursed his lips out and closed his eyes. "You wanna kiss me now?"

Matt shook his head and grinned. "Maybe later."

"Good. I'll run out and get some breath mints."

Nick crumpled up the paper from his sandwich and tossed it in the trash below his desk. "Is she going to be okay?"

"Yeah, she'll need to stay in bed for a week or so, then a neck brace for a while, but the doctor says she'll recover just fine."

Matt looked over at Tommy. "Could you do me one favor?"

"Shoot."

"Well, with Barzani still loose and this Russian in the area . . . I need someone to watch her while I help Nick. Someone I can trust."

Tommy smiled. He stood up and tossed his sandwich wrappings into the trash, then grabbed his drink. "It would be my honor, Agent McColm." He saluted Nick as he opened the door to leave. "Pardon me, Sheriff, but I have a security detail to tend to."

The door shut and the two of them looked at each other.

"You know you've just paid him the biggest compliment you could give him," Nick said. "Trust is everything in his world."

"Yeah, I know. Fact is, I probably trust him more than anyone besides you."

Nick's cell phone danced on his desk from the vibration mode. He answered, "Bracco."

"Please hold for the President of the United States," a women's voice said.

Nick twisted the phone away from his mouth and said, "Merrick."

Matt raised his eyebrows and nodded.

"Nick," President Merrick said over a speakerphone. "How are you?"

"I'm fine, Sir."

"Well, I have Hearns, Fisk and Himes with me today. We're discussing strategy over here."

Nick sat back in his chair and watched Matt swipe half of his sandwich and stare down at the map.

"How can I help?" Nick asked.

"Budarry has deployed fighter pilots over the western edge of Kurdistan."

"Near Karliova?"

"Exactly. There's also a tank and a covered truck on the way there right now. You see what's going on?"

"I can guess."

"Good. That's what I need to know. If the KSF headquarters is threatened by a severe attack, maybe even Barzani's family, would that be enough to dissuade Barzani from detonating a bomb here in the states?"

Nick sighed. "I wish I could tell you what you want to hear, Sir. But Temir Barzani has just murdered every single KSF soldier in his crew, including his longtime personal security guard. The man has no soul. Threats to the KSF or his family are futile."

There was no reply. Some distorted voices in the background muttered sounds of discontent.

"Well, Nick, that's pretty straightforward. That leads me to my next question. How close are we to finding Barzani?"

"Do you want the truth?"

"That bad, huh?"

"He's had six months to prepare for this moment," Nick said. "That's the part that bothers me."

"What are we missing?"

"We've got every available law enforcement officer on the street. I'm getting information emailed to me every five or ten minutes. We'll figure it out, Sir. I just need enough time."

"How does two hours and fifteen minutes sound?"

Nick looked up at the clock on the wall. That's when the president's speech was scheduled. "That sounds just fine, Mr. President."

"Nick, you've saved my bacon once before. Am I going to the well one too many times to ask you to do it again?"

Nick suddenly found himself sitting upright. "No, Sir, of course not."

"You understand I need to do what's best for the country, not necessarily what's best for Arizona."

Nick didn't need to respond to that. He understood the reference.

"You have my private cell number, right?"

"Yes, Mr. President."

"Good. Then use it, the minute you have Barzani."

"Will do, Sir."

"Oh, and Nick, do me a favor will you?" There was a smile in the president's voice. "Don't wait until the last minute, okay? My heart isn't what it used to be."

"Neither is mine, Sir."

Chapter 28

Matt was downing his third cup of coffee when he hung up the phone with Walt Jackson. Nick was barely keeping his eyes open, so Matt told him to take a ten minute cat nap on the couch. He'd let Nick go twenty since he was snoring in less than two minutes. Now, he went over and gave him a gentle kick.

Nick woke startled. His head jerked up, immediately grabbed his shoulder and winced from the unexpected jolt.

"Sorry," Matt said. "We have less than an hour."

Nick got up and went into the bathroom, leaving the door open. Matt heard the water running. A minute later, Nick returned with his hair sopping wet while rubbing it with a cloth towel.

"Where were we?" Nick asked with a yawn.

Matt was already on a knee organizing his duffle bag with the gear he needed. "I just got off the phone with Walt," Matt said. "One of Ken's goons just did a number on Semir and got him to admit their plan involved a giant flood."

"Why didn't you tell me?"

Matt got up and pretended he was about to slap Nick's face. "Wake up. I just got off the phone with Walt ten seconds before I kicked you. There's a helicopter waiting for us at the hospital to take us to Hoover Dam. We can still make it before Merrick's speech."

Nick threw his towel onto the couch, grabbed his cell phone from his desk and said, "Let's go."

As they made it out the front door, a Salt River Project truck was idling next to the Sheriff's car, side-by-side, the driver's side doors lining up. The SRP worker was leaning out his window and talking to Stevie Gilpin who was already behind the driver's seat of the Sheriff's car with a giant box next to him in the passenger seat.

Matt opened the back door to the Sheriff's car for Nick to get in.

Nick went up to the SRP driver and said over the noise of the loud diesel engine, "You're a little late for the party. We've already got things figured out. There may be a terrorist trying to bomb

Hoover Dam. You might want to warn any employees up there to stay above the water line."

The man said nothing. He did nothing. He simply rubbed his bald head and stared, like he was in deep thought.

Nick was almost in the car when he turned back and saw the man remaining still.

"Didn't you hear me?" Nick asked.

The man shut off his engine and the world became quiet.

"Are you telling me there's a nuclear weapon by Hoover Dam?" the man said.

"No, it's not nuclear."

The man nodded, but stayed completely unfazed.

"What's wrong?" Nick said.

"I'm the head engineer at SRP. And pardon my frankness, Sheriff, but I don't think you know what you're talking about."

That's when Nick's expression changed, like a hunting dog with his ears perked up. Matt had only seen the expression a couple of times in his career. He'd never questioned its genesis, but he knew enough to let it play out. He slammed the back door shut and joined Nick between the two vehicles.

Nick cocked his head. "What do you know about Hoover Dam?"

"A lot," the man said. "I know more about Arizona's dams than anyone in the country."

"Nick, we've got to go," Stevie said, urgently.

Nick waved him off. "Go ahead and go," he said. "I'm staying here."

Stevie looked at Matt and saw him nod his approval.

"All right, guys," Stevie said. "I'll keep you posted."

The car spit up gravel as it took off for the hospital.

The man got out of his car and shook hands with both agents. He was trim and clean-cut, with jeans and blue collared shirt. "Chase Benton," he said.

"Nick Bracco."

"Matt McColm."

"Now," Nick said, "tell me why I don't know what I'm talking about when I say Hoover Dam is about to be bombed."

"Well, it's just that Hoover Dam is over six-hundred feet thick. Made of the most durable concrete in America. What type of material do you suspect this terrorist is using?"

"Semtex."

Benton shook his head. "There isn't enough Semtex in the world capable of taking down Hoover Dam."

"How can you be so sure?" Matt asked.

"Because," Benton smiled broadly, "I did a thesis on the possibility of such an attack in grad school. It was right after September 11th and the next terrorist target was on everyone's mind back then. My theory concluded that nothing less than a nuclear weapon could cause it to crack."

The man's demeanor oozed experience. He spoke as if he were a professor addressing his students.

Matt felt a sense of anticipation building. He looked down at his cell phone. There was less than thirty minutes before the president's speech and Barzani's direct response.

Nick took the lead. "We found samples in the shoes of some of these terrorists which were compatible with water found around dammed water. Chlorine and a certain type of moisture which gave us the conclusion it was Hoover Dam."

Benton nodded. "That sounds plausible, but you may have the wrong dam."

"Here's the thing," Matt said. "We know this terrorist very well. Temir Barzani. He's not exactly going to bring down a dam just to cause long-term hardship on a community or even a state. Now, we did some research on this, and Hoover Dam would cause more destruction and loss of life than any other target. It's not even close."

Benton rubbed the back of his neck and looked up into the twilight. The sun was going down, both literally and figuratively.

"Let me ask you a question," Benton said. "Did you find any traces of copper in those shoe samples?"

Nick and Matt both looked at each other with wide eyes.

"I'll take that as a yes," Benton said.

"We didn't know what it meant," Nick said. "You do?"

The engineer grinned. "I have an idea. There's an active copper mine about forty miles from here and the water runoff tracks right by Roosevelt Dam. If someone were to walk anywhere near there, they would certainly pick up copper on their shoes."

Matt nodded. "But we looked at that and Roosevelt Dam didn't carry enough water to do enough damage."

"Yes, but what you didn't look at was what's below the dam.

If that dam were to be compromised, it would create an overflow of water too great for the next dam in Apache Lake to hold, so that dam would also be compromised and so on. Like dominos they would go down one by one."

"And?" Nick asked.

"And a cascade of water would rush down the Salt River with the force of a giant tsunami." Benton looked at both of the agents. "Are either of you familiar with Phoenix and its topography?"

Matt looked at Nick who gave him a sheepish shrug.

"Well, it's called the Valley of the Sun for a reason. It's a valley. We've done studies on this exact scenario. If Roosevelt Dam were ever ruptured, within four hours Phoenix would be under sixteen feet of water. We've estimated the loss of life to exceed three hundred thousand people. And that was a couple of years back when the population wasn't as large."

Nick looked at Matt. "Do we have anyone down there?"

"We sent everyone up north."

"Shit," Nick muttered. He pulled the hair on the back of his head. "We're screwed. We'll never get there in time."

"What if we get the helicopter to bring down some agents from up north?" Matt asked.

"What's the problem?" Benton asked.

Matt glanced at his cell phone. "The problem is we're on a time crunch. When the president announces he has no intention of removing troops from Turkistan, our terrorist friend is going to detonate a bomb to destroy Roosevelt Dam. That's almost an hour's drive. Nick's right. We're screwed."

"What time is the speech?" Benton asked.

"Less than twenty-five minutes," Matt said.

"Well," Benton said, pointing to the woods behind the office. "I know a back road which could get us to the dam in less than twenty minutes from this very spot."

Nick ran into the office without saying a word, then came out a moment later holding up a set of keys and pointing to a dark-green Sheriff SUV.

"We're taking the beast." Nick handed the keys to Benton and said, "There'll be no speeding tickets today, so get us there as fast as possible."

* * *

President Merrick sat in a barber's chair with a cloth sheet tucked into his collar to protect his suit jacket from getting messy. He stared into a large mirror while his makeup artist, Camille, dabbed his face with cotton balls. The room was empty but for Camille and Samuel Fisk. It was a small side room, well lit and just steps away from the podium he was about to take to address the American people. Fisk sat in a barber's chair next to him with his legs crossed.

"Eight minutes," Fisk said.

"Any news," Merrick asked for the third time already.

Fisk sighed. He looked down at his phone and scrolled his thumb across the screen. "Yes," Fisk said staring at his phone. "Good news. Barzani decided to give himself up. It seems he's afraid Santa won't give him any presents this year." Fisk looked up at Merrick. "Well, that's a good break, huh?"

Merrick made eye contact with Camille through the mirror. "See what I have to deal with all day?"

Camille smiled and kept busy wiping gauze across Merrick's forehead to even out the powder.

"Yes, Mr. President," Camille said.

Merrick ran situations through his mind like a chess player considering his next twelve moves and his opponent's reaction to those moves.

"Hey, Sam," Merrick said. "What if I announce a troop withdrawal from Turkey, but never actually act on it? I could buy Nick another twenty-four, maybe forty-eight hours."

Sam's face went sour with disgust. "The next time you begin a sentence with, 'What if,' I'm moving to Moscow."

"I'm just suggesting alternatives to our dilemma. There's no reason to get condescending with me."

"Yes there is. You're quite eager to sell your integrity. I thought that was the one thing you'd always leave intact no matter how broken our system had become."

"Yes, but is that any different than saying I won't cut taxes, then cutting taxes once the budget is presented?"

"No, that's why you haven't done that either."

Merrick tugged on his cloth sheet and ripped it from his collar. He quickly stood up, leaving Camille with a handful of brown cotton and a shocked expression.

"Listen," Merrick said, coming around his chair now and

facing Fisk head on. "I'm looking at this thing from every angle, okay? Occasionally I need to verbalize it and hear the words coming from my mouth before I decide what action to take. And when I do that, sometimes I just need you to listen."

Fisk sat perfectly still with no expression.

"Can you do that for me, Sam?"

Fisk said nothing.

Merrick turned to look in the mirror and twisted his head from side to side. "I think we're done here," he said.

No one spoke as he headed out the door.

* * *

They were rushing down the dirt road way too fast. Benton seemed to know the way and several times made quick, hairpin turns to avoid smacking into trees. The SUV bounced and skidded while branches kept slapping the windshield so hard, Matt actually flinched a couple of times from the passenger seat. Nick was on the phone in the back seat, trying to find the closest available backup.

When Nick got off his cell, Matt looked over his shoulder at Nick. "How

long?"

"Thirty minutes is the best they can do."

"We're only five minutes from the east entrance," Benton said, keeping

his eyes peeled to the narrow strip of dirt, while yanking the steering wheel back and forth.

Matt turned on the radio and found the all-news channel. They were discussing

the President's speech, making wild assumptions which were sure to boost the ratings. The announcer gave vivid descriptions of who was in attendance and estimated the president's arrival to be less than three minutes.

"All right," Matt said to Benton. "Tell us everything you know about this dam and where we might be able to spot Barzani."

"Well," Benton said, his eyes shifting ahead of him, "It was finished in 1911 and in 1996 we raised its height by seventy feet. In order to add to the original construction, a series of tunnels were built to give the workers access to the interior of the original design."

At the word "tunnels" both Matt and Nick had given the SRP engineer their full attention.

"Those tunnels are still intact," Benson continued. "The main opening begins behind a maintenance door tucked behind a cascade of oleanders. You'd have to be pretty well-informed to even know about the tunnels or their entrance. But if you knew what you were doing, there are a couple of spots where the old and the new parts of the dam converge . . . and . . ." Benton glanced over at Matt, seemingly measuring whether Roosevelt Dam might truly be in danger of a terrorist attack.

"Go ahead." Matt nodded, not wanting the engineer to lose his train of thought by bogging him down with a heavy dose of Barzani's skills with explosives.

"Well, if someone knew what they were doing, that's where the dam would be the most vulnerable."

"Okay," Matt said, "you take us straight there."

"That'll be easy. This road ends directly in front of those oleanders." Benton fished out a set of keys from his pocket while handling the steering wheel with one hand. He handed the keys to Matt, holding one key in particular between his thumb and index finger. "Here's the key to get in that maintenance door. Take the tunnel straight for about fifty feet, then veer left when you come to a fork."

Matt took the keys. He looked back at Nick and saw him texting on his phone.

"Anything?" Matt asked.

Nick shrugged.

While looking back, Matt spotted something out the back window which caused him to glower. In the distance, a tiny puff of dirt seemed to drift up between the trees behind them. The wisp of dirt seemed to move with a consistent motion. It only took a few moments for Matt to realize what was happening.

"We have company," Matt said, nodding out the back window.

Nick struggled to turn freely with his shoulder wrapped. "Shit," he said.

The cloud of dirt came from a set of tires charging up the road behind them. The vehicle was probably less than a half a mile away. Maybe forty seconds on the winding path they were traveling on.

"Could it be one of ours?" Matt asked.

"No," Nick said. "The helicopter was going to be the quickest to arrive."

Benton glanced at his rear view mirror. "It could be hunters," he said. "They're about the only ones who use this road anymore."

Matt and Nick both knew it wasn't any hunter. They also knew it wasn't Barzani either. The terrorist was ahead of them; that was for certain. So that left one obvious answer to the question.

"Here's what we do," Matt said, unfastening his seat belt and pulling the Glock from his holster. "Slow down enough for me to jump out into the trees and I'll take care of this."

"No," Nick said. "Too dangerous. He's a pro."

"Who's a pro?" Benton asked.

"How close are we?" Matt asked.

"It's just around this next turn, maybe a hundred yards," Benton said. "Who's a pro?" he repeated.

That was the last words spoken before the explosion lifted the speeding SUV and drove them into the trees. The velocity of the vehicle and the power of the bomb combined to lift the car into a rolling mass of dead weight. Like a meteor breaking through the atmosphere, momentum and gravity both conspired to stop its flight with a deafening collision.

Chapter 29

Matt felt his face first. A sharp pain. Then another. When he finally opened his eyes, Nick was over him, slapping him hard. Matt drew enough strength to grab Nick's hand.

"Stop," he said, his vision swirling with blurred images of tree limbs.

"You with me?" Nick said.

Matt tried to move and that's when he felt his left leg. "Ah!" Matt let out a sharp cry. He looked down and saw an image which didn't make sense. His leg went in a direction it wasn't meant to go. His tibia shot out from his skin sideways, the bone was exposed and glistening with cartilage and blood.

"Shit," Matt grunted, leaning his head back down and trying to gather himself.

"Stay put," Nick said.

Matt forced his head upright and saw the vehicle mangled into a stand of trees, smoke drifting from its frame.

"Benton's dead," Nick said. His voice was soft and urgent. "I'll be back."

"Wait," Matt said, taking in Nick for the first time since the explosion. Nick's forehead was bleeding, his shirt ripped, his arm sling gone. "What are you doing?"

"I need to find Barzani while there's still time."

"You can't, I need to come," Matt said.

"Don't be an idiot. Help is on the way."

"You can't," Matt gasped, but wasn't sure what he was trying to say. What he wanted to say was, 'You need me,' but one more look at his leg and he realized he was worthless.

Matt nodded. "Okay." He searched the ground around him. "My gun?"

"There's no time. Stay still." Nick raised his eyebrows. Matt understood. Whoever was following them was still back there. Matt needed to stay tucked under the cover of the woods and maybe he'd be overlooked. He wondered if he'd actually landed this far from the vehicle or if Nick had pulled him into the forest. Either way, he needed to let Nick go and allow him the slim chance of finding Barzani in time.

"Get going," Matt ordered with as much force as he could muster.

When Nick hobbled away, he looked like a peg-legged pirate stumbling between trees and finally following the road. They'd both known an IED was a possibility, but there was no time for caution. Nick was in the same position now. There was no time for caution and Matt worried he may never see his longtime partner ever again.

Matt leaned his head back down and tried to think of some way he could help. He felt completely helpless and his adrenalin kicked in giving him the strength to get to his elbows. Nick was out of sight and the forest was devoid of sound. Matt wondered whether his hearing was damaged from the blast or the aftermath had scared the animals into a stunned silence.

As these thoughts ran through his mind, a man crept out from the woods and into a clearing just ten yards away. He looked like an ordinary citizen without any striking characteristics, but for the gun in his left hand and the casualness in which he carried it. He looked down at Matt and seemed to regard him with a hint of pity.

"Today is just not your day, Agent McColm," the man said with a thick Russian accent.

* * *

Nick hurt everywhere. His neck and his legs were throbbing, but his left shoulder was shooting a pain so harsh, he had to lean over and force himself to breathe. He was a worthless wretch with limited mobility about to enter a terrorist's lair which had been set up months ago.

Somewhere nearby Nick could hear the Salt River flowing. Roosevelt Dam was on the other side of a huge hill and out of his view, but he could smell the lake. He spotted the stand of oleanders up against the side of the hill and immediately knew what he'd find behind them. The maintenance door. Then another thought occurred to him. The keys.

When he squeezed behind the bushes, he saw the door ajar. He didn't know how to feel about that. Like the spider offering the fly an open invitation. With his pistol out, he stood against the wall next to the door and pushed it open with the muzzle of his gun.

Then he waited. Nothing happened, so he got to his knees and peeked inside. It was dark, but the sunlight allowed him to see the brown corridor extending into the hillside. He was aware of the time and felt an unhealthy sense of duty nudge him into the tunnel.

Nick slowly shut the door behind him and allowed his eyes to adjust. The tunnel was large, maybe ten-feet wide and seven-feet high. It was lit with dim amber lights hanging along the wall which allowed him to see down the winding corridor. The temperature seemed to drop twenty degrees. There was a noise ahead of him echoing into the body of the tunnel. It was a man's voice. As his words reverberated off the walls, Nick recognized who was speaking. It was President Merrick. Somewhere, there was a radio broadcasting the President's speech.

Nick crept down the dirt path; a deep musty aroma forced him to breathe through his mouth. He followed the President's voice taking careful steps, heel to toe, his gun out in front of him.

Stiff-legged and panting from pain, Nick saw the tunnel split in two. The radio broadcast was coming from the left tunnel, the same direction Benton told him to take. He inched his way down the dirt shaft until he saw an opening on his left. It appeared to be an intersecting tunnel, but as he got closer, the President's voice seemed to amplify. The opening appeared to be more illuminated than the other parts of the tunnel and as Nick approached, he understood why. The opening was a room of sorts. A small cave with no outlet.

Nick suddenly felt claustrophobic. There was no turning back now though. He either found Barzani and stopped the terrorist from detonating a bomb, or he became another casualty of the KSF's pronounced death sentence.

The President was getting ready to announce his support for Turkey. He was glorifying past alliances with the Turkish people and offering his sympathy for the turmoil the Turks had to endure. It was only a matter of moments before Merrick would declare his unequivocal endorsement of the U.N. peacekeeping troops in Turkistan, leaving Barzani no doubt that his threat had fallen short of its target.

It had been so long since Nick cleared a room by himself, he felt naked. He and Matt had such a system down, such a smooth rhythm of checks and balances. Now he was forced to make a charge and gamble. The clock was ticking.

He leaned back against the wall and took a long breath. His

heart pumped so loud it made his eardrums throb. In one swift move, he turned into the opening and swept his gun across his field of vision, left to right, by the book, his gun lined up directly with his view.

The cave was empty. Nick exhaled. The room looked to be ten by ten and contained a wooden bench against the far wall. In front of the bench was a short, folding table, like something the kids would sit around for an outdoor party. On the table was a black portable radio with a single antenna sticking all the way up. The President had just given his word that America would never be intimidated by terrorist threats, nor would he ever negotiate with people who didn't respect America's freedoms.

Next to the radio was an ashtray full of cigarette butts. Nick didn't need to examine them to know which kind they were. The smell of stale cigarette smoke lingered throughout the small confines. He'd trained himself to listen for anything he couldn't see, but he never heard his attacker plow into him from behind and throw him against the cave wall. His gun flew loose from the impact and he found himself on the floor in severe agony. His shoulder had taken the brunt of the collision and he couldn't help but clutch the tender joint.

A tall man with a Mediterranean complexion and a weathered face picked up Nick's gun and sat on the wooden bench. He held up a pair of hiking boots, then dropped them to the floor to put them back on his stocking feet. There was no doubt in Nick's mind who was sitting in front of him.

"I have done a lot of research on you in preparation for this moment," Anton Kalinikov said with a Russian accent. "I am retiring after this job. My wife wants to live near a beach and I never disappoint my wife."

Nick's survival mode kicked in and he tried to get to his feet.

Kalinikov held up his hand. "Please do not act foolish, Agent Bracco."

For some reason those words resonated with him. It was incredible how easily Nick seemed to accept his fate. There was no time to reminisce. The only thought imbedded in his mind was the image of Julie's soft belly carrying the child he would never live to see.

The President's speech was winding down. His tone seemed to contain resolve, a commodity which Nick was lacking at the moment. He wasn't even sure he could get up without help, never mind mount a successful attack against a professional assassin.

Kalinikov leaned over and turned off the radio. "There's too much hate in the world." He shrugged. "I guess that's why people like me exist, huh?" He pulled a pair of purple gloves from his pocket and began to stretch them on his hands.

"I tagged your vehicles with a GPS device as soon as I drove into town. I thought your technology person would have discovered them." The Russian looked over at Nick with a mixture of confusion and pity. "You knew you were a target. Yet you were so blinded by the chase, you had forgotten to check your defense. That was a mistake."

Kalinikov gestured toward Nick's shoulder. "Your sutures have opened up."

Nick felt the wound and came back with bloody fingers. His mouth had dried up. He'd wondered why his assassin hadn't killed him yet, until Kalinikov produced a metal cylinder from his jeans pocket and began screwing it on the end of his pistol.

"In all this rush, I forgot to attach my silencer," the Russian said. "I guess we all get hasty at times, right?"

From the tunnel came a pair of footsteps rushing toward the cave. Kalinikov didn't seem to be affected by the sound. A few seconds later, Temir Barzani came rushing into the room in a cloud of dust. With his pistol out, he looked at the two men. First Nick slumped on the floor, then Kalinikov sitting on the bench, putting the finishing touches on his silencer.

To Kalinikov, Barzani said, "You?" He pointed to Nick and said, "Why is he still alive?"

That's when Kalinikov raised his gun and shot Barzani with the quickest move Nick had ever seen. A chest shot. By the amount of blood saturating the terrorist's shirt, it was obviously a direct hit on his heart. Not a difficult shot from the distance, but effortless and professional and with just a muted pop. Barzani's face held the shock all the way to the floor and it never left even after his life had expired.

Kalinikov moved quicker now, getting up and rummaging his hands through Barzani's corpse. "I put a tourniquet around your partner's leg," he said. "If he gets to the hospital within the hour they should be able to save it." He seemed to be finessing something from Barzani's pocket. Finally he came up with a narrow, metallic device and gave it a careful examination before placing it on the plastic table.

"That would be the detonator," Kalinikov said. "There is no timer, so your people should be able to defuse it rather easily."

The Russian must've seen the confused look on Nick's face. He grinned. "Barzani offered me money to kill you." He raised his eyebrows. "But the Turkish government offered me more money to kill him. A lot more."

Nick didn't move. His pulse pounded through his head like a steady drumbeat. He still anticipated one more shot to be fired.

Kalinikov put away his gun and wiped the dirt from his pants. "You're good at your job, Agent Bracco. It's the reason I followed you. I knew you would lead me directly to him."

The Russian folded his arms. "I also know you well enough to know you have no intention of going after me. It is why you are still alive. Anyone who mingles with the type of organized criminals you do, does not care about anything but the results. Besides," he looked over at Barzani's body. "I am now retired."

Nick watched Kalinikov leave the cave. His footsteps became softer with every passing moment.

"Oh, one more thing," Kalinikov's voice echoed throughout the tunnel walls. "Please thank your cousin for the drink. He was good company."

It wasn't until the maintenance door slammed shut that Nick realized he was going to survive. It took another five minutes for his breathing to slow down enough for him to attempt to get to his feet. He pushed down on his good arm, then decided against it. Somehow sitting in a small cave with Temir Barzani's decomposing corpse seemed like a satisfying place to spend a few minutes.

Chapter 30

President Merrick was back in his private office with a handful of his closest aides. The thin-screen TV on the wall was tuned to CNN and everyone had a beverage in their hand. It was the end of a long day and possibly the beginning of a long night.

Merrick sat at the end of the couch, legs crossed, reading the words scrolling across the bottom of the screen. The TV was almost always muted so the flow of conversation in the room wouldn't be interrupted. Currently, a commentator interviewed a Senator from Arizona who was concerned Merrick hadn't given the KSF's threat the respect it deserved.

"Idiot," Merrick murmured. His left foot tapped the floor nervously while he kept glancing at the digital clock on the wall. Every minute that passed without the words, 'Breaking News,' showing up on the screen, was a blessing.

He made eye contact with Fisk who stood holding a beer in his right hand and loosening his tie with his left. Fisk shook his head, letting Merrick know he hadn't heard anything from the War Room.

Next to him, Vice President Hearns leaned over and said, "You did the right thing, John."

Merrick nodded absently. "Tell me that after half of Arizona is underwater."

His Press Secretary Fredrick Himes came over with his head buried in his computer tablet. "The polls are in and fifty-three percent of the population agreed with your decision. Thirty-one percent in Arizona."

Merrick nodded. He was bombarded with statistics like that all day long and was practically immune to its relevance. He knew the poll taken tomorrow morning could be thirty points different, in either direction.

Now Fisk had a phone to his ear and nodded. "He's right here," Fisk said handing the phone to Merrick. He was beaming.

Merrick got up and took the phone. He instinctively walked away from the TV and sat on the corner of his desk.

"Yes," Merrick said, expecting to hear someone from the War Room.

Instead, a voice with a distinct Turkish accent said, "Temir Barzani is dead."

"Mr. Prime Minister?" Merrick asked.

"Yes."

Merrick looked at the wall clock. "It's past four in the morning over there."

"You are quite right, Mr. President. But our alliance does not fade after working hours."

Merrick saw Fisk on another phone call. He seemed engrossed in deep conversation. "We have no confirmation on our end Barzani is dead," Merrick said. "How can you be so sure?"

"Because I have personally made certain of this. Barzani will no longer be a threat to America. I want to thank you for the speech tonight. It was gratifying to hear you offer so much support to our great nation."

"Of course, Mr. Prime Minister."

"We do not want to be the friend who gets the Christmas card in the mail," Prime Minister Budarry said. "We want to be the friend who joins your holiday feast."

Merrick smiled for the first time in days it seemed. "I'll have a place setting reserved at our table for you."

"Good night, Mr. President."

"Good night, Mr. Prime Minister."

Fisk saw Merrick put his phone down and walked over with a sly grin. "I just got off the phone with Nick Bracco."

"And?"

"Apparently, while tracking Barzani, an assassin intervened and killed the terrorist for him."

Merrick squinted. "An assassin?"

Fisk nodded. "A Russian assassin."

"What?"

Fisk held up his hand. "Nick said he poses no threat to anyone."

Merrick cocked his head. "How can he be so sure?"

"He said he'd put it all in his report."

"And the bomb?"

"They have the detonator. Bomb squad is on their way. They'll be no explosions tonight."

"So who hired the assassin?"

Fisk looked down at the phone sitting on Merrick's desk. Merrick followed his gaze.

"You scared the crap out of him," Fisk said. "He went and did something rash. He was afraid you would use your speech to announce a troop withdrawal."

Merrick slumped back on his desk. Fisk reached into a nearby cooler and came up with two bottles of beer. He handed one to his longtime friend.

They clinked bottles and both took long swallows. When Merrick came down with the beer he held out his fist and received a fist-bump from Fisk.

"Thanks," Merrick said.

"Hey, of course."

Merrick put his beer down on the desk and slapped Fisk on the side of his shoulder. "I'm going upstairs to hug my kid."

Fisk smiled. "That's exactly what I thought you'd do."

Epilogue

10 months later

St. Thomas Church was a converted warehouse and one of the more popular churches in Payson, Arizona. While the outside lacked any real warmth with a corrugated steel roof, the inside had been renovated with thirty rows of brand new pews and padded kneelers.

Although the room was filled with flowers, the altar had a massive floral arrangement which had to be delivered in sections because of its girth. The card simply read, "Happy Baptism, to a special boy, President Merrick."

The fifty guests and family members crowded around Julie as she cradled little Thomas Bracco in her arms with a wide smile. He was wrapped in a soft white cloth and kicked his tiny legs in the air. Nick had his surgically repaired arm around Julie's shoulder and beamed down at his son.

Father Al Greco stood next to a ceramic stand holding a bowl filled with Holy water and addressed the guests with his left hand held high. "We are here to proclaim this child into the church of our Lord, who lives and reigns with the Holy Spirit and will bring this child into the Kingdom of God."

Father Al looked at Julie. "Who shall be the child's sponsor?"

Tommy squeezed between Matt and Jennifer Steele and stood beside Julie with a look of great satisfaction. "That would be me, Father."

The priest nodded. "Please take the child."

Julie handed her boy to Tommy.

Father Al said, "As the Godparent of this child, do you accept responsibility for raising him and helping him through his travels on this earth?"

"I do," Tommy said, smiling down at his Godson.

The priest guided Tommy to hold the child's head over the basin. Father Al dipped the metal bowl in the basin and gently poured Holy water over the baby's forehead.

"I baptize thee, Thomas Luke Bracco, in the name of the Father, the Son, and of the Holy Spirit."

A flurry of cameras and phones clicked as pictures recorded the ceremony.

Nick felt tears threaten to trickle over his eyelids. He clutched Julie tighter than he'd ever held her before. She whirled around to face him. For a brief moment there was pure ecstasy on her face. He wanted desperately to keep it there for as long as possible. But the report he had folded in his pocket screamed for his attention. He kissed her forehead.

Tommy turned and showed off his new Godson as the guests surrounded the two of them, gawking, and smiling and taking pictures from every angle.

Nick made eye contact with Matt and saw him sit down in a nearby pew. He let Julie loose to mingle and slid into the pew next to his partner.

"Are you going to tell her?" Matt asked, staring at Julie, who was glowing.

"Eventually," Nick said, leaning over with his elbows on his knees.

As Tommy walked down the aisle, Jennifer Steele put her arm around him and smacked his cheek with a kiss. In a mischievous tone she said, "Godfather."

Tommy grinned. "How about that."

THE END

If you enjoyed this book, the first chapter of the next book in the Nick Bracco series, *A Touch of Greed*, is on the following page:

A Touch of Greed

When the blood stopped oozing from James Braden's head, FBI Agent Ricky Hernandez knew his partner was finally dead. Hernandez was tucked behind a steel column in an abandoned airport hanger just inside the Mexican border. His partner was sprawled on the floor ten feet away, his body riddled with bullet holes from the ambush.

"Mr. Hernandez," the man's voice called out from behind him in a Mexican accent, "we have two kinds of soup today. We have chicken soup and we have screw-you soup. Unfortunately for you, we are out of chicken soup."

A roomful of laughter echoed throughout the empty chamber of aluminum roofing and corrugated steel walls. Hernandez judged about thirty men surrounded him with AK-47s, while Hernandez had an FBI-issued 9mm pistol with just one solitary bullet left. He stared at Braden's corpse lying there in such an unnatural position, his eyes wide in horrified shock. Hernandez's legs trembled. His left eye had an uncontrollable twitch. The desert heat was so viciously oppressive, his sweat-soaked shirt stuck to his chest.

The voice taunting Hernandez belonged to Antonio Garza, known as El Carnicero throughout the world of Mexican cartels. The Butcher. He was an infamous assassin with a legendary reputation for torturing anyone who crossed him. Including undercover FBI agents posing as drug dealers. Hernandez had seen the remains of the bodies Garza had left behind. Fingers, eyes, tongues, all severed and stuck inside the victim's mouth, while the body floated in a vat of boiling water. The assassin was known to have a doctor on hand to continuously revive the victim and prolong the torment for hours, sometimes days.

"Mr. Hernandez," Garza said, closer now. "I make you a deal. Come out right now and I let you speak with your family. You can say a proper farewell, eh?"

Hernandez was in shock, his mind numb to the statement.

"You can't be saved, so make your peace," Garza ordered.

Among other things, Garza was a chronic liar. Hernandez

was lured into Mexico while undercover, so there would be no rescue. He was out of U.S. jurisdiction. Then it hit him. He still had a minute or two to say goodbye to his wife. He fumbled into his pocket and pulled out his cell phone.

"I'm waiting," he heard Garza say.

Tears blurred his vision as he tried to find his Nicole's number in his contact list. He was bawling now, warm urine leaked from his bladder. Once he'd heard her voice, he realized he wouldn't be able to speak. He was wasting too much time just trying to gather himself. Then he saw the name just above Nicole's. Nick Bracco. Hernandez knew then what he needed to do with the remaining seconds of his life. He pushed the button.

"Time is up," Garza called out.

"Hey, Ricky," came the voice on the phone.

"Nick," Hernandez stammered. "Nick can you . . ."

"What's wrong?"

Hernandez's hands shook, tears crawled down his face. "Please tell Nicole . . ." he hiccupped and whimpered, "how much I adore her."

"Where are you, Ricky?" Nick demanded.

"Now!" the assassin screamed, a barrage of bullets exploded all around the agent as he shriveled up behind the column for protection. His legs were getting pounded by direct hits and ricochets.

"Ricky?" Nick shouted into the receiver.

The shooting stopped. The tops of Hernandez's feet were missing, only two toes stood out among the bloody stumps. Hernandez's stomach spiked up into his throat. "Nick," he uttered. "Promise me you'll kill him."

Footsteps came shuffling up behind him and Hernandez dropped the phone between his legs. He took one last look at his partner, then said, "I'll be right there, Jimmy." As he braced the tip of his pistol tight under his chin, the one thought which remained, the one glimmer of solace which contained him, was the thought that Garza would not survive long. Hernandez had an irrational rush of jubilation. Nick Bracco had been notified. Ricky Hernandez smiled.

Then he pulled the trigger.

* * *

Walt Jackson was considering going home. It was almost seven and his stomach was beginning to growl. He stood behind his desk, searching for a couple of secure flash drives he needed to take home, when his cell phone chirped. "Nick Bracco," came up on his display. As the Special Agent in Charge of the Baltimore field office, Walt was the head of an elite anti-terrorist task force simply known as, "The Team." Four of the shrewdest investigators the FBI had ever trained. Along with Nick and his partner Matt McColm, the team was split across the nation. Nick and Matt were in Arizona, while the other two worked out of the Baltimore field office. Nick Bracco was the lead agent of the group and rarely called to chitchat.

"What's up?" Walt asked, finding the two flash drives and slipping them into his pocket.

"Sorry, Walt," Nick said with a somber tone.

Walt's instincts told him to prepare for the worst.

"Tell me," Walt said.

"Jim and Ricky are dead."

Walt's pulse quickened. He felt lightheaded and plopped down in his leather chair with wobbly legs. He ran a hand over his face and looked at the floor. His new team was only six months old. They'd been grooming new members carefully ever since four of the original six members were murdered by a Russian assassin last year. Now the newborn group of four was down to two.

Walt had the overwhelming sense that he'd come too close to touching the sun and was now paying the price. He tried to control his breathing with mild success.

"You still there?" Nick asked.

"Yeah," Walt croaked.

"Jill and Nicole need to know."

"I'll take care of it."

"Sorry," Nick repeated.

"Damn it," Walt muttered. "Someone gave them up."

"Yes."

"Someone on our side."

"Yes."

"Who?"

"I don't know, but I will."

Walt took longer breaths while Nick patiently waited for him to recover.

"You took every possible precaution, Walt. There was no way to eliminate all the risk."

"No I didn't, or we wouldn't have two more dead agents on the team."

Walt's stomach tightened, while his head throbbed. He was clearly losing the battle with his emotions, but needed a clear mind. He needed to make the right choices or the damage could accumulate.

"Nick," Walt said into the phone, rubbing his temple. "You can't go down there."

"I know."

"I'm serious. Once you cross that border, you're alone. Completely."

"I know."

"I mean, these cartels, for crying out loud, Nick, they *are* the law down there."

"I understand."

Walt looked around to assure his solitude. He was in his office with the door closed, yet still knew enough to keep his voice low.

"You're going to need help."

This one seemed to stop Nick. Walt could tell his lead agent was surprised by his suggestion.

"You mean . . . Tommy?"

There was no other help Walt could've been suggesting. The CIA was constantly at war with his division and adding untrained FBI agents to the body count simply wasn't acceptable. Nick's cousin Tommy, however, had roots within a well-known Sicilian family which occasionally operated outside the law. A family whose information had been very instrumental in capturing terrorists in the past. It was a relationship Walt found uncomfortable, but the return on investment had been remarkable.

"Yes," Walt confirmed. "He'll have contacts which could be extremely valuable."

"Okay," Nick said.

"I mean, we can't afford to send shoes down there to muddle things up. The more agents we send, the scarier it gets. We use the surgical tactic we've planned. The smaller, the better."

"That's fine, Walt, but I'll need Stevie to bring some tech toys with him."

Walt looked out the bulletproof window behind his desk. The

setting sun cast a shadow over the few cars left in the parking lot. His wife probably had his cold dinner already wrapped and in the refrigerator. After thirty years of marriage, she'd still be waiting for him with a smile and a kiss.

"I'll have Stevie on the first flight out in the morning."

"Good," Nick said.

There was a silence while the two of them put their thoughts together. Walt wanted to tell Nick he'd hop on a plane and be there himself, but as he stared outside, he could sense the sun setting in too many ways. He owed it to his wife to be there. She'd seen too much action.

As if Nick could translate the silence, he said, "Stay where you are, Walt. You're more valuable to me inside the beltway where you can get decisions made." "

Walt took the cue and said, "Nick."

"Yeah?"

Walt squeezed his eyes shut. "Please. Be careful."

64114722R00115

Made in the USA
Lexington, KY
28 May 2017